'S

Ignacy Karpowicz

GESTURES

Translated from the Polish by Maya Zakrzewska-Pim

DALKEY ARCHIVE PRESS

Originally published in Polish as *Gesty* by Wydawnictwo Literackie in 2008.

© Copyright by Ignacy Karpowicz
© Copyright by Wydawnictwo Literackie, Kraków, 2008
Translation copyright © 2017 by Maya Zakrzewska-Pim
First Dalkey Archive edition, 2017

Library of Congress Cataloging-in-Publication Data
Names: Karpowicz, Ignacy, author. | Zakrzewska-Pim, Maya, translator.
Title: Gestures / by Ignacy Karpowicz ; translated from Polish by Maya Zakrzewska-Pim.
Other titles: Gesty. English
Description: First Dalkey Archive Press edition. | Victoria, TX : Dalkey Archive Press, 2017. |
"Originally published in Polish as Gesty by Wydawnictwo Literackie in 2008." -- ECIP galley.
Identifiers: LCCN 2016031191 | ISBN 9781628971637 (pbk. : alk. paper)
Subjects: LCSH: Mothers and sons--Fiction. | Terminally ill parents--Fiction. | Children of sick parents--Fiction.
Classification: LCC PG7211.A675 G4713 2017 | DDC 891.8
LC record available at https://lccn.loc.gov/2016031191

Partially funded by a grant by the Illinois Arts Council, a state agency
Publication subsidized by the Polish Book Institute

www.dalkeyarchive.com

Victoria, TX / McLean, IL / Dublin

Dalkey Archive Press publications are, in part, made possible through the support of the University of Houston-Victoria and its programs in creative writing, publishing, and translation.

Printed on permanent/durable acid-free paper

Translator's Preface

Translating a novel written in such masterful prose was challenging, and I make no claims to have done it full justice. Whilst I hope to have captured the "essence" of *Gestures*, the stylistic and culturally specific elements could not all be similarly expressed in the English language. For instance, in the Polish original, every chapter title begins with the letter *G*. Like the number of chapters (forty), which reflects Grzegorz's age, this brings attention back to the protagonist of the text, tying the character and the form of his story closer together. In an attempt to keep the same meaning of these titles, I was unable to follow the same strategy.

Cultural references to life as a child under Communism place Grzegorz's story firmly in a specific time and place. I have done my best to express this in my translation. I have kept the names of places and characters in their original Polish form to help situate the events that much more clearly in Poland. The hero is unmistakably shaped by his upbringing, and I hope that the importance of setting and culture in forming his character is as clear as it is in the original.

There are, however, universal themes dealt with in *Gestures* as well. Happiness, grief, guilt, death, loneliness, remorse—all these aspects of life will be familiar to a reader from any country. It is the battle of the individual with these emotions which, for me, constitutes the spirit of the novel, and it is this battle I have tried to translate. Of course, it cannot be forgotten that a translation is an act of interpretation and re-interpretation, and I am sure this is not the only way to read the original. For me, though, this emotional struggle, so poignantly expressed by Ignacy Karpowicz, and so accessible to readers of many cultural backgrounds, is what makes *Gestures* so captivating.

Gestures

BOUGHS

I DON'T REMEMBER MUCH of my childhood. Perhaps I don't want to. Perhaps I'm still too young. Perhaps there is still too far to go before the end. But I'm getting closer. Regardless of whether or not I want to. Every day is another step. Three hundred and sixty-five steps is a year. Every four years, I trip over a leap day.

With every year I learn, or at least I hope I do, how to be honest with myself. Exercises in honesty are far from being a favorite pastime. I'm not very studious in this subject. I have good intentions, but limited patience. I don't deserve more than a pass in honesty; and this only to encourage me to continue. I'm not sure if this is enough to go on to the next grade. Regardless of all this, though, for years now, step by step, I cover the same material.

I don't remember much of my childhood. First, I was born in winter. This is a fact: the date appears on my birth certificate, and the season in the stories my parents tell. First, I was born, but I remember nothing. I don't remember swimming. I don't remember my mother's water breaking. How my lungs filled with air for the first time. How I began to use my mouth to eat, because earlier I ate through my belly button. How my eyes first deciphered a shape. How my brain recognized a shape for the first time. A new word: "familiar." A familiar shape.

Second, I learned to talk. I don't remember my own baby talk. I don't remember my first words. According to my parents, it was "mama." Perhaps if I asked my dad when my mother was out of earshot, he would say "dada." I don't remember my first word, my parents remember for me, but they remember in their own way, each in a different room and a different past. If I were to pick my first word, based on my life experiences so far, it would be "me." Second, I learned to talk, and my first word was "me," even though nobody remembers. Me neither.

Third, I learned to read and write. I don't remember my first sentence. I'd have to look it up in the textbook that everyone was learning from at the time. I suppose that the first sentence I read featured Alice and a cat. And between two nouns there would be a verb, which—much later—gained some meaning in my life: "to have." Alice has a cat, perhaps; I don't remember.

I remember my father. He supervised my clumsy arrangements of letters, standing over me. Or maybe he wasn't standing at all, but sitting beside me? I was only a few years old, he was a few decades older. As large as a mountain, hairy, motionless. I remember spelling out: "c-o-r-k." "So what will it be?" my father asks. I'm afraid. My tiny brain and tiny body can't cope with this fear, because there is too much fear in relation to my weight. I'm afraid of the letters, of embarrassing myself, of my father's raised voice and hand. Most of all, I'm afraid of dessert—that, as punishment, it might be taken away from me. I'm afraid, but I have to answer, so I answer, before my father can repeat the question in a raised voice, his right hand above his head, fingers twisted by poliomyelitis or some other oblique blessing. "Cap," I say.

I remember that cork and cap. Or the cap and cork, I don't remember. I remember dessert. That cork (or cap) took away two Jaffa Cakes that I'd been waiting for since that morning. At least, I suppose I'd been waiting since morning. I suppose that the recalled scene occurred somewhere between five and six in the afternoon. That was the time my father returned home from work. But I don't remember. Did he feel ill, and decide to take care of me and my future, which was at that point, according to him, doomed to be analphabetic, as soon as I came home from school and ate my soup? I don't remember, I can guess, but I can't find the event among my memories.

I remember tomato soup. Mother made tomato soup at least twice a week. "Tomato soup is very healthy," she would say (and says still). "Tomato soup should be eaten at least twice a week," she would say (and says . . .). That's why I think that my mother made tomato soup at least twice a week. What she said (and says . . .) I consider to be a fact which sunk into my memory, though I don't remember. I hated tomato soup. In my memory, tomato soup is the soup of my childhood, eaten at least twice a day.

Tomato soup could be made in one of two ways: with rice, or with noodles. Rice and noodles taught me a certain emotional flexibility. When I sat over a cooling bowl of soup, staring at the red eye surrounded by white cream, with skinny snakes of noodles and a large amount of salt (I added the salt myself, crying over the bowl like a crocodile), I thought about rice. That really, I liked rice, because in comparison I disliked noodles so much. Sitting over a bowl of rice, I thought that I liked noodles. They are smooth and slippery. They don't get stuck in your throat. That's what you might call flexibility. It stayed with me for longer. For later.

Fourth, I learned that some people are forever, and some are present in my life only occasionally, and that I have no control over who falls into which category. My younger brother by four years turned out to be in the "forever" group; my grandmother was of the "only occasionally" people. My parents remember for me, and their memories are remarkably similar, how I stole the pillow from under my brother's head. Because they remember the same, and agreeing with one another is not their strongest suit, I suppose I really did steal the pillow from under my brother's head. I was probably not one of those who was made happier by the arrival of a new being in our house. Probably, I would have picked a dog, had I been consulted on the matter. Probably, I hadn't articulated my wishes clearly enough. If I mixed up a cap and a cork, why not assume that in more complex situations I didn't mix up more words?

So my brother forever, my grandmother only occasionally, and I—somewhere in between. Tomato soup forever, sometimes rice, sometimes noodles, and I—somewhere hovering over the plate. My grandmother only occasionally. During my childhood, I had two great love interests, which appeared simultaneously, I suppose, but I don't remember exactly: my grandmother, and a bitch named Teddy. And this is my fifth. And sixth.

Fifth, I learned that you can simultaneously love more than

one being. That loving one, for instance my grandmother, did not immediately exclude loving another, for instance Teddy. I also learned that those you loved might have different opinions on the nature of loving. Those I loved thought I could love only one individual, perhaps one other in addition to my parents. I could make a choice: my grandmother or the dog, and my parents.

Sixth, I learned that the answer to the question didn't depend on the nature of the question, but on who was asking it. For instance the question—who do you love most in the world?—left less opportunity for variation than the choice between a cork and a cap. That right answer was "you." But often, "you" wasn't enough. One had to be specific. Being specific meant: Mommy, Daddy, Granny—depending on who was asking. God forbid if one made a mistake and said "Granny" to mother or "Mommy" to grandmother or "Teddy" to father. But I managed. I learned to supply those answers that were expected of me. Afterward, a treat awaited me, usually in the form of sweets. Later, much later, punishment awaited me, I didn't know how else to answer, the untruthful "you" became as much a part of me as my own skin.

At home, I often heard that one learns from one's mistakes. That you have to get burned to remember, as if remembering was directly connected to temperature. Teddy was an old dog; in my eyes she was an absolute beauty. That's the Teddy I committed to memory. Recently, I helped my mother to go through some old things. In an old shoebox we found a few dozen photographs. One depicts a small smiling kid, and a dog is licking his face. The kid is me. So says my mother. The dog, ugly and skinny, twisted like the boughs of an old walnut, is Teddy. So says my mother. I remember Teddy differently, I don't remember myself at all. I believe my mother.

My old mother sleeps little, she moves with difficulty, but she remembers so much, she remembers for me. My old mother resembles an external memory, a flash drive. All you need to do is connect her to an old yellowed photograph, and her brain begins to show illustrations of the past. She speaks in short sentences, loses her train of thought, goes off topic and off that topic, too. My old mother rarely makes tomato soup, rarely leaves the house, and if she does, it's most readily on a trip to the pharmacy. "They have nice pharmacists there," she claims. I believe her. I believe my mother.

Seventh, there are questions that I return to. The more steps are left behind me, the fewer years that await me, the more frequently I return to those questions to which I cannot find a satisfactory answer. For instance: Did my parents love me? The answer is larger than a city, it has so many roads which change and entwine, crossroads that I've passed and which appear again, unscathed by a step. Until I finished high school, I had no time or reason to wonder about this matter. I told myself that they loved me the only way they knew how. The way they knew, they loved.

Seventh, there are questions that I return to. During my university years I lived, as I remember, more slowly. I studied little, I thought too much, or rather—I lay around. I would have done better, according to my father, had I studied more, and thought (lay around) less. My father was probably right. He never thought much, and despite this he still built a house, produced sons, lived to see his pension and a set of diseases. "An ordinary life," my father used to say. "A good life is an ordinary life," he said. I believe him.

"I'm tired, let's have tea, I need to take my pills," said my mother. We sat on the couch. The couch, younger than my mother, was living out its final years under our bodies. My mother didn't want to throw it out. She couldn't explain her loyalty to the piece of furniture. She would end any discussion about it with a cutting, "You should all just leave it alone." I looked around the room, searching for someone, who, perhaps even if it were someone in a photo on the wall, might explain her use of the plural.

I boiled the water and dropped a bag of green tea into the teapot. My mother believes in the power of green tea. Green tea is in third place, right after tomato soup with noodles and tomato soup with rice. I don't like green tea. The soup satisfied my desire for healthy foods perfectly. I would return from school and ask my younger brother what was for dinner. He answered twice a week: "O-D-M-S-D." Our Darling Mother's Special Dish.

For myself, I made decaf, also healthy, in the top ten of my mother's list, above Pharmaton Vitality pills and lecithin. On a rectangle yellowed with age and with a frayed edge stands a kid ("That's you," whispers my mother's memory), and an old and ugly dog is licking the kid's face ("That's Teddy, that dog, don't you remember?"). In a moment my mother will tell the story that I've heard so many times I can almost remember the events myself.

We lived in the country back then, in a wooden house left behind by my father's parents. My grandparents, with their younger son (my father was their elder one), lived in the house next door—the new one, made of bricks. This new house, large and rich, was the thorn in my mother's side; it got stuck under her skin and even tears of helplessness did nothing to weaken the foundations; it stood firm and refused to vanish overnight. My parents commuted to work to the nearby town, a few dozen kilometers away, usually on their bicycles, because the buses often broke down, and the drivers were drunks, which had a direct effect on the frequency with which the buses appeared, not to mention how punctually they did so. "It was Saturday," my mother says, and in a moment she will hesitate, asking herself: "Or was it Sunday?"

"It was Saturday. Or was it Sunday after all?" asks my worried mother. "Sunday, Mom," I say, even though I don't remember. I say it to make her feel less lonely. "Sunday," she decides, calmer now. "Your father was helping out in the fields, and I . . ." she falls silent. Something is wrong. Nobody worked out in the fields on Sundays. I'd forgotten. My mother ponders, raises the teacup to her mouth with a trembling hand. Something is wrong. I can see how her forehead wrinkles in an attempt to pinpoint the mistake which makes the whole story impossible before it even really begins. "Saturday, Mom," I say. She smiles. "Yes, son. Of course. It was Saturday."

Seventh, there are questions that I return to. These questions resemble places. I cannot give the answers, but I can say a bit about the questions. Questions-places. The places of my childhood and my youth, the houses I had lived in, the schools I had attended, weren't built with bricks, but letters. I combine these letters into words, I take apart the words into letters and—I think—I give the wrong answer. Instead of a cork, cap, instead of a cap—cork.

"Saturday," my mother repeats over and over, as if to convince herself. Father helped out in the fields, she cleaned and did the laundry, catching up on all the chores she had no time for during the week. And in the background my tiny brother, sickly and moody, burst into tears every so often. "Because he was so sickly and always cried," my mother says with honest regret, with, awoken from the past, chronic sleep deprivation. "But now he's healthy and never cries, and never visits," I have to bite my tongue to keep the words inside my mouth. I don't want to argue. We are, after all, sitting on a couch in a room where I'm merely a guest.

Then follows the part about her mother-in-law. My mother lights up with a new energy. She hated her mother-in-law as much as I loved my grandmother. It's hard to believe that her mother-in-law and my grandmother were the same person. We remember her so differently. Sometimes, rarely, my grandmother overlaps with mother's mother-in-law. In small events, in details, for a short while they become the same elderly woman. "You don't know, she never helped us, just took for herself, always for herself," says my mother, shaking her head. I don't know if this gesture is intended to disagree with her own words, or with the reality she had experienced. I don't know.

"If she hadn't always been taking everything," my mother continues quietly, "your father would still be alive." I've heard this accusation multiple times. I used to answer that if my father knew his own mind better, or even had better health, he would still be alive. This or a similar answer drove my mother into a rage, possibly tears. That's why I now say nothing, or I say: "Yes, Mom." My "yes" calms her down. Just another sip of green tea and she'll pick up the main story, about Teddy. The main story, which for my mother is a digression from her main story about her war with her mother-in-law.

"You could walk already. And I cleaned the house and did the laundry, chased your brother to bed, because he was always crying, and then I made the food and carried water from the well, because your father was out helping in the fields, and everything was for me to do, and you with legs, because you could walk already. My mother-in-law never helped, but your grandfather was a good man. He took you and watched you, an hour or two at a time. He was sick then and smoked one cigarette after the other. It was the cigarettes that were the death of him. I'm telling you, quit smoking, or they'll kill you too. They killed your grandfather, but my mother-in-law killed him first. She had health. She could smoke and smoke. But she didn't smoke. Out of cunning."

Eighth, I learned how not to listen. If I'm not all that interested in what my conversationalist has to say, I zone out, my thoughts run away with me to things trivial and unimportant: what will I eat this evening, have I bought cigarettes, once more I forgot to call . . . I don't listen, but my body does, in my stead. It has learned to chisel my facial muscles into a mask of an interested listener. It has learned to nod, and—I have recently realized—it has even learned to ask short questions. Soon, perhaps, it might learn the art of remembering the answers.

I think about the weather, a wet autumn, dark and cold. About the car, which needs to have its oil indicator changed. About the shrimp I no longer like the taste of. About the workers who never finished the new fence.

"So grandfather was supposed to be watching you, but he was sick. And he didn't watch closely enough. We were looking for you everywhere. Even your grandmother was looking. She couldn't find a plausible excuse to not look. We looked for an hour. We even checked the well, to see if you hadn't fallen down it. I cried, even more than your tiny brother. Because how could you have disappeared without a trace?"

I think about the weather, the autumn without light, sodden with dampness. From the window, two walnuts are visible. Most of their leaves have fallen and now lie beneath them, rotting. They will not be gathered and burned. There is nobody to do the job. My father is gone. My brother's not here. My mother's too weak. And myself? I'm no good.

"And we looked for you. We looked and despaired. Your grandfather finally said to let Teddy off the chain, to have her look too. Teddy stood in front of the doghouse and wagged her tail. And that was when I realized. I looked inside the doghouse, and there you were. Thank God. Your grandmother barely looked for you. She went to milk the cows. That's what she was like."

Two walnuts are visible from the window. Small remnants of leaves in places cling to the boughs. Sometimes, in summer, there's so much light in the air, as if the air itself were a sheet of glass with blinding lines, zigzags, ellipses. Now I'm looking at the opposite of summer, at the two walnuts, almost bare. The air is a sheet of glass, dirty glass. Besides, the pane I am looking through is dirty. My mother hasn't the strength to clean the windows. In this unkempt, unclear air one sees black outlines, zigzags and forking lines; the boughs of the almost bare walnut. I look at the tree's crown, but I see my mother's head, remnants of hair clinging to the skin. Skin with protruding veins, with round chocolate liver spots. My mother's skull looks as if it were decorated for a final ball. Covered in brown confetti and ugly sequins, which construct the outline of the final map, an incomprehensible record. "Mom," I say, "those walnuts need to be cut down."

PORCH

NINTH, I BELIEVE I SHOULD dig out all my memories from the past. I don't believe in psychoanalysis, psychology, psychiatry. From studies of humans, I believe only in a marginalized specialty—pharmacology. I have taken the advice of psychoanalysts, psychologists, and psychiatrists, but the true relief, short-lived and heavy as exhaustion, was given to me only by pharmacology. Mainly pills and tablets. There were months counted with the rhythm of colorful constellations on my palm, which I threw into my mouth and swallowed with water. Constellations of pills of different shapes: perfectly round, flattened like coins, elongated; of varying size: no larger than the head of a pin, than a bean; of varying color: the whites dominated, alongside reds and blues. I have never met with gray pills, as if gray pills hadn't the power to color a life. These multicolored galaxies of medications should dissolve in my stomach, give a healthy color to my body, my thoughts, my life.

Ninth, I believe I should dig out all my memories from the past. I believe that I need to name and organize past events. There is no other prescription that comes to mind, this is the final one in the prescription pad.

Fifth, I learned that you can simultaneously love more than one being. My first loves—my grandmother and Teddy—were not my only ones. I had, it seems, a certain predisposition to love. Iwona, three years older than me, lived six houses down, on the other side of the only road that ran through the village. Oleg, younger by a year, came to his grandmother's every summer and lived a field and two houses down, on the same side of the only road in the village.

I help my mother unpack the bags. We went shopping to

Tesco. I hate supermarkets: the kilometers to walk between the shelves, the lines to the till, the barcodes that refuse to scan. And the people, too many people, like at a football match. I hate supermarkets.

I unpack the plastic bags: a variety of cans, cartons, tubs, bottles, and jars. My mother doesn't eat much, she never has guests. Who, then, will eat all this? Who will rub the tubs of all these creams into their skin? Who will use up all the soap? Use up the boxes of detergent? "A friend said," says my mother, putting something on a shelf with her back to me, "that my hair will fall out."

I'm helpless against my parents. I'm forty years old, but I'm as helpless as a child. I stand with a can of decaf in my hand. I'm afraid to set it down on the table. It's absurd, this fear, I know. Decaf is really healthy, in the top ten of my mother's ranking, a can of coffee will not kill anyone. "I don't have much anyway," my mother says. The phone rings, and I free myself from the can. My mother runs to the living room. "It must be your brother," she shouts.

Iwona left behind a scar on my left knee. Iwona had dark hair and was the best of the boys at climbing trees. I didn't distinguish at the time between boys and girls. I think I sensed that the world was divided between those who were flat and hairy at the front and those who carried breasts. But this was a division above my line of vision: I was barely tall enough to reach my father's waist. In my world, everyone was the same. We were called children, in a calm voice, because raised voices used different words—brats, for instance.

I don't remember many of my toys. My mother remembers them all. She remembers how much they cost, where they'd been bought, what happened to them afterward. She has in her head a list of my brother's toys, mine, her godchildren's and grandson's. It's enough to say, "Mom, your godson Paweł, Christmas '89," and she'll find in her memories the price tag attached to the toy she'd purchased. She remembers so many details, and forgets to turn off the stove.

She returns with a smile, I know, because I looked at her out of the corner of my eye. That smile is meant for me, to cheer me up. That smile means: everything is all right. But that smile is as transparent as her skin, with the bones of her jaw and teeth visible through it. I don't need to ask who called. I cringe, because my mother's smile says: it wasn't your brother, but I'm doing fine.

I don't need to ask my mother about my first bike. I remember. Not the details, color, number of wheels (three, four?). I really liked that bike. Once, on a summer day, as a joke or out of envy, Iwona asked if she could sit on it for a moment and check the seat. "It's probably uncomfortable," she said, so I let her, and she started to cycle away. I ran after her. After her and the bike. She was much faster. I tripped over a stone and fell. I cut my knee deeply. I looked with surprise at the crimson which covered my calf and sandal. I don't remember whether or not it hurt. I remember that I started crying hysterically. Because something really did hurt; the first lie and betrayal, or perhaps it was the knee, I'm not sure. Iwona turned back. She dismounted and offered her hand to help me get up. We looked at each other like adults, her—willowy, dry, and clean; and myself—covered in tears, snot, and blood. I didn't take her hand.

"Why did you buy the shrimp?" I ask my mother, to keep up the conversation in the kitchen. In reality, there's nothing to keep up, for fifteen minutes now a word hasn't been said among the rustle of the plastic shopping bags. The fake heroic smile left my mother's face. She's focused on unpacking the food. "For you, son, you like shrimp." "Mom, I used to. That was ten years ago."

The bike stood beside me. I watched Iwona walk away, still covered in tears, snot, and blood. I felt humiliated. Of course, I didn't know this word at the time, the word "cap" was the highest level my vocabulary had reached (or "cork"), but that's exactly how I felt: humiliated. And in pain. I'd never thought that you can get as drunk as a lord on something other than booze. That you can, willingly, humiliate yourself, day by day.

"If you don't want them, I'll give them to Cesar," says my mother. Cesar is her dog, a calm German shepherd. He died two months ago, I took the body to be cremated myself. I don't know how to answer her. Sentences crop up that reveal the holes in the world. Sentences that don't relate to the present, or rather, don't relate to this present shared with others. "I'm going out onto the porch for a smoke," I say. I'm hoping she will start talking to herself and forget about the dog. She'll forget that she forgot that the dog is dead. Has been, for two months.

Fortieth, I shouldn't smoke so much. I throw on a jacket, but I'm getting cold anyway. The porch isn't big, but full of glass windows. In many places the insulation has been worn away and the panes tremble when there's a stronger breeze, they chatter from the cold like teeth. They haven't fallen out yet, probably because of the habit of keeping their place, or because of the dirt. My mother fought dirt for her whole life, obsessively washing, sweeping, dusting, polishing everything. There is no such verb or activity that's unknown to my mother if it might be of any use against her war with dirtiness. The dirt on the porch spoke more loudly than the failing memory of my mother's degeneration. She manages to keep things clean in the house, but the mess and dirt shine through the hygienic cocoon she has been trying to build her whole life.

The cigarette smoke irritates my throat. I smoke about two packs a day. Forty cigarettes. I shouldn't smoke so much since I've turned forty. I kill my body forty times a day, though it doesn't seem to feel it—from time to time, a stab of pain in the heart, perhaps. I light another cigarette off the last one. The sandy, worn welcome mat has insect corpses rolling around on it, almost like figure skating, where the figures are chosen by the wind. It's twenty years now that I've been sitting on the porch to smoke, looking through the windows at the driveway, garden, or road. Twenty years ago the windows were insulated properly, the welcome mat was brand new, my father could be seen in the garden while my mother was in the kitchen. I didn't sit on the chair, as I do now, usually I stood or paced. If there is anything that links these past twenty years—apart from the cigarettes— then it's my seventh.

Seventh, there are questions that I return to. I don't know how many of these questions there are, I've never counted them. Too many—this probably isn't a mathematical analysis. For instance, this question: what am I doing here? I've been asking myself this for twenty years, smoking one cigarette after another. So many answers! Put simply: I smoke, visit my parents before my finals, I see the optician, I bring something with me from Warsaw that my mother asked for, it's my father's birthday, I need to return some money. A river of shallow, surface answers that flows to the garbage heap. What, then, am I doing here? Sometimes, months would go by during which I didn't see my parents, but I always returned eventually. What am I doing here? Perhaps, simply, I just am. But am I here because I can't live without my parents while they live?

The doors squeak. "Don't sit out on the porch too long, you'll get a cold," says my mother. I put out the third cigarette. I had just lit it; it would have lasted another five minutes. My mother shakes her head disapprovingly. "You should have finished. It doesn't matter what kills you, the cigarettes or a cold," she jokes, now she only allows herself jokes of this sort, dry and deadly serious.

Iwona left behind a scar on my left knee. Oleg didn't leave me anything. At most, some sunny, shape-shifting mark on my memory. Oleg was Belarusian, he lived near Grodno, he came to see his grandmother every summer for a month or two. And we spent this month or two together for three or four years. I don't remember much, we spoke a lot in a strange language, our own, inaccessible to others. I forgot that stretch of time, the part where our childhood lies, the rules of that love and friendship. I suspect we created our language based on our knowledge of Polish, Russian, Belarusian, and *trasianka*. And lone German words. The Second World War left not only buried explosives, but also foreign phrases sown in the memories of our grandfathers. These macaronic phrases attracted us in a special way, fascinated us more than any shells we might dig out from under the moss in the woods. These relics of times not so long gone exploded against the roofs of our mouths. I don't remember what meanings we attributed to them, but I know they were the most important words, defining our relationship and the whole world.

Near the river grew a wild pear, the only one in the field. The field, regularly trimmed by cow tongues, resembled a purple freckly face because the cow tongues avoided the purple flowers on their long, leafless stalks. The pear gave birth to tiny, tart, and unhomely fruit. "Unhomely" is probably the only word that has remained with me from those years, it indicated an object more frequently than it did an individual. For instance, Oleg's aunt was "unhomely." The boughs of the pear composed themselves into something of a bed, into which it wasn't difficult to climb. We lay beside each other and talked or just lay there, eavesdropping on the conversations of others: insects, cows, the river, leaves. The old pear turned out to be the most homely place in an unhomely world. Until, one summer, Oleg didn't arrive. I don't remember that summer, I don't remember my disappointment or surprise. I suspect I felt something, but I don't remember.

Seventh, there are questions that I return to. For instance, this question: what am I doing here? Maybe I'm waiting for my mother to die? I imagine her death, I can visualize her funeral, but my imagination goes no further. No matter how much I try, I cannot imagine what might happen after the funeral. Even the conversation with my brother that we have always "left for another time." We have a lot to accuse each other of, which is why I once left this conversation for "another time." And so it stayed.

It would be good to talk soon, to give us all time to tie up loose ends. I won't call. The very thought of the conversation makes a knot of my stomach, until I hunch over and put my open palm on my torso, trying to massage the pain away. My left hand hits the table and a pile of old newspapers falls to the floor. This porch, surrounded by glass on three sides, has something in it of the unhomeliness of an aquarium. "I'll be back in a minute," I tell the closed door.

NEWSPAPERS

Tenth, I'm addicted to newspapers. I like newspapers in all paper forms. I like the internet too, but I hate internet editions of newspapers. I cannot imagine a morning without coffee, a cigarette, and a paper in my hand. I mean, I can imagine it: the yard of hell, a cold porch in purgatory. I like newspapers because they draw you away from all that's important and permanent. Newspapers are out of date before I even buy them in the corner shop. They tell you about the world of the past. That's why I find newspapers touching; I'm touched by the belated hurry, the outdated time of the present, and even—if I'm having an off day—the poor quality paper. Turning the pages, I'm unable to get rid of the sense of affection; here I am touching the world, my finger tracing the tsunami columns, my finger leaving a colorful smudge on the politician's photo, the coffee stain alters one of the Baltic borders or destroys a stupid sentence—depending on what it is I'm reading, and how clumsy I am when I move my coffee cup.

I arrived two months ago. I left the comfortable flat in the old, renewed building in Stary Mokotów, I got into the comfortable car and came to the large, empty house that my mother lives in. I hadn't seen her in a few months, probably not since Christmas. I spent Easter in Spain with some friends, and then I was busy with work. Although this was only a few months ago, I can't remember what it was that took up so much of my time. Was I writing for the Teatr Współczesny, an adaptation of John Banville's *The Sea*? Was I editing a crime novel of mediocre quality and high outlay for some publisher in Kraków, which is now of slightly better quality and lower outlay? Was I a judge in some festival? Probably, I was busy with all of that, I don't remember.

During those months, dried up and empty like a snake-skin, I pretended I had time for nothing else, and it (pretending) was made easier by my efforts to keep my timetable from allowing even such distractions as coffee with friends. During those months my mother called twice, I remember. I remember, because for the twenty-two years of my separate, more or less independent life, my mother called only rarely. She called about specific things, no sentimental stuff, no "Why do you never call?", no "I miss you," nor "Come home," no indication that she'd broken her leg. Our relationship was businesslike, proper and limited to purely professional issues; renewing my grandparents' tombstone, a new boiler, a cousin's wedding, insurance payments. I took up the position of the responsible, though elusive, son, and she the position of senior manager in an institution known as Mother's Partnership.

The first phone call caught me right before a movie. I couldn't talk, I asked if it was anything important, she said it wasn't, I said I'd call her back, then I turned off my phone and watched the movie; today, I don't even remember the title, though this was only a few months ago. "I can't talk," I said. This wasn't true: I could have walked into the hall and given her a few minutes, at most I would have lost an ad or two. I preferred the lie: "I can't talk." I didn't call back. If it wasn't anything important, I repeated to myself, I won't call. I won't waste any energy on unnecessary conversations. I really did think that.

The second phone call, about a month later, I picked up in the car. Part one of the conversation: my question of "Are you all right?" For twenty-two years now the answer is invariably: "Yes." I'm more used to this response than I am to my morning coffee; I think if she said "No," I wouldn't understand, or notice, or hear. Part two of the conversation: her question of "What's the weather?" and my reply, encompassing a range of linguistic and meteorological phrases, never exceeding fifteen words; it's happened that I told her it was snowing and only later realized that I was in Morocco; I didn't mean to lie to my mother, I just didn't pay attention to what I was saying. Part three of the conversation: I tell her in a few sentences about how busy I am;

part three lays the groundwork for part four. Part four of the conversation: my question of "What's new with you?", which should be understood as a command for her to immediately get to the point, because (see part three) I have no time. Part five of the conversation: a concise piece of information from my mother about whatever it was that forced her to make the call, although my mother understands that (see part three) I have no time. Final part: a solution to the problem and—consequently—dissolution of the conversation.

Once I told my coworkers at the theater, as an anecdote, what parts comprise my conversation with my mother. After a few months, I heard one of the makeup artists say to an actress, "Mr. Part Three is here."

The second phone call, about a month later, I picked up in the car. The conversation ran smoothly and without surprises until, and including, part three. "What's new with you?" I ask. My mother replies, "Cesar died." Part six: "Mom," I say, "I'm really sorry to hear that, but what can I do about it? I'm in Warsaw, I'm working, call someone who can take the body to be burned. Really, I won't be driving two hundred kilometers just to do that myself. I can't talk anymore, I'm driving, I'll end up paying a fine for talking to you. Just do as I say, all right? Bye then."

Eleventh, I hate phones and phone calls. I have a deep dislike of phones. A few years ago my therapist, a waste of time and money, joked inelegantly that when I was young I must have been raped with my first cell phone. Or something along those lines, I don't remember. Until this day I'm not really sure what he meant. That when I was younger nobody even imagined such a thing as a cell phone could exist? Or perhaps something else? Some joke on the level of the first cell from which I developed? I don't know. Clearly, our sense of humor was incompatible, and that's why he couldn't help me.

Seventh, did my parents love me? Twenty-two years of contact through phones has not brought me any closer to an answer. Maybe I wanted to hear some "love you" or "miss you"? Maybe I wanted to hear it, but I could have said it myself.

I don't remember where I was driving or what I was doing

that day when my mother called the second time. Instinctively I felt something bad had happened. Perhaps I talked to her for so short a time because conversations with her were always painful, in not a very obvious way. Painful because limited to purely practical matters, maybe. I don't know. I know that however one might describe these conversations, I'm equally responsible for them. Equal responsibility sounds hilarious, but nobody would understand this hilarity, and definitely not my therapist. Equal responsibility, so equal risk. My mother risked absolute loneliness, myself—a nervous breakdown. Equal responsibility and equal risk. Hilarious.

I returned to the flat in the evening, tired and restless. I drank a glass of whiskey. The alcohol failed to have a calming effect. I drank a second glass. It reaped no results. I tried to keep myself busy with something, but I couldn't focus on anything. That's when I listened to my voice mail. I never pick up the landline, but I pay for it anyway, out of habit, and once a week I listen to my voice mail. "Hi, son, it's me, Mom," my mother clears her throat, searches for words. "You're out, I just wanted to say that Cesar died. Goodnight then. Goodnight."

The restlessness and worry plaguing me the last few hours, since talking to my mother, intensified as a consequence of both the message and the alcohol. I sat at my desk in a comfortable armchair, with the third glass of whiskey in my hand, and I stared at the phone. I had to unbutton the collar of my shirt. I remembered simultaneously a number of things. My mother's first phone call, from a month ago, that I never returned because she had nothing important to tell me.

I repeated this out loud. "No, son, nothing important." I think I'm drunk. For twenty-two years, and she never called without a reason. And if she called without a reason for the first time in twenty-two years, then she must have had a reason that I just failed to hear.

How old is my mother? I counted: sixty-five. How many years has she got left? That I couldn't count. How often do we see each other? I couldn't count, I kept making mistakes, it turned out that a hand has too many fingers. How often? Once a year, perhaps twice. How many square meters in the house in which she lives? One hundred and ninety. How many people live on one hundred and ninety square meters? How many? One.

This emotional mathematics was painful, these exercises in the geometry of feelings. Years, meters, meetings, people. Like an equation that's difficult to solve. Like a painful result that's difficult to accept.

Suddenly, I understood that which I'd always known. My mother has been absolutely alone for the past five years. Doing nothing. She lasted five years. Cesar died.

I sat at my desk in a comfortable armchair, with the third glass of whiskey in my hand, and I stared at the phone. I pressed the button. "Hi, son, it's me, Mom," my mother clears her throat, searches for words. "You're out, I just wanted to say that Cesar died. Goodnight then. Goodnight." I pressed the button. "Hi, son, it's me, Mom," my mother clears her throat, searches for words. "You're out, I just wanted to say that Cesar died. Goodnight then. Goodnight." I think I got drunk. I listened to the message many times. Tears ran down my cheeks. This was the only way I knew how to cry: silently. I could be simultaneously crying and talking on the phone. Nobody would know that I was crying. Even I find it hard to believe in these tears. "Hi, son, it's me, Mom," my mother clears her throat, searches for words. "You're out, I just wanted to say that Cesar died. Goodnight then. Goodnight."

I erased the message. That's when I heard the date and time when it was recorded. I checked if the date and time were set correctly. They were; a four minute difference between that and my cell. I didn't manage to move the armchair away from the desk. I threw up.

I shoved my head under a stream of cold water in the bathroom. It sobered me up within moments. I'd sobered up two minutes previously, at my desk. My mother had left the message two days ago.

I didn't want to get into the car straight away. I shaved, my hands trembling slightly. I took a long bath. I waited until the water cooled off and took away the unnecessary degrees from my body. I had hunched over from the cold, which is why drying myself off took almost fifteen minutes.

I examined my face and body carefully in the mirror. I didn't rush; I'd lost so many years that I could let myself not rush now.

My body was in not at all a bad shape and form for a forty-year-old. A bit of fat on my stomach; I worked hard on it, breaking through the stubbornness of my metabolism which insisted on burning all the fat and leaving me with nothing for winter. That little bit of a belly is the only cuddly part of my body; the rest isn't cuddly.

My face, a smooth mask of expensive creams, looks younger than might seem from my birth certificate. One needs to look carefully to notice the tiredness and destruction, but it's only a matter of a trained eye.

Then, I got dressed. It was after two in the morning. I packed a large suitcase. I cleaned up my vomit. My mother loves sweet things, or at least she loved them when we still knew each other. I remembered the chocolates that I had brought back from Brussels with me the previous week. They should make her happy.

I was ready to leave by four. Sober, though tired. At this time, the journey from Warsaw to Białystok should take two hours, at most. Risking stomach cramps, I drank a strong espresso. I waited another fifteen minutes. Nothing was happening. At four forty-five, I was sitting behind the wheel. Twenty past seven, I parked the car in front of my mother's house.

The metal wing of the gate had been pulled down, looking like a wounded bird, I had to struggle to lift it. I left the gate open. I didn't want to fight the uneven hinges. It was a good thing I hadn't forgotten the keys my mother had given me two years previously, "just in case." I realized what she'd meant, saying drily "just in case." Not a situation like today, an unannounced visit had not been taken into consideration at the time. The "just in case" was meant in the final case, the last instance.

Two, no, three days had passed since my mother left the voice mail, since Cesar died, if she called without waiting first. After so many days, the corpse should be decomposing, smelling. But

I couldn't smell anything. My sense of smell is not the most sensitive. How I describe my sense of smell is also the best way to describe myself.

I couldn't turn the key. I always get the directions mixed up. Which way to lock, which to unlock. I mix right and left to the extent that I don't know which political parties are on which side of the Center. I mix them up to the extent that if the hands on a watch started moving counterclockwise, I wouldn't notice. Really, I wouldn't notice; perhaps I'd just be a bit happier. That's why I don't use the watches that have hands. They give me no power over the hours. That's why I use digital watches. Time is less complicated, it doesn't flow with no direction, it just jumps from one number to the next.

The air on the porch is musty, damp, like it would be above a still and old body of water. I wonder if my mother's asleep. I don't know her routine. I don't know that much about her. I haven't slept all night, exhaustion sticks my lids together in a pleasant way, so different from the stickiness caused by pills.

I walk along the long corridor to the kitchen, I take out a carton of milk from the almost empty fridge. I pour it into a glass. Milk with bits, gone off. I don't call "Mom." Perhaps she really is asleep. I go into the sitting room. I'll wait.

I notice my mother. She sits in an armchair, motionless. She doesn't realize I'm there. I didn't announce my arrival, so I haven't arrived. I stare at my mother, or rather at a strange woman, fat, who resembles my mother. I haven't seen her in nine months. She's changed a lot. Or maybe I'm the one who's changed?

I stand in the door. My mother is staring at something. I follow the line of her gaze like a tightrope walker who's afraid of what he might find at the end of the rope. It's a good thing I'm really tired. Thanks to that, all I notice at the end of the line is an object, just an object. My mother is staring at the phone.

"Mom," I say. "I've come." She doesn't react. Maybe during the last empty years she's heard such noises often. She'd turn her head in hope and find it dashed against the empty wall of the room? Maybe she doesn't believe in such words anymore. She awaits a specific sound—the ring of the telephone. That sound has never let her down. For five years, it hasn't been heard in this house.

"Hi, I'm sorry I didn't call," I say loudly, too loudly. My mother rips her eyes away from the phone. She smiles at me, but she's taken aback. The surprise doesn't let her find the right words. Any words. That's why I help her and, walking closer to the chair, I come up with a story about a meeting at the university, that I couldn't really say no, so I came because we haven't seen each other in a while—something along those lines. Something along such slightly absurd and nonsensical lines.

I lean down to kiss her cheeks, she has such dry skin, smooth, smells nice—I make a mental note—which means she still looks after herself. She leans on my arm and gets up, with difficulty. I keep talking, I don't stop, out of fear that my mother might decide to be honest and explain what she'd just been doing. For instance, that for years now she'd been willing the telephone to ring.

We go to the kitchen. "You're probably hungry, son." "I ate on the way, in a bar," I lie. "Good, because I didn't know you were coming, I didn't do any shopping."

"I'd love some coffee," I say. "What time is your meeting?" she asks. What meeting? Oh, right, the university. I lie that it's probably the day after tomorrow. "That's Sunday," says my mother.

We take the coffee into the living room. We talk about nothing, with fragmented phrases, words without a context, among the used up furniture. Eventually, I ask what happened to Cesar's body. My mother seems awkward, embarrassed, as if caught *in flagranti*. *In flagranti* with death.

She remains silent for a while, clearly flustered. "I didn't want . . . I dragged the body out into the garden, under the chestnut. I wanted to dig a grave, but something cracked in my hip. When I was pulling Cesar. He's probably still lying there . . ."

"Did you see a doctor?" I ask, in the voice of a worried and responsible son. How easily I switched to this official tone: here is the daughter-business (or son-business, really) calling mother-business, please take care of yourself and attend a medical examination immediately. "No," she replies. "I called, but you know how it is with public healthcare, they told me to wait two months."

"You could have gone privately," I say, slightly irritated. I try to stay calm, but it's difficult to break a habit that's lasted years in just a few minutes. My mother makes a face: "For private appointments you have to pay."

I feel all the blood rush into my head. My ears burn, as if just rubbed with snow. It never even occurred to me that she might not have the money. Once a year I asked if she needed any, but she always said no. Well, she always said that I needed the money more than her, and I interpreted that to suit me best. I guess that makes me a pretty poor interpreter.

Again, math. My mother's pension, how much can that be? One thousand złotych? Less? And the expenses of the house? Heating? How much is that? The fridge is almost empty, I'm remembering now a few cheap cans of pâté and sausages.

We're silent. "I'm going to the toilet," I say. I sit on the toilet seat and stare at the little shelf. A bitter contrast. The shelf holds expensive perfumes and lotions that I'd bought her myself for birthdays or Christmases, the shelves in the fridge hold only the cheapest pâté and sausages made of ground up bones, dyed pink.

Seventh, there are questions that I return to. For instance: how could this have happened? Are my observation skills lacking? My inability to converse? My self-involvement? I don't know. I have failed the empathy exam many times. I was only ever able to empathize with myself, and only a little.

I flush the toilet and wash my hands. A new bar of soap, "Olive," probably the cheapest in the shop. The towel is clean, hard, and used like a dishcloth.

I convince my mother to take a walk to the shop. We leave. I watch her close the porch door. I know this ritual. The grinding sound of the lock, the hand pressing down on the door handle twice, walking down a step, a twist and another checking of the door handle. "It's closed, we can go," she says.

To my surprise, she doesn't head in the direction of the gate, but to the back of the garden. Maybe she wants to show me the spot where Cesar is rotting? But no, she follows a path she probably made herself through the grass and to the fence, she stops at the place where two of the rails are missing, leans down and squeezes through. I follow her, not understanding anything. Has my mother gone crazy from loneliness? Once on the pavement, I can't keep silent any longer and I ask her why she doesn't use the gate. People usually use the gate.

"The gate doesn't work," she says. "I don't have the strength to go pulling on it. This is easier."

I don't answer. Our conversations were often like this. One of us would say something, the other doesn't pursue the topic further.

In the shop, my mother automatically reaches for the cheapest items, but a moment later, maybe because of me there, she picks some of the nicer ones. "I'm buying today," I say. My mother used to love to do the shopping. I throw loads of things into the cart, and my mother gradually lightens up and more boldly picks the things she wants, not looking at the price. She's as happy as a girl.

Even with my mother's help, I wouldn't be able to carry all the bags home. We took a cab back, even though it was barely a fifteen-minute walk. At the sight of the open gate, my mother jokes: "Isn't it so difficult to pay me a visit?"

GRAVES

IT TOOK ME A LONG TIME to get used to cemeteries. When I was younger, I couldn't grasp the concept of a cemetery. A cemetery is a sort of city, inhabited by dead people. A city as alien as one can imagine. The negative of a city. I was afraid of cemeteries. I didn't understand that, according to the living, the dead also need some space.

Almost my entire family "lives" in the cemetery in Gródek. That means the dead part of my family. I remember one tombstone from that cemetery. An ordinary tombstone, like many others. What was unusual was the headstone, or more specifically, the writing on it. Although I was a kid, I understood that under the surname two dates were engraved: that of birth and that of death. I also understood that first, one is born, and then, consequently, one dies. I understood that you could count the amount of years someone had lived. Step one: the four numbers of the year of death need to be subtracted from the four numbers of the year of birth. Step two: the two numbers of the month of death need to be subtracted from the two numbers of the month of birth. Step three: the same should be done with the numbers indicating the days.

I learned math at cemeteries. I learned subtraction. It was at cemeteries that I understood the existence of negative numbers. I thought it all very logical. If here lived people who no longer live, then here is also the place of the numbers which are not.

My grandmother took me to the cemetery often. There was always a lot to do by the graves. Flowers were planted, watered, weeds were pulled. The little footpaths were cleaned, benches fixed, headstones washed. There was always something to improve, fix, change. The dead, just like children, were always ruining something. At first I was bored, but then I began taking pen and paper with me. I wrote down dates and played with subtractions. The easy part was always the first step—subtracting years. The second step wasn't so easy. Death in month 02, birth in month 12. I wrote down 02 - 12 =. I stared at the paper as if entranced, not understanding anything, until I got a headache and I started to cry. My grandmother rushed over to see what was wrong. I didn't know how to explain. She bought me an orangeade. Drinking it, I understood, in the first epiphany of my life, that one must switch the numbers around: 12 - 02 = 10. Ten, the number that is not, because I'm at the cemetery. I began to laugh, loudly.

At home my mother, surprised at my interest in math, unusual at my age, or specifically my interest in subtraction, which was awakened in a place where awakening anything or anyone was not usually desirable, patiently explained the workings of years, months, and days. I understood that the ten that was not, had to be borrowed. One had to be taken away from the number of years lived. This saddened me because it seemed too unfair. A negative number of months and such a high interest rate, which took away a year's worth of life!

My mother spent an hour in the bathroom, I worried that she had fainted. Eventually she came out, the smell of creams wafting around her smiling face. I don't know who was the author of this smile: her face, her hand which dragged the lipstick along the skin of her lips, my imagination? I didn't know what to think, which is why all I said was, "You look beautiful," even though she didn't. In recent weeks she'd lost weight, but she still had the same amount of skin as she had before. The skin hung loosely, especially on the cheeks, above her eyelids, under her chin, it hung like dishcloths; unclean, stained with little defects, moles, the threads of single hairs; dishcloths that someone had hung on a skeleton. My mother didn't look beautiful, but her appearance was touching. "Sometimes a lie is better," she responds.

We get into the car. I help her fasten her seat belt. Seat belts save the lives of accident victims, young victims, flexible ones, because the old ones like my mother couldn't reach far back

enough to grasp the belt made of—making the feat that much
more difficult—slippery material.

We don't drive quickly. My mother fears speed. "I'm in no
rush to get to the cemetery," she jokes, trying to tame her fear,
which grows along with the average speed we are driving at. She
jokes because, I know, she would like to find herself as quickly as
possible at the grave of her husband. Contradictory desires and
only one body, such equations cannot be solved.

My grandmother took me to the cemetery often. There was
always so much to do. She cut, watered, weeded, and I wandered
from one grave to the next with pen and paper. I counted the
years lived, the months, and days. I thought my work was so
much more significant than what my grandmother was doing;
as important as the job of a postman; I was also delivering mes-
sages, and from the other side at that.

From one grave to the next, sweating form the effort and with
a bottle of orangeade, I never paused in my algebraic passion.
My work drew me in, all this writing and subtracting, equations,
some linear and some squared, with an equals sign like a tombstone, and—something which caused the hairs on my forearms
to rise up—all the pluses written everywhere. I subtracted some
dates from others, and the homes of the dead, as if just to be
controversial, decorated themselves with plus signs. The vertical
line was definitely too long, but there was the horizontal line
going through it, as if crossing out the excess length of the first.

Now, when I think about it while driving along with a silent
passenger, an old woman who is my mother, I find my interpretation of the Christian cross funny, especially the manner in which
I dealt with the horizontal line, *scabellum pedum*, symbolizing
the fate of the criminals crucified next to Christ; for me it was
only a correction of the mistake made by those who filled the
graves with the wrong signs—plus signs. I turned into the country
road toward the cemetery. I am so amused by this memory that I
cannot hold my laughter in. My mother looks at me and smiles
sardonically: "You always reacted a little oddly when it came to
cemeteries. I was hoping you'd grown out of it, son."

I drag the bag with my mother, full of candles, cloths and

some liquid to clean the stone, and two large flowerpots with white chrysanthemums. My mother, limping slightly—the badly healed bones of her right foot cause her some pain—regains some confidence once we pass through the cemetery gates. At the cemetery she's in her element, she leads unfalteringly along the small footpaths, from one grave to the next, candle after candle, as if following a string, starting with the distant relatives, until finally we reach my father's grave, shining black marble and gold letters, decorated with leaves and twigs from the wild pear that grows nearby. My mother's name and date of birth are also engraved on the tombstone. The only thing missing is her date of death. My mother notices the direction of my gaze. "I could ask for the year to be engraved. You'd just add the month and day," she says.

I place the flowerpots on the bench. I take out a candle from the bag. "I'm going for a walk, I'll be back soon," I say. Leaves rustle underfoot, as if I were walking along a path of snail homes; people don't care for tidiness like they used to. I get a bit lost, the last time I was here was five years ago, for my father's funeral. There it is, the magical grave of my childhood. Now, I can read the names and surname. As a child I dealt well with numbers, both Arabic and Roman numerals, but letters always caused me problems. A lot of work and determination had to be put into deciphering the cork or cap which guarded the entrance into the world of words.

Under the tombstone lie the remains of two women. Mother and daughter. They died the same day. There would be nothing unusual about this if it weren't for the dates. The mother, Lidia Popławska: b. 1937-03-02, d. 1960-07-12. The daughter, beloved Ania, no surname but with the adjective "beloved": b. 1960-10-15, d. 1960-07-12.

This grave fascinated me, it appeared in my dreams, I couldn't stop thinking about it. Mathematics of the highest level, a heavenly equation, a symphony of dimensions. These dates accompanied me my whole life. Even now, having lived for forty years, I feel an almost feverish liveliness, because my material body is standing before a mystery enchanted into stone. I stand before the grave of Ania, beloved Ania, who died first, and then was born.

I told a friend once, a serious and wise theologian, about the unusual dates on this tombstone. He thought about it for a long time, I thought that perhaps he'd fallen asleep, which happened on occasion, but he brightened up suddenly, his eyes lit up with a boyish glee, and he burst out with: "The mistake of creation," following this with laughter.

Twelfth, I feel great at cemeteries, it's a family thing. I inherited this ability from my mother, as she did from her mother, and so on, following the thread to the origins of our genealogy. As I realized from the stories, this ability was typical of the women in the family. My grandparents, my father, and my brother saddened in the presence of graves. But not my mother, or her mother, and this unsociable skill seemed to have only strengthened itself in me.

After forty-five minutes I return to my mother, the autumn chill bitingly reminding me about the presence of my body. My mother hands me the bag with the burned out candles, old flowers, dirty cloths. The grave is cleaned, the final resting place mirroring its surroundings for the last time. My mother's calm face, red from the wind and effort, is relaxed. "You've got everything nicely sorted here," I say. "Nicely," replied my mother, carefully navigating between a bench, the pear trunk, and a tombstone, "though it's a bit of a tight squeeze."

GAMES

Ninth, I believe I should dig out all my memories from the past. I don't believe that the past will miraculously save me. I don't believe we can win this game that we play with ourselves. I know only that it hurts. I got a paper cut yesterday. I cut the skin on my finger with a page from a novel. *Death in Venice*. It's difficult to believe in the southern, golden, transparent death when there is a dirty autumn and two bare walnuts behind the windowpane. Walnuts in Polish have "Italian" in their name; I think the person who named them has a very specific sense of humor, focused on details. I don't know if the Romans worshipped a god who was responsible for details, for the unimportant situations, the makeup artist of events. I don't know, but I felt a malicious kind of satisfaction as I watched my blood drip onto the pages, sticking them together. Paper cuts hurt in a very specific way, on one hand they are rather unobtrusive, somewhere between itching and stinging, somewhere between irritation and unimportance, and on the other hand there is the painful consciousness that something so small and insignificant demands so much attention. Just like the memories of bygone days, insignificant and without a continuation, but organizing subsequent years in a chronological order, as uncomfortable as dental floss. It's difficult to believe in a sunny death when through the window you don't even have stars, or the beach, but just two walnuts. It's difficult to believe in death at all, when a stupid page alone can bring out the exhibitionist tendencies of a body, bleeding in such a touching, meaningless way.

Tenth, I'm addicted to newspapers. Before I learned to read, I mastered the art of using newspapers, probably in the same way as my peers. I was born and raised in Communist times.

35

I'm the child of my parents, obviously, but I'm also a child of deficit. Everything was lacking, from sugar and flour to fridges and washing machines, one had to get in line for anything at all, get tickets to be able to buy anything at all, and the occasional bonus bottle of vinegar. The tickets were made of paper. There was nothing, everything for the tickets, tickets made of paper, that's why there wasn't enough paper, especially toilet paper. Instead of producing toilet paper, people produced newspapers.

Tenth, I'm addicted to newspapers. Before I learned to read, before I put the smudged lines into sentences, I learned to carefully scrunch up the quartered *Tribunal of the People*. I didn't know that the hygienic act stops being a fight against shit, and becomes a fight against the system. Toilet symbolism.

I accompanied my parents on a visit to my godfather once. My godfather exists in my memory not as a person, but as a place. A very specific place, and also one outside of time and deficit. I received a Soviet tank, metal with a red light in a patchy, olive-green camouflage—my mother's memory is a mine of details—but without any batteries, which of course disappointed me as much as anything. I asked where the bathroom was. About fifteen steps from the house. I left, angry at the lack of batteries, though careful to avoid the chained dog that was circling the doghouse, monochromatic and barking.

In the outhouse I found a different world. I couldn't smell the smell of excrement. My sense of smell, stunted and afraid, became subordinate to my eyes. Walls of smooth planks of wood, painted with oil paint, were covered with photos from floor to ceiling. I'd only ever seen anything similar in an Eastern Orthodox church, such occupation of space. On the walls, as in an original comic, pastel figures of the saints in golden aureoles told the Holy Scripture, raising their gazes toward the heavens, where Christ Pantocrator reigned; strangely elongated as if pulled toward heaven, with bodies as flat as the folds of their clothes, they didn't resemble the kind of people I knew. There was also a story told by dozens of colored figures, ranging from white to black through all the shades in between, in all possible positions, though usually depicted in portrait form, in a range of sizes, from small rectangles to calendar-sized illustrations, on paper of varying quality—among the cheap sheets glistened postcards from countries so warm I felt the blood fill my head, making me strip my shirt as well as my trousers (which I'd already done).

And so I stood, naked, underage, flabbergasted. Hundreds of eyes looked through my body, hundreds of nipples and breasts invited me to play a game I learned the rules to—only up to a certain level, let's say the medium one, though perhaps I flatter myself—many years later.

Tenth, I'm addicted to newspapers in all paper forms. I find newspapers touching, even those unread, lying at the publisher's, and those that have degenerated into pieces and now fly around on streets, and the old ones from the basement, soft from dampness and time, and those with desperate covers that make you think the world is ending; apparently colorful *Fakty* and the late *Super Express*, the weekly *Wprost* and defeated *Przekrój*.

I agreed with my mother that we'd go the next day. She didn't want to. Why pay for a private visit when the public health service will find a doctor who will say the same thing, just two months later? Why know tomorrow when you can wait calmly?

I drove her, walked her to the door of the office, went to the waiting room filled with strangers, then walked outside. I sat down on a bench. There was a newspaper sticking out of a bin, rolled up, looking like the pointy end of a Cornetto. I lit a cigarette. I shouldn't smoke so much. What an awful autumn, where water collects in every object, omnipresent dampness, even the lighter flares up only reluctantly. An awful autumn.

The doctor said that the tests would take at least an hour. It was almost ten. I walked through the hospital gates, across the road, and into the coffee shop Hortex. They were only just open, the radio was playing, I took in the interior with regret; a mixture of McDonald's, a waiting room of a three-star hotel, and the display of a suburban jeweler. I ordered a coffee and ashtray. The coffee was rank, but warm. The ashtray arrived after fifteen minutes. What an awful autumn. I put my phone on the table (the doctor promised to call once the tests were finished).

The radio declares breakfast with poetry. I would prefer

scrambled eggs, but "we don't have that," the waiter informed me, so I'm eating with my ears:

> *Little mother in the nest of the chair*
> *Through an entrance of the trunk and sap*
> *You made it to a chair*
> *But so little that the cat sees a mouse*
> *Sooner than he'd see you*
> *And the black seed of the sunflower*
> *Is clearer against the night sky*
> *More clearly whispers of sleep*
> *To the open eyes a drop of the thunderstorm*
> *None of the philosophers suspected*
> *That someone so little could exist*
> *The mathematical equation*
> *Provides more support for those still surprised*
> *Than the invisible twist of your head*
> *To the one who asks for you*

The phone rings, quarter past ten. Eleventh, I hate phones and phone calls. I hesitate between the buttons; green for answer (definitely not), red for ignore, or put the phone on silent. One of my bosses is calling, a director at the Teatr Współczesny, and out of respect to him I just put the phone on silent.

A child is jumping on one leg out on the sidewalk. Hopscotch, I think that's what you call it. I don't remember. Games were never my strong suit, just like my memory. I have so many not strong suits, so many that I feel like a very wide person, stretched out by the ability to burn water (that's what my mother once said; I'd burned the tomato soup) and to find a loophole in everything (also my mother's words), through a lack of any manual skills and sense of responsibility (this was my father's), to "remarkable shortsightedness and cowardice" (a quote from Katarzyna, my first love).

What an awful autumn. The coffee is rank, already cold. The breakfast is not very nutritious, I didn't even hear whose work I was digesting. They don't have any of today's newspapers in the cafe. None of yesterday's, either.

I used to play pick-up sticks with my grandfather. I almost always won. My grandfather didn't have a very steady hand. "Are you shaking so badly because you're worried about moving?" I asked him.

My grandfather spent hours with me, made sandwiches; with butter and honey, with cream and sugar. He also swore horrendously and smoked pipes. Swore and smoked. I also swore plenty when I was a child. That's what my mother remembers. I need to believe her. She's the only source, and almost impossible to check, though her body is being checked out right now so the adequate fix can be made so she can last long enough for another checkup.

"What fucking move?" my grandfather asks. "Into the fucking grave," I reply, surprised at my grandfather's ignorance; the whole family was talking about it.

We also played draughts. I almost always lost. Limb flexibility was not as important as brain flexibility. My grandfather never went easy on me. "When someone is inferior, they fucking lose," he'd say, shoving all his pieces off the board (mine were already off, lying defeated by its side).

Twelfth (number 12.1), my grandfather taught me to think that inferior people lose while superior people win. That one shouldn't go easy on anyone, children or the elderly. There are discounts along the way, for instance. But life refuses to go easy on anyone, the bill has to add up and even out.

My parents played cards, they started late in life, three years before my father died. I caught them at it once in the sitting room. They were sitting at the table, my father with a beer, my mother with a glass of liqueur. They were playing war. My mother was cheating—that is, she was letting my father win. My father's body was losing the game against life, especially on the cardiology front; the central piece (the heart) worked reluctantly, and the net of veins was regularly faulty, which showed in the purply patches across my father's skin where the blood had flown outside of its designated path, like schools of fish whose stomachs glittered. My parents' game of war was strange. For their entire lives they were really at war, day after day, morning until evening; my brother and I couldn't stand this civil war in which we were used as bargaining chips by one or the other side. And now (then) I was looking at my parents in the sitting room, at a war taken into the world of queens, kings, and jacks. What a calm war this was, so full of love. I felt as if I'd caught my parents in an intimate situation. I reddened and left the room.

Twelfth (12.2), my mother showed me, by cheating and letting my father win, that superior people often lose, usually because of themselves. My mother, to be fair, never expected my brother or myself to be the best. Our failures—and there were quite a few—she accepted with understanding and respect, which makes one think that she must have lost more than once in full consciousness of what she was doing.

I order another coffee, though the first remains in its cup almost untouched. I look around my unfamiliar surroundings. We used to come here with Kasia, back in high school. I would invite her for coffee and ice cream. Then we'd go to see the orchestra, which was close by, a five-minute walk, and we'd hold hands, like children. I don't remember what the interior of the cafe looked like twenty years ago (more). I didn't pay attention to the tables then, the chairs and walls. I paid attention to her, she laughed often, and her right eyelid would droop slightly, which made her look rather eerie, but I also found it rather—touching, maybe? Like a tired, beloved teddy bear.

The waiter brings my coffee, he seems irritated. The radio serves second breakfast:

> *The journey divided between horses and people*
> *Then between horses and saddles*
> *Then between people and helms*
> *Then between forelocks, muzzles, and legs*
> *Everything was carefully divided,*
> *It was a well thought-out division*
> *That came about from a lot of confusion*

The phone rings: it's the doctor, we don't speak for long, the results will come in in two days, my mother is waiting for me in the hallway. "On my way," I say.

"I think everything's fine," says my mother. I go into the office to talk to the doctor. It's one of my high school classmates. I don't remember whether we were friends. It doesn't matter today, I paid for his time. Clean-shaven, full face, golden-rimmed glasses, his entire being bursting with optimism, which—if this was his natural state—could inhibit the delivery of bad news. "I don't think there's anything seriously wrong with your mother," he says. I find it difficult to believe him, I don't believe people who are bursting with optimism, but at the same time I want to believe him, because we are talking about my mother.

I remember a joke from a drawn-out show about a patient and doctor. The latter says to the former: "You have cancer." The patient responds angrily: "What do you mean, cancer?! Last week you were saying it was gallstones." The doctor: "Well, yes, stones, and a crab hiding under every one."

I'm remembering this joke about the doctor because I'm at the doctor's. It's because of my imagination; "You have a remarkable imagination," Kasia would say drily. And she'd say so because I associate water with water, perhaps tap water, because I associate games with games, perhaps losing, because I associate death with death, and if I really try I might also think of a cemetery, flowers and skeletons. "That's very original," Kasia would say drily. I would defend myself by saying that my imagination was just shy.

Then I learned to hide the fact that I made such obvious and uninteresting associations. Hiding is a game with very simple rules. And you always win. Someone asks: "What do you think of . . ." and you pick the word that you think fits the situation least. For instance: "What do you think of when I say shoe?" You think about this and dismiss: a hole (in the shoe), a story (seven-mile boots), the Italian Peninsula (shape of a boot), putting effort into something (a goody two-shoes), etc. And then you say multiple sclerosis, for instance.

As a scriptwriter and director at a theater I had to pretend that my imagination was fresh, original, unique. I had to pretend, because people got it into their heads that a scriptwriter and director could be ill or miss deadlines, but under no circumstances might he think the same way that members of the general bread-eating population do. Bread eating makes me think of bread, perhaps also salt, but I'd respond with daisy, for instance.

Then all you have to do is figure out a way to connect these two nouns (they're usually nouns). Bread and daisy: bread fell out of the bag onto a jar that just happened to hold some daisies sold by an old woman. A shoe and multiple sclerosis: I can't get out of my head how difficult putting on a shoe is, with the shoelaces slipping out from between fingers—the disease would start from the feet.

Simple, don't you think? A game easier than war. And, you can cheat. And you always win. And it's gross.

On the way home my mother tells me a joke, probably one she overheard in the waiting room. A patient (elderly and deaf) says to the doctor: "Excuse me, doctor, but did you say that I look like an aristocrat?" Doctor: "No, I said you have prostate cancer."

I laughed to make her happy, my knuckles whitening against the steering wheel; I didn't find it amusing. My mother never told jokes.

GATHERINGS

THERE WASN'T MUCH difficulty in rearranging my few responsibilities. I can work (write, read) in Białystok as well as Warsaw. I'm not tied to a place, just my laptop. The magic phrase of "personal things to take care of" was very useful, it worked like a spell to silence any potential resistance (and curiosity). I forgot that everybody is entitled to a personal life. Still, these calls exhausted me. My mother is in a good mood, preparing dumplings. We don't talk much. We don't know how. We watch TV.

I came over to my mother's a few days ago, we go over the terms of our cohabitation. This process occurs outside of us, outside of words, we are careful, focused. We are professional, methodical, and delicate. My mother is happy that I'm with her, though she doesn't show it. She never was a hysteric.

My mother is aware that I'll stay as long as it takes. Whatever that might mean. On Sunday, she didn't say a word about the meeting at the university; the meeting I had forgotten about. I don't have a good memory, I shouldn't lie. My mother is perfectly aware that I'm here to pay the debt that has been growing for years, especially in the last five years. She's aware that I think so, which is why she's trying so hard to reach a balance, though delicate and brittle, the least embarrassing balance possible.

Our cohabitation over the last few days has been according to the unspoken agreement in which—we both know—it will be difficult to have ends meet. Me: I want to be a good son, to understand exactly why I'm the person that I am, and not a parallel version of myself, I want to enter again the city in which I grew up, with the knowledge that one doesn't go into the same river twice. My mother: she wants to hear somebody's voice, she wants confirmation that her earlier decisions had not been mistakes, not fully, she wants to help herself, but also me—in some atavistic move, a paroxysm of motherhood and knotted genes.

My friends, I had real friends, bought a hovel in Myscowa, in the Lower Beskids. We spent our summers there together. There was a masonry heater in the kitchen, awaiting a stove fitter, and every evening when Zuza lit the fire, smoke emerged from every crack. In the kitchen there was a large table that organized the space and, along with the heater, our summer life. There were also two windows, two doors (to the hallway and bedroom), and a ceiling lamp. When twilight arrived, we lit the fire, turned on the lamp, but no one closed the windows. At the table, we drank hot milk and played cards or dice. Sometimes we read, sometimes we worked. The lamp attracted insects. There was a spiral hanging from the ceiling to which they stuck. Huge mosquitoes came, along with pearly butterflies and moths, fuzzy and heavy. Groups of insects chaotically arranged in space, around the lightbulb, throwing upon the walls, ceiling, and floor fluttering, restless shadows. We played cards, *makao*. Into the middle of the table, right onto the stack of cards, small brown balls began to fall, like a miniature hailstorm in the wrong color. A moth got stuck to the spiral, warm and fluffy like a comforter. This moth, struggling, possibly sensing impending doom, was bombarding the table with eggs. From her swollen body quick series of brown bullets erupted. These balls, funnily enough, were supposed to carry life, not death.

My mother resembles that moth. I'm ashamed of myself for thinking this way, but my mother resembles that moth. She's incomparably more elegant and less forthcoming, she tries to control her reactions and feelings, but she's as afraid as that insect. She struggles helplessly, stuck to a spiral trap, which turned out to be her life. She spreads her fingers, pushes dishes from the table, sometimes she stills, perhaps thinking, perhaps gathering her strength. She's afraid that I'll leave the house and her struggle will have no witnesses, and at the same time she's ashamed that there is still someone here to see her struggle. If this is what dying looks like, I'd like to give it a miss.

I don't sleep well, not since my arrival. Nothing new. I've

had various periods of insomnia. After a few sleepless nights I lay down my weapons. In the first phase, which lasted for about a week, I compensated for the few hours of sleep with many glasses of whiskey. The end result was the same, and there was even added value, a stash of bottles for the nights that followed, for another attack of insomnia. After a week I capitulated again. Alcohol, no matter how carefully I did my sums and pretended that everything was all right, did not replace sleep. In the second phase, drunk and so very tired that there was no chance of sleep, I went to a doctor, or rather an acquaintance who was a doctor, who gave me strong sleeping pills. I paid and thanked him. Then, I spent a few hours on the couch, looking at the boxes of medicine, dazed and exhausted. I was afraid of pills, because I knew what happened after they were taken. I waited until I capitulated for a third time and swallowed a bunch of pills.

The dumplings are tasty. My mother cooks well, the only imperfection on her chef's honor came from the tomato soup. I ate three dumplings, my mother had half of one. "I have no appetite, son," she explains herself, clearing the table.

"Maybe we could watch something on TV?" I ask and, without waiting for an answer, turn the TV on. These careful sentences we utter, all cocked ears and skittish, aimed at each other or ourselves, resemble the movements of chess pieces. We do our best to not take out any belonging to the opponent, but—let's be honest—at some point there won't be enough empty squares and a sacrifice will have to be made. That's what the game is about, there's no escaping these rules, no space: the chessboard doesn't stretch, and you can't always just leave the room.

After the earliest years of my life, which were spent in the country with my grandparents, my parents made the decision to move to Białystok. I was starting school in a year's time. They didn't want to send me to a country school, they wanted my next step to be taken in the big city. And there was my mother's hatred of her mother-in-law; my father gave in. This hatred, now decomposed and wiped out, cannot be forgotten, because it was often the last straw that tilted the scales. Rumors, mountains made from molehills, and mostly the new brick house inhabited by the in-laws and their younger son; that house was the bone of contention, the cornerstone of hatred between my mother and her mother-in-law; that white house my mother could not stop visualizing; the house, like a thorn in her side, stung and sent streams of tears down her cheeks to accompany her nonsense complaints. My father gave in.

My parents bought a third of a large, one-story house that had been built before the war. In later years, when the government stopped taking an interest in the exact number of square meters owned by every individual citizen, as long as these didn't include communal areas, my parents bought the remaining two thirds. Only then did the thorn in my mother's side dissolve; the brick house of her in-laws, smaller and lacking the history, inspired only pity.

I don't sleep well, not since my arrival. Nothing new. I sit in my room just as I did years ago. Not much has changed. The same dresser, desk, swivel chair. The same bed, lamp, window. I spend the evenings sitting in my room on the first floor, my mother is watching soap operas on the ground floor, and I stare at the white screen of the computer. In reality, we see the same thing—my mother, colorful pictures, and I, part of an empty A4 page; we see the same thing: nothing, we've both got the white blindness. The items in my room bear signs of wear, in this I resemble the furniture, lamp, and clay flowerpot: I bear the same signs.

I don't sleep well, not since my arrival. I try to convince myself that it's just stress. I haven't reached for alcohol. I'll wait until tomorrow, until Monday. On Monday we get the test results. "I don't think there's anything seriously wrong with your mother," said my old school friend. He, if I recall, was never the best student. He rarely knew the right answer.

On the first day of high school we had to introduce ourselves to everyone. I remembered only two people. Aneta, who muttered her surname—"Can you repeat your surname?" asked the form teacher, and the class erupted with laughter—and Kasia. We sat in the chemistry lab, our form teacher taught Chemistry. I can't picture the faces of my friends, but I remember the room.

I think objects remain in one's memory more easily than faces. Objects don't move, they don't gesture.

After an hour of tension, during which friendships and enmities were forged, in the chemistry lab, where we were going to spend a lot of time in the coming four years, we were let out to go home like a defeated army. I don't remember quite how it happened, but I walked Kasia home. She didn't invite me in for tea, decaf coffee, or cake. She didn't say that she has a younger sister, but no father. I walked briskly away for a few blocks and when I was sure she couldn't see me from the window I sat down on a bench. I had to relax.

I don't remember September first of that year. I imagine a warm and sunny day. Or maybe it was cool and the rain was only waiting to surprise passersby, while I sat and feverishly thought of my first day at school and first walk with a girl from the first year of high school?

I pressed my fingers against my eyelids, lightly pushing my eyeballs back into my head. Against a dark background, as if on a sheet, bloomed bright, white-gold patches. These patches changed shape and color, as if I were staring into a strange flame. A flame that reached my labyrinth and imbalanced me. That was the first of the pleasures I discovered. I didn't discover masturbation until much later, it didn't bewilder me so much; I preferred to occupy my fingers with my eyelids.

I pressed against my eyelids, sitting on a bench at a safe distance from Kasia's window. After a moment blinding flowers grew in front of me, I couldn't smell them, my head tilted backward as if moving away from the starry groups that, both suddenly and unsurprisingly, were born before me and—simultaneously—inside me.

The items around me bear signs of wear. My body, especially my spine and eyes, have their best years far behind them. In this room the only thing that seems new is the white A4 on the computer screen, with a long and unwritten future before it. The word document, new, though created six months ago: gestures.doc, sonia.doc, button.doc, the name changed while the contents remained the same, the format of the file (doc)—still the same. The format still reminds me more of the doctor than the document.

BUTTON

FIRST, I WAS BORN. Fifth, I learned that you can simultaneously love more than one being. Tenth, I'm addicted to newspapers. What can one conclude from this list? What?

We were over an hour late. My mother was complaining, she changed her clothes three times. Four times. The colors didn't match, the materials didn't match; the matching colors and materials didn't match the weather, and eventually a button fell off. My mother took her sweater off. "I need to sew the button on," she said. She never sewed buttons back on in clothes that were on someone at the time. She was afraid one could sew one's mind shut. "Hurry," I growled, "please." Her slowness and indecisiveness irritated me. I thought that she was doing it on purpose, for all the years of waiting, and I was close to swearing. I stopped myself with the utmost difficulty, my jaws clenched so tightly I was surprised the bones didn't crumble. My mother found a needle and thread. She stood by the window, fruitlessly trying to slip the thread through the eye of the needle. I lost count of how many times she tried, and still the thread missed the eye. A she-camel entering Paradise. I was observing her coldly, she was glancing at me, trying to discern whether I was only angry or already furious. My mother knew that I hated being late. She was glancing at me like some small, frightened animal. I don't know what she saw, but she said, helplessly letting her arms drop: "I think I'll just wear something else, son."

She stood by the window, she was afraid. Droplets of sweat shone on her temples. She was afraid of going to the doctor's. I had forgotten that my mother was afraid of hospitals, offices and doctors. I'd forgotten.

I walked over to her, took the needle from her hand along

with the thread. "We have time, Mom. The doctor can wait," I said. I slipped the thread through the eye, and only then did my mother relax. "Thanks, son," she said.

I don't remember how it began, what started it. Did one of us make a gesture, unintended? Did someone else make a gesture in our place, and we were left with no alternative but to bend our heads together in conversation?

Gray tiles on the floor, painted walls (or were those panels? Real, or just resembling wood?), a line of uncomfortable wooden benches under the windows. I can't reconstruct the building of my high school. In my head the building isn't a place, it lacks details on which one might lean, even such broad details as the color of the walls. High school is not a place, just a four-year cutout from a timeline. Time doesn't have walls, colors, a smell.

We were, Kasia and I, good students. Usually As, less often Bs, boring behavior which on a report meant praise. After passing the first year Kasia and I went to the park near the Branicki Palace. We sat down under the bridge, crumbled crackers, and fed the ducks. Kasia didn't look at me, she was leaving the next day to an aunt in Germany for the whole summer, so she avoided my gaze. She was looking at the school report: "Exemplary behavior," she read in a sad voice. Her two-month absence hurt me, for now it was only a potential pain, I didn't know how to enjoy our last few hours together. "You're going to your aunt's even though you don't want to," I said. "That's really exemplary, a perfect mommy's girl. It's a well-deserved grade." She waited for my anger to dissipate. "The only things I do that are exemplary are those I don't actually want to do," she broke off and looked straight at me. "The things I do care about—well, with those I barely pass with a C." My anger evaporated when it met her words, just as milk steams and evaporates on a hot surface. There was no smell of burning. Kasia had summed up our first difficult year of school, and simultaneously—as I understood it—revealed her feelings toward me. "I'd flunk you," I told her, and then we kissed for the first time.

When Kasia laughed, her right eyelid drooped, as if its owner didn't know how to laugh and look at the world with both eyes at the same time. A pair of eyes that knew how to look is definitely too much to retain good humor.

When we kissed, I closed my eyes, tightly, almost so much they hurt, wanting to erase the whole world. The big wide world, full of buildings and caught in a net of roads, pipes, telephone and power lines; populated, full of people. When we kissed, I closed my eyes, desiring complete blindness and solitude; desiring Kasia's lips, because they turned out to be the gates that led to the place I most wanted to go.

I was always a loner. "A sociable loner," Kasia used to say. I searched for solitude among people, in others. Quickly enough— this is my thirteen—I realized that four empty walls are just four empty walls, a used up allegory of solitude. Thirteen, I learned that real solitude can only be found with another person. Kasia was the first "other" person in my life with whom I felt solitude in an almost perfect way. That's why I suffered so much when we weren't together, I hated the holidays that we almost always spent separately.

I don't know how to express my concept of solitude. I trip over words. I trip over time. High school, Kasia, and our thoughts are prehistoric. In order to find them one must, with trowel and brush, hire an excellent archeologist. Yes: when memory and therapy fails, the only thing left to do is to find an archeologist who, with trowel and brush, like a neurologist, will examine our reactions, our unfeeling nerves.

I think this was my line of thought: one is always alone, out of fear he attempts to form a relationship with another to defeat loneliness, which at the end of the day never works; that's why one must find a person who, in your company, will always feel solitude; and when two such people meet, united in an understanding of solitude, they feel bittersweet happiness, because they know that they find peace in the other person, a peace that comes from accepting the laws that are impossible to break.

I think that's how I thought, but I'm not sure, because my reasoning now is a reconstruction of the reasoning of the past, of an archeological site where new discoveries await every day. "With you I feel I'm really alone but nevertheless, that I'll manage to happily live my life," Kasia said once. "Promise me you'll never leave."

Of course, I promised.

I spent a long time talking to my old classmate, my mother waited out in the hallway like an incapacitated adult or child. Some of the tests had to be repeated, results were rather worrying, he said, only to add that there was nothing to worry about. I don't think I'll ever understand the medical dialectic: thesis, antithesis, and synthesis in white coats sounds like thesis and antithesis leading to a prosthesis.

We agreed that the following morning I would bring my mother for a second day of tests that had names as long as diseases. This pro forma invoice could astonish both by the number of items and by the final pricing. "You'll have an empty house starting tomorrow," my old classmate joked. Optimistic, in golden frames. Something tells me I didn't like him.

"You see," my mother says when I stop for a red light. "There wasn't any reason to rush." Automatically I reach for a cigarette, but I don't light it. I try not to smoke when I'm around my mother. Indeed, we still don't know what's wrong with her body, there wasn't any reason to rush, we are no wiser. We are richer in assumptions and feelings, as bright as this last autumn has been. "The button," the word erupts from my mother as if from the middle of a conversation, which she was probably having mentally with herself. "A button with a loop."

CLOSET

Fourteenth, I don't have any control over my own memory. My power is less than an illusion. I'm tempted to say that I manage my life as well as I do my memory. My life is slipping away between my fingers, my memory is slipping away from my brain to attack the body. My entire body is marked with metastases.

I drove my mother to the hospital in the morning. We were two hours late. Before my mother got dressed, she checked that the colors and fabrics matched. On the bed in the bedroom she arranged human figures from her clothes: skirt, shirt, cardigan, tights, scarf. Every few moments she would switch one part of clothing for something else. A blue silk shirt was replaced with a woolen beige one. "What do you think," my mother asked, "Do they match?" We were playing a game, wasting time. "I think that skirt clashes with the cardigan," I said. My mother corrected the flat, bodiless figure on the bed; trousers appeared that pushed the cardigan back into the closet. We were playing, I didn't want to take away the pleasure of completing an outfit, a pleasure only increased by my presence. We were wasting time; two adults and a closet full of clothes.

It was almost like spin-the-bottle. Someone spins the bottle, and its neck (once it stopped) points toward the person you then have to kiss. If someone doesn't want to kiss, they have to take off an item of clothing. It was like the childish game of spin-the-bottle, just an adult version, a corrected version, conservative. Nobody kissed or undressed, the consequences extended only as far as the mannequin stretched out on the bedclothes in the bedroom. This figure created from clothes, flat, waiting for my mother's body to give it some dimension, saddened me, though I tried to hide it. It was this, no more than this, that would be left by my mother: her body would rot alongside that of her husband's, and I would be left forming her shape with the clothes she used to wear, and a foggy memory that hid her body.

I remember one game of strip spin-the-bottle. Middle school, three girls and myself. The girls were embarrassed to kiss each other, so after only a few spins of the bottle they weren't wearing much, while I felt a strange warmth spreading through me under my clothes. I don't know how that game might have ended, maybe we would have entered Eden and tried the forbidden fruit, if one of the girls' mothers hadn't walked into the room. Instead of the forbidden fruit we got a taste of loud yells full of words I wasn't allowed to utter myself if I wanted to be able to sit down comfortably without wincing.

I remember one game of strip spin-the-bottle. There was a string of people turning eighteen that year. We were on the cusp of the adult world, with final exams and college ahead of us, and then a responsible life forever. I don't remember whose birthday it was, where, when. I don't remember. We were sitting in a circle, about ten of us, almost-men and almost-women, after consuming quite a few bottles of alcohol and having smoked many packets of cigarettes. Heterosexual correctness which chose losing an item of clothing rather than kissing someone of the same gender, was broken by two girls from my class at a point when they were wearing more skin than anything else. My two friends kissed each other right in front of our eighteen-year-old, adult eyes. Two women in underwear, perhaps also socks. Two almost naked women, kissing each other far more than the rules dictated, with hands buried in hair and saliva mixing in mouths. I saw magazines brought over from Germany before, and kissing women inside them, but my kissing friends didn't resemble those women at all. These were lips I knew from whispered test answers, but they were silent now; these were hands I was used to seeing spattered with ink, but they were busy doing something other than writing now; these were breasts usually hidden under layers of clothing, swinging openly.

That game, if I recall correctly, didn't have any social repercussions. But that's not all. I would like my film of memory to stop right now, at the kissing girls, but I don't control my memory (my fourteenth). My memory has escaped my brain.

One of the guys spun the bottle, I was wearing jeans, a belt, underwear and socks; enough to safely participate in the game for a long while yet. The bottle pointed toward me. I thought that the guy—I didn't know him much better than just knowing his name, he wasn't in my class—would take off a sock, but he reacted differently. Maybe he was made bolder by the girls, maybe it was the alcohol. I don't know. He didn't take a sock off.

I remember quite distinctly what he looked like, our classes had PE together and we shared a changing room. PE lessons didn't prepare me for what happened next. He didn't take a sock off.

Having chosen an outfit, my mother busied herself packing a suitcase. Clean underwear, cosmetics, a book (*Loneliness Online*). Slippers, crosswords, pajamas. "They're too old," my mother decided after examining the pajamas. We went to buy new ones, decorated with blue flowers. We were two hours late.

"Mom, I'll come back tomorrow morning," I say. "Call the house phone if you want." My mother is thinking hard about something. "Son, I forgot to pay the bill for the electricity. It's under the napkin on the fridge. Under the napkin."

Fourteenth, I don't have any control over my own memory. I remember not the things I would like to. I would like things to be different than how I remember them, and not when I do. Syllogisms and other tricks, taken out of a hat like a rabbit, are long gone.

I'm lying naked on the bed in my room, imagining my mother lying in her new pajamas at the hospital, blue flowers on a turquoise background. This large, malicious house is not letting me get warm, it defends itself with damp walls and cracks through which the heat escapes. I lie naked, the only one in this large house, it's so cold and wet that even the ghosts have given up, and I think I have as much life in me as there is in the human figures my mother constructed on the bed a few hours ago.

My life is slipping through my fingers, not only mine, but also, probably, my mother's; my memory has escaped my brain to conquer my body. My entire body is marked by metastases. I don't know what's responsible for memory, maybe some cells that are similar to red blood cells with patches of hemoglobin? Of course memory has no color, it doesn't have an indentation and isn't round. Memory cells have escaped my brain, have reached my blood and are traveling to different parts of my body, where they create new lumps, memory-created metastasis.

There is a white scar on my left knee, courtesy of Iwona. There is a thicker bit of skin on my chin, a mark from a dog bite. On the inside of my thigh are two shining brown spots, caused by matches. My right ear sticks out more, it was used to pull up the rest of me by older classmates and teachers. Kasia's image imprinted on my cornea, a mirror image, so when she laughs it's her left eyelid that droops. Lips burned with the touch of other lips. In the shrugging of my shoulders there's a feeling of helplessness, which I copied from my brother.

If it wasn't for my body, this ruined map, there wouldn't be much that I could remember, really.

GEOGRAPHY

THE GEOGRAPHY CLASSROOM was in the basement. Through tiny windows we saw feet, maybe hundreds of them, before even switching shoes for slippers. When the owner of some feet dropped something, we might have been lucky enough to spy his face, but this didn't happen often; in winter there was a shadow of a chance that someone might slip and fall—then the entire body of that person would stretch out like a worm, divided; the head in a hat in one window, the body in the next, the feet in the third. Such (rare) falls, not too serious, broke the monotony of the lessons, at least in winter.

Our teacher, quite young, was a homosexual, according to the rumor—this was never confirmed. What surprised us most was that he looked and acted normally. For a teacher, he looked and acted normally. Maybe he had mood swings. One of the girls summarized it quite accurately: "A homosexual is a man who acts like a pregnant woman and is obsessed with the capital cities of African countries." We weren't always careful with our words in the classrooms, for instance the word "normal." A normal teacher, a normal person.

Geography was always either the first or last lesson. We sat in the back row, close to the cupboard with globes and atlases. I liked geography lessons and simultaneously I hated them, the one lesson during which I sat next to Kasia. I couldn't pay as much attention to her as I might like because I had to be careful; the teacher (we called him the gaygraphy teacher) asked questions out of the blue, especially about capital cities: Madagascar, Antananarivo; Ghana, Accra; three mistakes, a fail on your record.

We sat together for three years, whispering the right answers to each other during tests, in the first year I'd squeeze her hand

57

under the table; in the third I put a hand on her thigh, or she did on mine. In the first year I didn't know that the capital of Equatorial Guinea was Malabo, in the third I remembered that Ouagadougou was the capital of Burkina Faso, Upper Volta, "land of honest people" in Moore and Dioula.

I remember latitudes and longitudes. The Prime Meridian, going through Greenwich, the Equator, the longest latitude, and then the Tropics, of Cancer and Capricorn. I was born in winter (Capricorn), Kasia was born in summer (Cancer). Even though I hated geography, or maybe because I did, I was the best in the class: I had to learn everything at home so I could spend the lessons focused on Kasia.

I don't remember how it began, what started it. Did one of us make a gesture, unintended? Did someone else make a gesture in our place, and we were left with no alternative but to bend our heads together in conversation?

Already during the first month we were drifting in the same direction, and then we just got closer and closer, pulled together by currents of school breaks, we were linked by gazes and whispers of classmates, tied together by tea and snacks in the cafeteria. We didn't have that much control over it. "You know," Kasia said, "we're like two whales dumped on the beach. Nobody else is in sight. We'll die together."

We didn't die. At least, not together.

After a month we began to write each other daily letters, and the longest were created over weekends, I learned to like Mondays. We realized that it's easier to write some things down than to say them out loud. Paper is so much more patient that a conversationalist of flesh and bone. Paper forgives misunderstandings, though it points out spelling mistakes. Misunderstandings complicate life, spelling mistakes only lower the final grade.

We exchanged pieces of paper daily. Kasia had remarkable handwriting, which leaned to the right as if it represented determination; the spaces between the lines, even on a blank page, were even, like rays of sunlight broken by blinds.

We were silent at times, moving through the corridors in such a way as to minimize the contact between us, but our silence and the complicated, separate movement from lesson to lesson wasn't caused by arguments or mutual aversion. We had our pages, our secret that everyone knew and laughed about. We needed solitude. "Like a desert needs rain," Kasia said once, and her right eyelid drooped.

I directed six plays, they all got good reviews and awards and, as it turned out, brought in quite a lot of money. Thanks to them, among other things, I can afford such luxuries as private health care for my mother. In each of my plays I tried to convey happiness, because unhappiness seemed too easy a theme. Usually, in life I pick the easy road, and compensated at the theater by picking the most complex topics, and to this day I think happiness is the most complex of them all.

Fifteenth, I don't like geography. I don't like the capital cities of African countries, lateral or terminal moraines, and especially recessional moraines. I hate maps: the ones on the wall, at which we were questioned (my teacher's favorite cities were faded by the constant rub of the ruler he used to point them out with); technology roadmaps (the horror of moving from one city to another, a journey which only looks straightforward and safe on a map); pocket maps (always in the pocket of the wrong jacket); old and new; all maps.

"Who do you want to be?" I asked Kasia, an ordinary and important question, teenagers always ask this question. "If it were possible, a psychologist," she replied, and then hung her head.

I don't have the nature of a traveler or discoverer. I know what I like. I'm not interested in what's around the next corner, though I am interested to see if I find what I've remembered is behind the next corner. People like Arctowski, Nansen, and Magellan are eerily alien to me, cold. My curiosity of the world, similarly to my sense of smell, seems to be muted, it has firmly set and not very wide borders. Kasia turned out to be the only exception.

I don't see her very clearly in my memory. My mother keeps my photos from high school somewhere, but now she's in a hospital bed and if she's thinking of anything at all it's that she hasn't paid the electricity bill, which is under the napkin on the fridge.

We spent almost four years together, and I remember more clearly the woman who sells me my bread. It's not fair.

Kasia was slightly taller than me. She moved heavily and clumsily, carefully, as if the pavement might decide to pull a prank and move out from under her. She didn't break things too often. When she broke a teacup at my house she said, embarrassed, "Call me Grace." Kasia always resembled a big animal. Docile and too intelligent. She resembled the huge Epigoni, a crumb from the old times, a living fossil, a wise and elegant fragment of the past or prehistory.

It's absurd what I'm about to say: I think I fell in love with Kasia before I met her.

I was attracted by one other thing: the secrecy or emptiness, it's impossible to distinguish between them.

My phone rang. Eleventh, I hate phones and phone calls, but I picked up because it was my old classmate, who's now a doctor. A clean-shaven face with golden rims was calling. We agreed to meet that evening at the Attic, to remember together the old days. I haven't the slightest desire to spend any time with Golden Rims, but tough, I gave my mother into his care and soon I will need a new prescription for sleeping pills. I'm good at doing the things I really don't want to do.

Her hair was always cut short for a girl in those years. It reached halfway down her neck. I had the courage to ask why she didn't want a more feminine hairstyle. "I don't like being extravagant," she replied. "I'm not going to pretend that I'm any prettier than I am."

Fifteenth, I don't like geography, especially maps. Staring at a map, I feel as if I'm looking into a mirror. I see my own face, not always carefully shaved, tired and older, always older. Staring at a map, I don't see the threads of roads, motorways, and railways linked by dots of cities like the skeleton of a house made of modeling clay and matches. Multicolored and entwined lines, connected by splotches of cities, resemble an intricate net of veins; winding kilometers over which time travels. Staring at a map, I see the diagram of passing hours, minutes, and seconds.

City A and city B, always linked in such a way that one takes a wrong turn, never arriving at the intended time and place.

IF I HAD

IT ALL BEGAN WITH the drooping right eyelid. Kasia laughed, the eyelid drooped.

I wore glasses since starting school. My parents noticed late that I didn't notice things. I gave a few demonstrations, quite spectacular. For instance, once by the well I found an old gray tube. I decided to pull it under the stairs of my grandparents' new house. The tube bit me. It turned out to be a grass snake. For instance, my godmother paid us a visit once. I was mixing sugar into the tea, the tea spilled onto the platter and then the tablecloth. I got a beating. For instance, while watching TV I would twist my head. The heroes of Westerns hung from the sky like Superman.

In our first year, Kasia didn't wear glasses, in the final year— jam jars that made her eyes look so big the rims were filled with her black pupils, and the color, bits of green, appeared only on the edges, like a curb surrounding grass.

Sixteenth, there exist in my head some happy events, a series of potential events, that I didn't help make real. That series begins with the words "if I had."

I liked tickling others. Before tickling begins to hurt, it makes you laugh. I tickled Kasia, she laughed, her right eyelid drooped. Her stomach stopped reacting first, my fingers slid off it like water off oilcloth if you blew hard enough.

If only I'd asked Kasia at least once to bring me something from her summers in Germany.

I didn't sleep, stretched out on the bed in my recovered room, staring at the ceiling; in three hours I'd be meeting my old class-mate in the pub known as Attic. The lines on the ceiling were interpreted by my brain as histopathological pictures from a kaleidoscope, sometimes as spiderwebs, sometimes a rose window, which had little in common with solar symbolism.

If I'd broken my word and went over to Kasia's at least once, unannounced and unexpected.

I had to overcome the numbness and go to the bathroom. Another two, three days I might manage to cheat my body, replacing sleep with a cold shower. Then alcohol or sleeping pills. Unless the increase of unnecessary, extra hours will stop, the hours will fade into darkness, darkness will seep into my skin, my skin will go numb, and I'll sleep.

The bed is smaller than I remember, though I haven't grown much over the last twenty years and I only weigh a bit more. I don't know any item or place that would resist the shrinking of this world; everything seems smaller; the clothes, hallway, garden, mug, desires, everything.

In order to take a shower, I have to reach the edge of the bed, let my feet drop to the ground and find the slippers. The bed is smaller than I remember, but the area of the bed is the most flexible thing, malleable and easily stretched between people. When I wake up next to someone whom—I think—I love, the bed is the perfect size, the mattress ideally springy, and the edge within reach. When I wake up alone, if I'd managed to sleep at all, the mattress is uncomfortable, too hard but also too soft, and the edge enhanced by the bedsheet is too far away. I need to go through the cold, unnecessary centimeters, reach the other side, the carpet onto which my room spat out my slippers, always narrow, with sand embedded in its fibers.

If I'd found in myself more humility, somewhere.

I shave; I learned to not notice my face. It's not that difficult. All you need to do is carefully follow the blade: cheeks, chin, around the lips; fragments, a puzzle that should not be put together. It's not that difficult. I just don't have any manual talents.

Then aftershave. It should soften, but stings instead.

If I hadn't searched for hidden meanings in everything Kasia said, and just accepted what she was saying.

My skin doesn't like cold water, it needs time to get used to it. A new place and different water dries the skin, it peels, resembles a white-pink paper sprinkled with paper confetti. I also need time to get used to it. A lot of time. A long time. I don't have a talent for adapting quickly, for reacting promptly.

I hate surprises (seventeenth).

A fresh shirt and jeans, two hours before we're scheduled to meet. I ordered a taxi for half past seven. I don't have anything to do. I wait for tomorrow and the test results. I wait for a message, whether my mother's body has passed the test for usefulness, and if not, then after what sort of preparations will it be allowed to sit the test again?

I could lie down, I'm patient, I've mastered lying down to an A+. Like in any sport there are injuries: from professional lying down my spine has stretched into a straight line, it's difficult to find the shape of a flattened s, it hurts often, doesn't let me tie my shoelaces, and sometimes cracks menacingly.

Cesar's body, my mother's German shepherd, I pulled myself. It stank, it had expanded. I had to pull it by the paws, because the fur was coming off the skin. Then I loaded the body on a wheelbarrow, pushed it into my trunk. I washed my hands and checked in the phone book where I could burn a dog that had been my mother's keeper of secrets for fifteen years; she didn't have another, she didn't go to confession.

I argued with Kasia in the third year that we knew each other, our first serious argument. "I think we've grown up," said Kasia, with a note of bitterness and sadness in her voice. "We're arguing like adults." "Yes," I replied, angry and scared. "Next thing we'll be behaving like adults too." "Unfortunately," said Kasia, "this time you're right. Unfortunately."

The pub Attic on Lime Street hasn't changed, though I didn't remember the interior clearly, only from some night from years ago, so if they had replaced the tables, for instance, I wouldn't have noticed anyway. A dark and smoky atmosphere, it suited me well; we wouldn't be able to see much.

I'd arrived a few minutes too early, I hate tardiness, but my old classmate and now Doctor Bank Account Leech was waiting. I didn't recognize him because he was wearing civilian clothes: jeans, a checkered shirt and zip-up hoodie. He slapped my shoulder in greeting. In response, I wanted to punch him.

A shirt that isn't quite done up under the neck means informal mode. I order a beer and we sit by the table, two forty-year-olds, relaxed because the collar doesn't throttle the neck, and the wife or fiancé isn't in the room. I'm beginning to regret I wasn't late.

The conversation develops in a monotonous rhythm. He, Paweł, that's his name, tells me what our other classmates are doing, and all one can hear is the cry of babies born too early and ordinary problems: bills, diseases, and infidelity. I told anecdotes from the big city of Warsaw. He, Paweł, talks about his life, composed of a family (in the wallet he has a photo of his wife and daughters), career (with specializations that sound like a knife being pulled across glass), holidays in warm countries: "Morocco is the best, but not in summer. There aren't that many Russians and the prices are lower."

I drank three beers, I wanted to go home. "I left the best until the end!" exclaimed tipsy doctor Paweł Drenasz, that's his surname. "Kasia works in a hospital with disabled children. She's a psychologist," he said. "What Kasia?" I asked, too quickly. "What do you mean? Yours, from high school." I said my good-byes, I hate surprises, I caught a taxi.

If I had known *this*. If I had known *this* twenty-something years ago.

In a 24/7 liquor store I bought a bottle of whiskey. It's a good thing the salesman didn't ask for a prescription. Or: please show me your cardiogram, the heart is indeed broken, a bottle a day and not more because instead of healing you'll only drown. Or: please show me your encephalogram, oh, the brain waves look shaky, low amplitude, a bottle a day and no more, because instead of sleep you'll find the Grim Reaper.

If I had is not a conjunction that introduces a conditional. *If I had* is a noun, it's a place and time in which I'll never be, but which I know very well. The walls of potential houses and seconds recording potential events I have gotten used to long ago, the difference between what I have and what I might have had doesn't hurt, not me.

GENETIVUS

"I'M WALKING IN A DRIZZLE on an empty stomach." We were sitting on an overturned pine trunk after dinner. On a small field, close to a grassy airport from which bowlegged biplanes took off (Any-2), and light golden orioles. The day must have been warm and sunny, I don't remember. But since we were sitting on a trunk, since planes were taking off, the scene must have occurred in summer. My stomach remembered what we ate: cutlets with fried cabbage, and where: at Kasia's. "You always knew how to express yourself," I replied.

We did the simplest things, Kasia and I: we walked and we sat, on benches and trunks, in parks and estates, in sunshine rather than rain. We drank tea, ate dinners, smoked cigarettes in secret. We wrote letters to each other, we talked both outside and inside, we had conversations in many languages: words mostly, but also touch, careful and controlled, also lips and tongue: speleology of the mouth, an examination of the roof, and the bones which supported it, and eyes: eyes, tongue, and lips—the architects of our kisses, the engineers of our shared hours.

We did the simplest and most accessible things, Kasia and I, we used only common verbs, the everyday and iterative verbs. Our body parts and those responsible for speech didn't recognize one-time or perfective actions, we didn't say: exploded, escaped and abandoned, emigrated, forgot, died. One-time verbs, perfected actions, and spectacular ones divide people, I think we understood that and so decided to live in an imperfect world, in a common world, written with a lowercase letter, without an end, like dinners and unfinished homework, like tests and slices of bread falling to the floor butter side down, like a star: make a wish.

Often, we uttered sentences that didn't match the situation, context, surroundings. In the first months such sentences slipped off the world and fell onto the bedding below, but sometimes they clung to reality and questioned it. "What's the nominative of drizzle?" asked Kasia.

"Drizzle, or rain," I replied, though I didn't know. "In old Polish anything that fell was feminine. With time, drizzle became rain." Kasia laughed aloud, she liked listening to scholarly disputes, as long as those who were disputing had no idea what they were talking about. "Copernicus was a woman," Kasia said, "but rain too?"

Eighteenth, my love for Kasia is eternal. It's eternal for a simple, grammatical reason. My love for Kasia is an imperfect love. My loving Kasia is eternal because no prefix can make it perfect. My loving is eternal because it's always present.

Eighteenth: it's funny that eternal love has reached such a far place, the eighteenth numeral. Why not first, second? Why not a bronze medal? It's always about the podium. Is it because at eighteen I became responsible for my actions?

Sometimes I have trouble working. I can't read. The letters in a word run away from me, like c-o-r-k, words in a sentence push away from each other, as if there were as many poles as words, sentences split up paragraphs into splinters, paragraphs break up pages into impossible-to-make-whole fragments, and pages put a text into a coffin: there's nobody left to nail the pages to the stake decorating the text. I can't write. Instead of sentences, groups of words form, "sunny" is hidden by "cloud," "they went" trips and falls as if after an amputation, "on the trunk" suddenly becomes "on the little trunk."

Sometimes I have trouble working. My work doesn't require me to be physically fit, quite the opposite, the more pain, the imperfect kind that interrupts a gesture halfway, the pain that's still present, written in the not-too-high register, the better: I can add characters to my own stiff spine, they'll be trembling like a caught insect until they'll freeze with opened feelings and motivations for all to see on the floorboards of the stage, an adaptation.

But sometimes I have trouble working, I can't read or write. I spent four years of high school in a class specializing in biochemistry, I wanted to be a doctor, and three months before exams, after breaking up with Kasia, I exchanged my dreams for others. I battled through college at the theatrical academy despite my parents' disappointment.

Seventh, there are questions that I return to. I return to some questions, important and unimportant ones, with or without an answer. For instance: what is the nominative of drizzle? About two years ago I asked a friend to send me the largest Polish dictionary. A truck arrived, fifty volumes of *Practical Dictionary of Modern Polish* edited by Halina Zgółkowa. "Drizzle" is the genitive case, a living fossil of the nominative "drizzle," an ammonoidea from the olden days that has lost its way in the oceanic flowing of language and has become "rain." *Practical Dictionary* . . . isn't practical at all, it takes up shelves; only the tenth volume has words starting with *d*.

That's how we spent our time, counting airplanes and parachuters, complaining about the yellow cheese in our sandwiches and our younger siblings. We talked about things farthest away, about elephants who said goodbye to their dead, about whales singing love songs, about Chinese whispers.

Seventh, there are questions that I return to, questions that have answers which never change. For instance: why did I pass my exams but failed in my love for Kasia? Our love was eternal because it was imperfect. An action that keeps happening cannot end, grammar doesn't allow a different outcome. Only that which is perfect occurs in time: in the future or the past. That which is imperfect exists in the present, it never ends and is never fulfilled. And still, despite that, despite grammar and dictionaries, I made our love extraordinary, or rather: an exception.

Whose—the genitive case supplies this information, it's the most frequent case, the most hopeless and permanent.

What if I was born into a tongue without the genitive case? Would things have happened differently? Would I have what I don't have?

"And what will you say about 'empty stomach'?" asked Kasia. "That it's rarely welcome," I replied.

GONG

I ACTED LIKE A CHILD without his parents. My father really did leave on the longest journey, five years ago. I sat in the living room with a bottle of whiskey and a packet of cigarettes. I drank and I smoked, I turned the TV on. The TV replaces company, for lack of a teddy bear or fluffy cat I use the TV: a teddy bear isn't manly, and a cat has to be fed so it won't die. The pictures before my eyes flare brighter and then dim, they describe the whole world, they can't conquer the thirty-two-inch rectangular boundary though.

I drank and I smoked, with a book on the table that I wasn't going to reach for, before me starvation in Africa and a bowl of crisps. To choose from there's the asymmetrical war with terrorism, a cabinet of ministers, a PhD given to someone in a toga who says his goodbyes to the world with the words: "Ladies and Gentlemen, what a great honor!"

I don't feel sleepy, there's less and less liquid in the bottle. I'm acting like a child without his parents. I'm not waiting for friends, though. We won't be partying until dawn, we won't be rushing to clean.

I've been sitting like this for a few evenings now. Each similar to the last. During the day I watch the workers who are putting up a new fence. During the day I try to work, which means: I turn on the laptop, hours pass, I turn it off, and my back creaks as if from hard work. I visit my mother at the hospital with fruit and newspapers, cosmetics and underwear, I talk to Paweł D. and two women who are in the same room as my mother. I pay the bills, pick up the phone when it rings, and exchange the same sentences: "Personal issues," I say, "I'm sorry," I hear the startled answer, as if personal stuff was as improper and embarrassing as syphilis used to be; in the world of Big Brother nobody suffers from personal issues, nobody has personal issues, perhaps in the bathroom behind closed doors like gastric trouble, a matter of excretion.

It's autumn, the sun warms other parts of the globe. Behind the thick walls and double-paned windows I can hear the hum and scream of seagulls. Of course, the sea doesn't hum in Białystok: cars, the running water called Białka that's the color of milky Mazut, the ghosts of Pasmanta factory, machines in hundreds of dentists' labs.

The drawn-out tests are not a particularly calming matter. I appreciate medical inquisitiveness: taking cells, liquids, x-rays and MRIs, the camera eye in inaccessible places inside the body, contrast, and so on. I appreciate it and I pay. I pay so as not to hear that it's not good, though there's nothing to worry about. I appreciate the monochromatic pictures and the colorful ones: the spine of a christened woman, the brain of a wife, the histo-pathological image of a widow, the entire catalogue, the complete album: photos, unfortunately all separate. Parents, husband, sons, are all missing.

I don't talk to my mother about the tests. We talk about the fence, the new pajamas, and diet after which the patient has to, sooner or later, end up on a drip. "It's not a diet, son. They're starving me," my mother complains in a whisper, glancing around to see that nobody's eavesdropping.

Such are the days, I make myself face them, I try and improvise as best as I can. My improvisations are few and far between.

Such are the nights, a bottle and the TV, a few hours of broken sleep, brown as the rivers of a tropical river.

I wait until the doctor calls to tell me to come in. I will sit opposite the desk on an uncomfortable chair, so much so that it's difficult to stay in it for longer than fifteen minutes.

"Son," my mother repeats, weary and exhausted with the surrounding aseptic atmosphere, "I'd like to come home now. You're probably not cleaning."

Sometimes I want to respond: "Mom, I often wanted to come home too." Of course, I keep this to myself. My mother also keeps a lot to herself. For instance, she didn't say once: "I can see that you're drinking." "You're probably wasting your life away." "You should iron your shirt properly, and not sit there with all those creases, aren't you ashamed?"

Since I came to Białystok, I haven't been sleeping well, if the bits of hours, tough minutes of nightmares, can be called sleep at all. I don't sleep well, the smallest thing irritates me. My condition is my age, in the middle; my spiritual state is not as fresh as breath can be, mints don't help; I would describe my state as stable: stably unstable, the biggest threat are the details, the oil pressure indicator, for instance.

This hum seeps through the walls and the cracks in them and makes me furious. The hum of a potential sea, maybe this house stands at the bottom of an ancient ocean? Maybe, quite possibly, why ever not: I'm drunk, wet, I'm leaning back on the couch at the bottom, I lift the glass full of alcohol to my lips, my hand raises itself, like the limb of a drowned man is moved with each wave.

This hum seeps through the walls and windows, through bones, to spread beneath the roof of my skull like a banner of a manifestation for some niche cause. My skull resembles the shell of a snail, a crumbling house of thoughts, empty and spacious.

This hum, broken by the screams of seagulls, won't let me rest. The seagulls are real, they moved to Białystok with me. Nearby there's a fish-processing enterprise: waste, fish heads and fins, the skin of fillets, scales—it all ends up in the stream and feeds generations of seagulls that have never seen the sea. The stream is so polluted, thick with the leftovers like Monday's soup, that it wouldn't be difficult to walk over it, an easy miracle that wouldn't surprise anyone. Wanting to impress the audience, Moses would have to be brought over so the waters might divide like the Red Sea.

The monotonous hum breaks the rhythm of my breathing, my heart trips and loses its step. Noises don't stop me from sleeping: roadworks, jackhammers, screeching neighbors, or hoovers. Noises that are quiet and monotonous: a dripping tap, a window that hasn't been properly closed, a gas stove that heats up water for nobody, the humming of a fridge, all this takes sleep away from me.

I bought the sleeping pills yesterday. Paweł D. was useful, I can dig out an oval bit of sleep from the silver packet, swallow down sleep with water, and let it dissolve in my stomach. Gradually, minute after minute, my entire body will drink lead and stop reacting.

Seventh, there are questions that I return to, questions that are immune to interest rates, or perhaps conserved within those rates, drifting behind me in a jar. For instance: what am I trying to drown in the bottle? The first answer is smooth, for public use: I'm worried about my mother. But that's not the truthful answer, it's the one used for the photo shoot in *Viva*, written in bold. I'm indeed worried about my mother, I worry in the guest room, but for naught. My worry hasn't found anything to stabilize it in the external world of facts. I know that it won't be good, that's what my parents taught me: expect the worst, it will allow you to live life with some amount of contentment.

I worry about my mother, about her body. My worry takes on the form of bookkeeping, eerily enough. I would like to make sure that before it disappears we can even out the columns under "has" and "owes." Perhaps I'll get a loan on good terms and pay off interest: each year she's sacrificed I'll buy back with a paid bill, my studies at the theatrical academy for the hospital bed, the wars fought with my father over money for me I'll return through the MRI, and so on, motherhood taken into the grip of usury.

Seventh, I return, I return to questions: What am I trying to drown in the bottle? Why does blunt sleeplessness catch me? Why now?

Worry for my mother would look great on paper of good quality, preferably semi-matte. Makeup artists could correct the contours of dark shadows under eyes, they would get rid of the red lines that span the whites; the hand of directors would cross out everything that's unnecessary, that's ambiguous, that nobody would pay for without a movie or glamour bag.

But, I'm afraid, the reply is different, it would peel away from the expensive pages. I drink because I can't sleep. I can't sleep because my classmate, my golden-framed doctor Paweł Drenasz surprised me, and I hate surprises.

My classmate, on whose face pimples have been replaced with a brown net made by Moroccan sunshine, my friend of shoulder-slaps told me Kasia works in a hospital with disabled children. That she's a psychologist.

It's not fair.

When we broke up in the last year of high school, three months before exams, we knew, Kasia and I, that it would be forever. Statistics wiped out the future. Kasia didn't have a chance of living longer, she had no right. The doctors were worried and unanimous.

It's not fair.

I would have been prepared to get the most beautiful flowers for her grave, but I don't know how to be happy that the grave turned out to be a miscalculation, that the only earth moved to bury Kasia was in my own head.

My outrage hums under my skull like a beehive, I'm happy that Kasia is alive, and simultaneously I can reap no joy from her living.

I buried Kasia scrupulously. For over twenty years she has lain in a double grave: her and her guardian angel, motionless, outside of the world. I could suffer in my spare moments, and cry over our love. This suffering seemed to me to be real and convincing—I am, after all, considering my profession, a profession of gestures. I believed in my suffering, I got used to it, and now it turns out that it was a fake, a decoration.

If I'd known that back then, if I'd been wiser concerning my future those twenty years ago, if I'd believed that fiction might step into life upon occasion.

I've never forgotten Kasia. I couldn't, and I didn't want to. Every woman, and there were never many, had to be compared to Kasia, and had to lose, because the odds were never even. A rigged match, in one corner a body while in the other—old photographs. Paper cuts through skin easily enough.

Round one: we get to know each other, the first steps, always in the right direction, with the chemistry transforming the world into butterfly wings, delicate tickling in the stomach, the fresh taste of morning coffee and newspapers like the straw bedding on the concrete floor of the butchery. Gong. Round two: contemplating my lover's face, guessing wishes, candlelit dinners with wine, mesmerizing nights composed of countless hours which would be missed later. Gong. Round three: she moves in with habits and phobias, with graphics for the walls and suitcases for the wardrobe. Gong. Round four: all is well, small desertions and compromises, kisses and sex, including oral, we make love just as one might tend a vegetable patch, without any larger emotions, what counts is the result and regularity. Gong. Round five: suddenly we awake in one bed, the other body lies within reach and simultaneously outside of it, a nameless body. Gong and a break, for instance a trip alone somewhere, for instance a beach and the Grand Hotel in Sopot, a lot of iodine and time which dilutes the poison. Round six: familiar walls of the Warsaw flat, familiar graphics on the walls which serve as a reminder of the suitcases in the wardrobes; there's nothing left of round one except for blurry memories and tickling in the stomach which causes breathlessness quicker than it does happiness. Behind the compromises and daily desertions not much is visible, but we talk: drawn faces, expensive restaurants, it's worth it—we make the decision together. Gong. Round seven: we're made for each other, that's the verdict reached at an expensive restaurant in candlelight—I fear the judge didn't pay sufficient attention to the arguments of both sides; we are made for each other, though we cannot create the conditions under which past mistakes might be forgotten; we are made for each other, we have mutual friends and access to each other's bank accounts, and our difficulties are all temporary. Gong. Round eight: the temporary difficulties don't pass, we grit our teeth and save our lives, trying to recover an old rhythm, asking each other for time and granting that time. Gong. Round nine: in the time we've negotiated from each other we try to find the reasons for failure, we count wounds and wear them proudly. Gong. Round ten: it's the end, the suitcases need dusting, graphics need taking down, walls need repainting, we need to walk away from each other like civilized people, call for a taxi or a friend whose shoulder we might cry on, look through photos and tear up a few. The judge takes our hands but raises neither as a sign of victory. We've both lost. The audience, our friends and strangers, nobody is satisfied. The ring needs cleaning: sweat, blood, and words—those uttered and those spat, those thrown carelessly and now tangling our feet, those thrown up with dinner and murmured in sleep.

The answer to my seventh doesn't wait at the bottom of the bottle, it doesn't bulge like a lonely island rising from the bottom with the last drop instead of a coconut. Alcohol helps to tame time, it softens the past and blurs the future.

I have learned to bear pain in the evening, pain that is as dulled as my mind, a common pain, though common painkillers (no prescription needed, always by the till near the chewing gums) don't help.

Everybody has a safe haven in which they can hide. Some house that is falling apart since granny died. A park bench. Some place in the brain. A memory or a dream. Something.

My haven is made of glass. The glass bears a sticker. The sticker bears information: how old the golden liquid is (most often this is twelve or twenty-four; my apostles, occasionally seen in double). My body tolerates alcohol well, better than it does a lack of sleep or an excess of questions.

My haven is a point of reference, reference to nothing, in which I don't have to do anything, time in which I fall asleep, fall asleep for real or just imagine I do: my fingers find no grip on the glass walls, I fall to the bottom and hold the bottle island in an embryonic embrace—the glass "nothing" and the transparent "I'll quit tomorrow," which deform the world, and a TV remote nearby, sprinkled with cigarette ash.

WILLY

ON THE SUBWAY IN TOKYO, employees in white gloves push pas-
sengers into the train before doors close. I also wear white gloves,
I push my own thoughts, phobias, needs together to get to the
next station: from one honorarium to the next, from one job to
another; consecutive stops, bewilderingly similar to each other,
skipping a year every once in a while.

I used to always await the bedtime story on TV, there were
stories I liked: Reksio, Filemon the Cat, Pyza (on Polish roads).
Flint and Mushroom, the first metrosexuals according to a later
article in *Cosmopolitan*, heroes which in primary school I mixed
up with the place Żwirki i Wigura, our Czech neighbors, the
Magic Pencil. Bolek and Lolek. And Maya the Bee.

I adored Maya the Bee, she had stripes and antennae. My
grandfather, worn out (according to my mother, who so believed
in tomato soup) by fags and my grandmother, had an apiary.
Not too large, a dozen or so beehives in the old orchard behind
the barn, zone zero, children shouldn't go there. I was, according
to my mother, an obedient child, on easy terms with personal
hygiene. That's probably why one day I found myself in the
old orchard behind the barn. Obedient children can be utterly
unpredictable.

My grandfather would come out of the house, sit on an old
bench and breathe. Sitting and breathing consumed him entirely.
Ever since I can remember, he had a round, swollen face. He
didn't drink alcohol because he couldn't. His lungs would swell,
or was it the pleural cavity, I don't remember, and the inner
swelling affected his body as yeast might: the stomach resembled
the face, and the face would sway with the whistling breath like
a balloon. A chubby grandfather: a body in rubber boots and

a jacket, denim pants sewn multiple times with multicolored threads that resembled light exiting a prism.

My grandfather would sit on the bench. My grandmother would be working in the homestead, my mother worked in Gródek, my father on various constructions sites, to the honor of the Polish People's Republic. Chickens could all be approached in the same way while turkeys would threateningly bear their red necklaces, Teddy would be padding around by her doghouse awaiting freedom from the chains and a pat on the head. Everything moved of its own volition and on its own legs or another way.

Only my grandfather was left out of the yard chaos, only my grandfather didn't have to work, like a living saint. He sat on his bench, worn out from asses and years, he sat and breathed, smoked and waved away my desires to lose another game of checkers or win one of pick-up sticks, which lay on the floor like a scattered bale of straw, colorful and with symbols; Poseidon's trident, an arrow, a fantastic plastic letter somewhere between alpha and omega.

Only my grandfather hovered above the bench amid cigarette smoke, round and pink like leavened bread. When he was sitting there calmly, when the whistling air filled his lungs and gray threads of smoke left his nostrils and—I would swear it—his ears, when the halo that belonged to every living saint glimmered in mica crystals in the white walls of the house, I would sit down by his feet. And wait. Wait for two things.

First, for a fit of my grandfather's coprolalia. He would begin to swear, going as deep as the world's roots, even further, beyond that. He swore cruelly, I don't remember any bunch he created, or ribbons he used to tie together the most unlikely words. I don't know what brought on these attacks: illness, the expected move to the cemetery, judgment of one's life? I don't know, but I felt as if my grandfather talked with winged messengers, that he was at least their equal, that the heavenly gates opened at his "fuck." "Welcome," the winged would answer.

Second, for the bees. My grandfather would be covered with bees. One only had to wait. The bees liked to sit on bare skin the best, though they avoided the face and neck, perhaps they were bothered by the cigarette smoke. The bees didn't sting my grandfather, and even if one did lose its stinger in his body out of carelessness, the body never swelled; my grandfather would take out the stinger and pick up the bee which would buzz, torn apart, dying as if it were human, without a higher aim, or the heaven which it had on a daily basis, insignificant, individual, and with transparent wings. Then, my grandfather would shake his head—maybe my mother gets this gesture from him—"Silly, silly," he'd say, emphasizing the last syllable. And then he'd swear.

I had hypochondriac tendencies, inherited from my mother, I guess. My mother shed hypochondria as one might shed old skin, about fifteen years ago when it turned out she was diabetic, or maybe it was atherosclerosis, I don't remember. Imagined illnesses were no longer needed. I was cured of hypochondria while on the beach. I was sitting with my partner, it was, I think, round six, gong, or round eight. We had drunk two glasses of red wine each. She was explaining to me how it was worth it and we loved each other, and I was thinking of the calcium tablets I never took: I was allergic to red wine. I wondered if my face would be covered with red spots, while she explained that it was worth it—gong!—"and" we loved each other, perhaps "because." I realized I would happily trade my companion for a glass of calcium.

In *The Adventures of Maya the Bee* I hated one of the characters, the mouse Alexander, I always thought he was gray and arrogant. As a mammal, he ruined the harmony of the insect world. He simply didn't fit in, but he took up so much space it was impossible to ignore him. Along with his talkativeness and glasses, even the spider Thekla, playing the fiddle, seemed nice and not so very dangerous. My therapist, a waste of time and money, said that I saw myself in Alexander. My therapist, the opposite pole of a good sense of humor, said that as long as I don't like the mouse, I won't manage to deal with my issues.

I used to always await the bedtime story on TV, there were stories I liked: for instance Aquarius Szuwarek and Spider Topik. Rumcajs and Professor Balthasar Sponge from the land of rain (today this land is dry, and instead we have thrillers and high-rise buildings). Teddy bears: the honorable invalid of the Polish People's Republic (Miś Uszatek) as well as the imported, from the West, pervert (Colargol), who refused a polar bear. Mole said, "Ah, yo." The wolf never caught up with the hare, just as the magazine *Kraj Rad* couldn't cope with upper-class five-year-olds: over one hundred percent in the norm, but the shops were still empty.

The black and white world was charming, it appeared before sleep, and then appeared the TV Rubin and colors, as well as General Jaruzelski who announced something. I didn't understand anything, I thought that the bald figure, similar to Miś Uszatek and the mouse Alexander, was apologizing to the children for the lack of a bedtime story. My mother listened, the puppet read, the flag hung, the snow fell, my mother cried. "Don't worry, Mom," I said. "We'll manage without the bedtime story somehow."

I promised myself, when I counted fewer years than fingers, that I would never stop watching those bedtime stories. I promised Kasia: I will never leave you, we'll die together. I promised the bottle it would end up in the trash, and I promised myself—peace and sleep, my mother—support. I made a lot of promises in my life. I feel a fatigue sometimes, as if I had kept all my promises, so many promises.

I walked through the gate, zone zero and myself; the obedient child. In the fenced orchard stood a few gnarled apple trees, with branches twisted with age and weather, just like an old person is twisted with arthritis. Harvest time was long gone, the trees would make for poor kindling, they only cast a shadow, a shadow of the second or third type, not very thick, poking holes in the sloping tops of the beehives, which were green, but I don't remember.

The bees were used to people, that's why they had no reaction to my trespassing. They did their own thing and I did mine: I sat by one of the beehives and watched. I spent a long time following the chaos of crossing paths, the workers returning to the beehives and flying out to the fields, the movement of wings and legs, and I talked to the bees as my grandfather did: "Silly,

silly," with an accent on the last syllable. And then I decided to tidy things up.

I began to arrange the bees in straight lines, but they didn't like my commands much, and the rows began to have holes as big as holes in cheese.

The bees stung me while I screamed, probably from fear and pain, I don't remember: "It's a miracle," says my mother, "that you survived those bees and your own stupidity." I was barely saved, though I don't remember the pendulum of bee poison that swung within me, from "to be" to "not to be" and back again. I think I must agree with my mother, in the broader context, that it was a miracle—to survive one's own stupidity, a miracle, but a common one.

I don't remember the consequences of that decision, that attempt to control the chaos by force. I was allergic to bee stings for a long time, but not to honey, I avoided that orchard. I don't remember.

Adults tell children stupid things. About storks and brothers (sisters), for instance. Adults ask children stupid questions, probably only to see how far the tongue can stretch. Who do you want to be when you grow up? For example.

First, I wanted to be my grandfather, which seemed to amuse most adults, and then I wanted to be the postman, to which adults would smile, and then I wanted to be Willy, which made adults visibly awkward and embarrassed.

Willy had stripes, antennae and wings, rarely used. Willy had faithful friends, for instance Maya, who was also a bee. Willy liked to sleep and eat. He was a drone. He got into trouble, and he was dragged out of it by his friends, and then he dozed for a week somewhere within the cathode ray tubes, only to awake— reluctantly—in the next episode of the bedtime story.

I didn't understand why the word "drone" had negative con- notations. Probably because of human anger and cruelty. Because everybody would want to be a drone, they were just too embar- rassed to admit it.

I wanted to be Willy, a drone bee. Dreams, though, sometimes come true: not exactly as we intended, perhaps, but they do.

ELSEWHERE

What I remember from my short stay in one of the African countries is a postbox. Letters were divided into three categories: abroad, capital cities, and elsewhere.

I don't like to travel further than a few blocks away by car in a familiar city, nevertheless I had to change continents from time to time. The theater, it turns out, knows no boundaries, though the same cannot be said for audiences.

In the house in Stary Mokotów I knew, it seemed, where I was (capital cities), but here and now (in Białystok)—I don't know. Sometimes I think it's abroad, that I've crossed the border, a visa has been stamped in my passport, without a photograph or my signature. Sometimes I think I'm elsewhere; somewhere outside of the order I have grown used to.

The customs officer should ask about the journey: "Business or tourism?" In reply, I'd mutter some word. Tourist, perhaps: I want to visit and touch the places of my youth. Or business, for instance: I have a deal to make, you know, I need to keep an eye on my mother, or rather, her death. "How long are you planning on staying?" would be the follow-up question. That doesn't depend on me, dear sir, the doctors have us trapped; at most just over a year. "Enjoy your stay," the customs officer would say.

I had someone come and clean yesterday, the rooms and bathrooms shine. I didn't let them touch the porch or my mother's bedroom. I had two pills last night. I lay on the bed and waited. It's these actions that I excel in. Sometimes I forget what I'm waiting for. And where.

I'm afraid of chemical sleep. I never remember much after awaking. All my muscles ache, my eyes are dry, as if I'd just witnessed some horrors. The pharmacological fairies don't want baby teeth anymore, they leave no gifts under the pillow, all the presents they bear are lead and mercury, radioactive elements, and chemistry.

I woke up before midday. Before my first coffee and cigarette (on the porch) I have to apply some eyedrops to rub away the chemical blindness. My brain was as tired as if I'd just finished work; memorized theories and a useless bibliography. For the first time I remembered that I'd been dreaming, I even remembered the dream.

Around me there were bad people in long, colorful cloaks and Eastern makeup, something like the Three Wise Men who gave Christ his first gifts, Demis Roussous on the festival in Sopot, and Ewa Minge in golden leggings. I had to rise up and laugh, and only then would the bad people fall apart into pieces and I'd regain my freedom.

I hate dreams (my nineteenth). I had to pick up my mother in the late afternoon (after four). In pajamas, slippers, and a jacket I went out into the yard, to the postbox, to get the papers.

In the office is a desk, and behind it sits my old classmate Paweł and his current friend, whose face is, for a change, worried. A comical pair in white lab coats, Flip and Flap, Sancho Panza and his donkey. Paweł speaks first, while the worried face only offers an occasional cough and takes off its glasses, wiping them into a chamois cloth probably for the sole reason of wiping holes into the glass. I don't understand much, but this is what it should be: a summary of the tests, columns of numbers, the current state of medicine, names of organs mixed with Latin. "My dear sirs," I interrupt them, "All I know how to say in Latin is 'fuck'." "Grzesiu," Paweł says tenderly, "that's a very fitting word. I couldn't have said it better myself."

The first page displays another revolution in the Ukraine, soon they'll run out of colors. I can't ignore that first page. I don't care about the Ukraine, blue or orange, I don't even care about the road by which this house stands, but I force myself to read. I found only one punctuation mistake, not much for a revolution. I always start with the first page. Then I throw out the inserts and local edition. I end up with the main one in my

hands or on the table in front of me. I make myself another coffee. A real one, not instant crap. The last page is occupied with
sports. In a month or two, the ski jumping season starts. Last
year they were writing that the Polish Eagle flew one hundred
and fifty meters, he won first place. One hundred and fifty isn't
much for an eagle. If it had been a kiwi bird or a potato, then
I'd understand the fuss.

I used to begin reading with news, both domestic and international. Then, I'd begin with the culture section: critics and
events. Then, I began with opinions, but when I stopped having my own opinion about most things about two years ago, I
moved my interest (which I don't have much left of) to science
and gossip. Now, though I'm not old, I look for hourglasses
like a knight (though not all do) searches for the Holy Grail.
Rectangles drawn in a thick black line calm me down. Name
and surname, title and profession (husband, father, friend), the
hour and place of the funeral, condolences or contact to those
in mourning (family, publisher, company).

I like cemeteries, I feel great at cemeteries (twelfth), that's why
I try to visit at least one when I go somewhere. I walk among
the tombstones, the paths resemble those in parks, but there are
few lovers. I read the dates and captions, as long as the foreign
language is not so foreign that I don't understand anything. I
think it was in Cartago, a small town in an insignificant country
of Central America, I read the following: "Here lies Mario, a
good husband and father, a terrible electrician."

I looked through the pages, burned my mouth on the coffee,
nobody that I'd known had died. I look through other papers
too, different people die in different newspapers. Very rarely does
the same person die in all of them. In the tabloids, there's no
place for death, sometimes only a spectacular noun on the first
page: rape, crash, murder.

My mother really has lost some weight while on the hospital
diet, she doesn't look too bad. On the way I tell her about the
workers who work so slowly on the new garden. "How long are
you going to stay?" she asks. "I don't know," I lie. "I can work
here, and I could use some peace and quiet." "Then, son, I think

you've got the wrong city."

The economy is developing more slowly than was predicted, but faster than expected. Sometimes I get lost in the columns dedicated to economics. I don't understand much, I'm familiar with individual words perhaps, but the phrases make no sense. I know what "to buy" means, and "to sell."

"I don't plan on giving up," my mother says quietly. "Everything will be okay," I lie. "You've always managed." "Don't take it personally, I just wanted to warn you, since you're staying," my mother says drily, not looking at me, or at the road speeding by the window, only at her shoes—my mother's bent head, the eyes of the best hygienist in Białystok, who, in the past, never missed any dust.

This isn't a pleasant conversation. I'd like to get back to the house now. I'm beginning to sweat and feel nervous, just like I used to before exams. When we stop at a red light, the tension rises as far as the roof and creaks like before a storm, charged with electricity, pine freshener, and mutual reluctance.

I glance at some of the supplemental sections: "Tourism," "Large Format," "High Heels," "Culture," "Your Network," "@tom." I like reports the best, those describing common events and ordinary lives, with a couple of photos taken in natural light, blurry, artistically messy.

My guts twist in pain, my body shrinks from it and shrivels like a plastic bag in fire. I have to shut my eyes tight, hoping my mother won't notice. But she does. "I'm sorry, son," she says, "I'm just pissed off that I have to die." My mother never swears. Suddenly we both begin to laugh, each of us for a different reason. The cars behind us begin to honk.

Of all the supplements in all the papers, I most like those devoted to books. Reading reviews, real reviews rather than summaries of a few sentences paid for by the editor, relaxes me. Real reviews have a beginning, middle, and end. Some of the reviews miss the middle.

I take two bags out of the trunk, I talk to the workers for a while, my mother turns the key in the lock. I know this gesture, the quiet click, the slight dissatisfaction and irritation on her features. My mother's lips tie themselves together at the sight of the ashtray in the porch, full of cigarette butts like a hedgehog full of spikes. She looks into all the rooms and bathroom. "It's clean," she says.

ACCESSORIES

FOR HER SEVENTEENTH BIRTHDAY I decided to buy Kasia a belt. We went to the accessories shop on Lime Street. The shop was doubtlessly expensive, while we were dressed in rather cheap clothes, so the young assistant looked down on us. I asked shyly about the price of a brown belt, while he replied in a manner that made no use of numbers: "Too much for you," he said, not taking into account my parents' high salaries. Kasia theatrically glanced at the shelves, full of bags, belts, purses, and turned to the assistant. "I take it your shop was inherited," she paused, "from your parents."

We walked out, and later could not stop laughing, a laughter that pushed tears to our eyes as a teaspoon of lemon juice might. "There's your present," I said. "Yeah, and it was cheap. Get me a casserole." "Happy birthday," I replied.

I don't think I ever laughed so much. I don't think I was happier in high school than I am now, but I certainly laughed more.

I began to trust my own body. My body behaves like a slipper. A slipper freed from any authority. I can convince myself something is good for me, but instead of snot on the tissue I see blood. I push away the necessity of confronting someone or something, trying to lead an ordinary life, and after a month I end up in the hospital with a body covered in spots for no apparent reason: I try to hide something, and my body rebels, oozing pus. My body wins. I trust it. I have no choice.

It's funny as well as paradoxical that my body is my highest authority and best friend, without which—literally—I wouldn't survive. I feel at times like a huge, two-legged tautology.

My body takes care of me, in a way. But the fruits of this care don't grow immediately. For instance, I would make friends with someone important, who held in their hands the fate of my career; I made friends and convinced myself that this person was both interesting and honest, and after a few weeks, on the day of signing a contract, I couldn't get out of bed and would throw up with bile and pneuma. The latter evaporated, the former decorated the toilet.

I don't know if Kasia is smarter than me. Nobody carried out any tests, and our average grades were comparable. I do know we stimulated one another, though. We were stimulated by situations and classmates, hot dogs in the canteen, and the mediocre and loud concerts at the Philharmonic in Białystok. Rain or snow, annually surprising the road service. Parents and siblings.

"Your deepest desire," I said, "tell me." Kasia thought long and hard, I thought she wouldn't reply. She often didn't reply, not straight away. That was the difference between us: I talked to find the answer, she only responded once she'd thought hard about the words. "To live somewhere," she began, "far away but with people, to live cautiously and not fall into debt, to have no mortgages to pay off. That, nothing more."

We studied at an elite high school, at the dawn of an independent and democratic reality, the "third." Independence, democracy and republic didn't mean as much to us as a biology test (desired grade: A). The world was composed of various levels: ours was small, the high school named for A. Mickiewicz, and there were other, larger ones, with votes, decommunization, and long words that we got used to in Polish class: nothing erases the meaning of long words better than the Ministry of Education. "Joseph Conrad isn't bad either," Kasia says, "drifting toward warm islands, then he gets drunk and he's right, perhaps he has moral depression with the help of his heroes, but without any deeper, dire consequences." "Kiss me," I replied.

My mother appreciated the clean state of the house, she unpacked and brewed some green tea, only then noticing the scattered newspapers in the living room. Collecting them together into a neat pile, she said angrily, like she used to: "Dear Lord, when will I finally get some peace. They come to visit and make a mess." I only just managed to stop myself from responding: I could pass along the message from the doctors. My mother will go to heaven. Not because she was a good person: she still is. My mother will go to heaven as a technical worker: nobody will clean the blue tiles as well, won't wear out her joints into clouds, and so on, similes, metaphors, and a tombstone.

I used to think that with age details became smaller, harder to notice. That a person doesn't notice the toothpaste has no cap, when his or her generation goes deaf the phone is impossible to hear too. But that's not true. Perhaps the details are more difficult to catch, obviously eyesight deteriorates, but suddenly the details matter more.

Kasia and I liked to talk about cheesy things, fakes, because we lived in an artificial world: the blearily remembered communism had fallen and capitalism spread like wildfire. Growing up at a time of historic significance isn't as fun as it sounds; the continuity of experience is brutally severed, advice of aunts and uncles is utterly useless, one belongs neither to the old generation or the new, and feels aversion toward his or her peers, if he/she feels anything at all. To grow up in a moment that spans years, when history is written with a capital letter and determines the money in one's purse, isn't all that.

Perhaps I'm wrong, but our only safe haven turned out to be other people. I hid myself in Kasia, and she in me. No ideology or demagogy: a saved body kept in another.

"The tackiest literary heroine?" I ask. "Sofia Marmeladova," replies Kasia. We disagreed as to what was superb, but we had the same views about what was unsuccessful. Our favorite scribbler was Dostoyevsky. Only years later did I realize he was also a theologist; taking the works out of a literary critical context and putting them in a theological one, a reader might be lightheaded with delight. But Sofia Marmeladova from *Crime and Punishment* could not be saved. Perhaps only an encounter with the paper Werther, young and suffering, might awake the human in her: where pages rub against each other there appear sparks; it sounds like the statement of a survival textbook or literary theory.

It's funny, but the heroes of novels chosen by the Ministry of Education seem as real to me now as my classmates of those years.

Ryfka is naked and red haired, like Aneta. Janko the Musician lived about two houses down, and his talent was much exaggerated (I heard). The Paul Street Boys didn't like me, though I liked them. Wokulski, the miser and private entrepreneur, had red hands in the vegetable garden near Foundation Street. The Great Improvisation turned out not to be so great after all, though better assayed than the improvisations of the unprepared Paweł when asked questions in Geography class.

What seemed tangible sometimes became as real as the constructs and concepts that one had to memorize; the upper lip of a friend with its first fuzz is as tangible as the later *Four Quartets* by Eliot, or rather earlier.

"The tackiest concept of happiness?" I ask. "Her and him, with children, until death tears them apart in a family house," Kasia replies. Then, she bursts out laughing. Her right eyelid droops, as if telling me this isn't real. That happiness is easy to laugh at, but worth experiencing.

My mother has drunk her tea. I don't like green tea. Green tea is very healthy, in third place, and it tastes like it's healthy: it tastes like nothing. I'm a child of deficit and healthy nutrition, because what was unhealthy was too expensive. Sometimes, for my father's name day or my parents' anniversary of their wedding vows—well kept—my mother would buy something small: Tic Tacs; I didn't know they were only two calories. The Tic Tacs made me think of a favorite novel: *Tapatiki*, volumes I and II. The sausages manufactured by Tulip, for instance, in pink plastic and an elegant can that was later used for pencils and crayons. Colorful crayons. To every color gray was added to make the world easier to draw.

My mother drank her tea. She's been drinking green tea for years. Her body tolerates green tea, I think it will survive chemo and radiotherapy. I'm irritated. I can't find a comfortable place for myself, so I go upstairs. "I need to work," I say. "If you must, you must, son," my mother replies. "I'll clean up this syphilis."

"The tackiest literary hero?" I ask. We are sitting in Kasia's room, on the seventh floor. There's decaf coffee on the desk and cake on the plate, and cockroaches dance in the chute. Kasia thinks for a moment, then replies in all seriousness, slowly: "That would be you." I begin to tickle her, we end up on the bed. We laugh, mechanically: the truth can be amusing if you tickle it.

"I'm not worried about your brother," said my father a few months before his death, like a financial adviser might say when assessing the assets and liabilities of a company, "but I do worry about you. We didn't raise you right. Nobody will give you a glass of water." "Dad," I replied, "what would be bad is if nobody gave me a glass of whiskey. I'll manage without the water." "You see, that's exactly what I mean. Seemingly you keep your head, but you'll die alone."

That was, I shamefully admit, the deepest conversation I had with my father, friendly, as if we liked one another. He died, I stayed. Alone, but out of choice; I pay for the drinks with a tip, so I never wait long, and the bartender is faster than my mother. And he smiles.

"What are you most afraid of?" I ask. "Tickling?" she replies, to add later: "Probably loneliness. That I'll be abandoned. And you?"

"That I'll bet on a horse that will get out of my control and then buck me off."

"What does that mean? Tell me, or you'll get no cake!"

"I'd like to attain a level of simplicity and freedom, so that my decisions wouldn't depend on my parents or you. Absolute freedom of passing sentences and making choices."

"Only a man could think of something so stupid," quips Kasia. "Even if you're only potentially a man. I never gave up my flower . . ."

"No, you haven't," I say, lying on top of her, while the decaf steams on the desk, the cake lies motionless, and the cock- roaches keep dancing. Then I close my eyes and we kiss, I see bright colors which simultaneously push me away from Kasia's lips while also not letting me leave the thin, pink layer of skin, tasteless, like dry ice cream. "Maybe today?" I ask as my hand drifts down her body. She laughs. "The flower's on my head, you idiot," she says, grabbing my head. We laugh so hard that I fall off the bed and Magda, Kasia's younger sister, looks into the room curiously.

Sometimes I read interviews with renowned psychologists. They talk about life within 3,000 characters. Apparently, you can talk about childhood in two ways. Either as a lost paradise. Or a hell on earth, always present. I wonder which category of remembering I fit into better. Probably neither.

I wasn't any happier then than I am now. The only upper hand the past might have over my present is homework. I did it all and knew the answers. The difference is merely a technical one, without any emotional coloring.

"I'm happy with you," I say. "I know," Kasia replies, "But that will pass. Tomorrow we have a Chemistry test. Moles and crap that I can't figure out."

I couldn't find enough support in people, so I tried to get addicted to substances. Everything comes down to biochemistry, really. It took a long time for me to get addicted to cigarettes. I failed with drugs, they change consciousness too much and I don't like that, I never had the courage to try heroin that supposedly opens up heaven's gates. Alcohol serves a purpose; it stands in place of sleep, aids digestion—a relaxing massage after a hard day.

I sat in the room upstairs in front of the computer screen, my first computer. I called it Bobas in honor of Stanisław Lem. My parents paid for the computer. I should have been studying, I had exams in two weeks, but I was playing some strategy game. I could hear the row downstairs. My mother arguing with my father or the other way around, from a practical point of view the order of that didn't matter, it can be alphabetical.

They argue about what they always argued about. The spread of topics isn't too large, but the strategy and tactics are full of insinuations for all of them, full of dramatic gestures, brave charges, and attempts to gain anticipated ground. My mother as regal as Caesar, my father as small as Bonaparte. My parents are like two superpowers, my mother bearing the kitchen and pot, my father the bedroom and (in his final years) the remote. It's a draw. They keep each other in check, the final victory is impossible, the rule of guaranteed destruction applies: that's all they can offer one another.

Subject one: my mother isn't economical and spends too much money. Subject two: her mother-in-law. Subject three: me and my studies. Subject three joins subject one: I'm the most expensive thing on the list of monthly expenses of my mother; my mother, as if my father's dick had nothing to do with my creation. My father never accepted my choice to become a stage director instead of a doctor, too much money that he has to earn. I can hear from downstairs that I'm wasting my life (which might be explained by my young age, for instance) and his money (that cannot be explained at all). It's a hopeless case, I'm studying and I cost a lot, with no chance of a good position and pay in a respectable and timely fashion, that is, right after graduation. It's a hopeless case: my mother, to draw, will have to join subject three with subject two. This is risky, as my father reacts allergically to allusions about his umbilical cord not being cut, he twists in anger around his own belly button like a crazed omphalopsychite. Joining subject three with subject two gives my mother five points for tactics and courage: a draw, my father, extremely irritated, slams the door only to come back that night, drunk. While drinking with his friends, I have to admit, my father does eventually remember I am his son, and that the money he throws away by paying for my education will be his ticket into heaven. I never thanked my father's friends.

I tried participating in one of these rows, once. Defending my own positions, I supported, I thought, my mother, but I withdrew quickly. I woke up the next day in the Warsaw flat, while my mother—next to my father. My help turned out to be of mammoth proportions. I don't like household pets.

I went down into the kitchen. My mother was reacting to the stress, throwing food into her stomach. Her eyes were rinsed with tears, and she was preparing tea or some herbal drink. "Get out," she said. I'm a master of ricochets. I always get hit, but I got used to it now.

"A mole belongs in the wardrobe, next to the naphthalene," I say. Kasia was weighing my hand in her own. "Perhaps, but you should go now, I need to study. For moles in the wardrobe

I'd get grounded." "And you'd fail the class," I said happily. "I doubt it," she said with that strange, slow, unidentifiable note of something in her voice.

We say goodbye in the hallway, a stolen kiss in front of Magda. "I'll get you the belt when the shop closes down," I say. "Keep the accessories with your gallantry," she says. We laugh, and the door closes. I look at the wood-like surface with a peep-hole, which won't betray if Kasia is looking at me or if she's sad that we won't see each other until morning. I won't see Kasia until morning, in a few hours, morning; I'll study and I'll sleep; such empty hours, the wrong breaths in the house, the wrong hand on the door handle to the bathroom, anatomy of the eye in my biology textbook—I see nothing.

MOUNTAINS

I ALWAYS ROOT FOR THE UNDERDOG. It sounds great, might bring a tear to the eye. I rooted for the underdog maybe because I counted myself as one—so, I rooted for myself, clever, but unconscious, pushed into shadows.

Shadow. It's a word that begins with the wrong letter, rather it should be "ghadow," that shaded my childhood. I dreamt of the cycling incident and Iwona, in my dream only one thing differed from reality: the people and objects all had double shadows. I conducted experiments in the yard, after waking up, but there was always only one shadow, or none at all. In my dream, four legs bent on the stones in a street, the stones slipping away from sandaled feet. Some night, instead of looking at the ground, I looked into the sky and saw two suns.

One day I was watching a documentary about World War II on a black and white TV. It was afternoon, with an absent season: battles on the Pacific were grainy, like fragments of the *Blair Witch Project*, a rising sun on the Japanese flag resembled the pupil of a dark eye, and the dark rays were like samurai swords. First the Japanese did the killing, at the start of the documentary. At the end, they did the dying. Like obverse and reverse. Paweł and Gaweł. In one house.

Americans dropped two atomic bombs on the empire. Two bombs saved the war and cemented the shadow: saying this, I'm as far away as can be from describing reality metaphorically. The documentary showed photographs of Hiroshima (Nagasaki?), an ordinary wall, and on it a darkly filled silhouette of a human. A figure appears, yellow, though black and white. "That's my grandmother," it says, pointing at the wall. Then it talks about how the bomb exploded, and her grandmother's body was in the way. The grandmother evaporated in a split second, throwing only a shadow on the wall, that's all. Then I heard other stories, that the wave tore clothes as well as skin. My imagination was stimulated by the less bloody image, the person immortalized in a shadow, turned into their own shadow.

Thinking about a person who's very different from me, I don't have to rely on my imagination, my brother is (was) right beside me. He's red haired and freckly, short and stocky. Me: brown hair, fair skin, tall and anemic, no characteristic markings. My brother had endless energy: first he was always sick and drove everybody crazy with his crying, then he was always exercising, running, swimming, taking karate classes, then he was building his home, working and studying, having a family, still exercising, running, swimming, and capoeira. And me? The stem of the word "run" was only familiar to me in the context of an upset stomach. When exercising, I was best at minimalizing the amount of energy used so as to survive the following twenty-four hours. I never had the courage to build a home, a family, have a child.

My brother doesn't sleep more than four or five hours per night, while I need as many to fall asleep and wake up. My brother shines with health and vitality, me—with bile and potentially a sense of humor, according to Kasia. My brother finds time for everything, I have to make choices.

My brother spends money sensibly, I don't. My brother is honest and has rules, I haven't, and if I'm not too dishonest that's only because I've had no opportunity to be so. My brother uses "colorful" language, I barely ever swear.

My brother knows what and why, he makes decisions quickly, I doubt and put off for tomorrow what I should have done yesterday.

Despite all these differences we've both managed to survive and achieve, at least in the material sense of the word, success.

When we were adult enough for the four year difference to dissolve, we tried to become friends. It didn't work in words, but there were some actions that helped our relationship: going to the cinema in Białystok, New Year's Eves spent together in front of the TV, bonfires with sausages in Siemiatycze. These were side gestures, another form of displaying loyalty, a synonym of brotherly love, a euphemism.

Twenty-first, I have a problem making decisions in real life, as if all my decision-making was exhausted at the theater: there, I don't have this problem, though, sometimes, I make the wrong ones. In life I first go into denial, waiting for something to happen to save me from this responsibility. Only when held at gunpoint, physically exhausted, I choose, because I have no choice.

Zuza says she likes to live with a razor at her neck.

I don't.

The only place where I'm happy, because I'm free of the responsibility of making decisions, is an old hut in Myscowa. For the last twenty years I spend a month of the summer there, sometimes longer, always with Zuza. Sometimes someone visits: her son with a new girlfriend, our friends who also own the place. Neighbors drop in too, and from time to time a cow looks in the window.

An ordinary home: there's electricity, water in the well, a wood stove, a bath in the stream. A bedroom, hallway, kitchen that is also a living room. A day, twenty-four hours, where time for everything is found. Hours count the time, organizing it, but they don't describe how quickly it passes by. A day in the mountains is late compared to time in the city, just as the vegetation in the mountains is late: July is only the end of spring.

Zuza gets up first, makes coffee, opens the windows and door, smokes a cigarette, has breakfast. I get up around ten, repeating her gestures: lifting the mug with coffee, tapping the ash of my cigarette, reading newspapers that are years old and have miraculously evaded the fire. We sit at the table or in the doorway and look at the hills and fields. "The Lower Beskids really are low," says Zuza. "You're right," I say, "they're not very high."

Our closest neighbor, Mrs. Józefa, who supplies the milk, butter, and eggs—ten minutes and three streams away. The closest shop is an hour's walk, open in the mornings and evenings with a break to work the fields. The closest post office, and in it newspapers and weekly magazines—three hours' walk. The closest town is Jasło, an hour on the bus. The world is huge.

We sit in the doorway, coffee and a cigarette, in stretched out pajamas with holes and teddy bears, paled from sunlight, there's barely any color left.

There's no internet or phone. To contact us, one must come specially or send a telegram: the post office works, the postman has a motorbike.

We sit in the doorway, information from the world reaches us rarely because it must be carried up, and I rarely feel like a three-hour walk. "What if the world ends down there?" I ask. "I'm putting the kettle on, do you want more coffee?" Zuza replies.

All the objects around us are old, saved from the trash: the chairs with uneven legs, chipped plates, aluminum cutlery which is worn thin from use, orphaned plates from dinner sets. There are objects that seem to have no use in the hallway, but we don't throw them out, we can't. We don't talk much, and only about trivial things. Our sentences resemble the objects, tired, old, always beginning with a lower case letter, the dot above "i" blurry and pale like a fly's shit, even our names look different, zuza and grześ. Names aren't necessary anyway: we live alone, she is her, I'm me (he's him, I'm me, she thinks). Two people. It's a lie that in paradise only Adam and Eve lived. Names weren't needed. Paradise is a place where there isn't anything that isn't necessary, a place without capital letters: her and him, that's just right, it's enough for a lifetime, even an eternal lifetime.

"Thanks," I say, taking the chipped mug. "It would be great," says Zuza, "we'd have nowhere to go back to."

GAZ-67

I think it was June when we went for our first picnic. Not too far away, close to the airport. We had a thermos with iced tea (from my mother) and sandwiches (from Kasia's mother). We had a blanket and two books. Kasia took *One Hundred Years of Solitude*, I had *The Woman in the Dunes*. I couldn't read, the sun was as blinding as grains of sand. I lay still, happy, because I was both alone and with Kasia. I lay like that for at least two hours. Kasia got up from the blanket: "I see you're in your element," she said drily.

My mother was cutting the carrot. Carrots are healthy, almost as much as decaf coffee, you can't dissolve it in water perhaps, but that's OK because you can't cut up decaf.

"Is the *Dunes* in the title a shortcut?" asks Kasia. "What do you mean?" I asked. "From 'blown up,' for instance," she replied. "What's going on in that head of yours?" I asked. "I don't know," she muttered, lying back down. "And I don't think it's my head."

Cutting up the carrot, my mother cut herself, deeply. She covered the wound with a dishcloth, I got the first aid kit. She put a bandage over it. "Aren't you going to disinfect it?" I asked. She was sitting on a chair, blindly staring at the orange circles. "I asked you to cut the carrot," she said. "I asked you, but you never listen. Never." I didn't respond: "I wonder who I get that from?" I went out onto the porch.

"What's you're *Woman* like?" Kasia asked. "About six times shorter than your *Solitude*," I replied. Kasia picked up both books and set their spines against one another. "Maybe about five times," she said. "Definitely not six."

I take a long drag of my cigarette. The ashtray is full of butts resembling a spiky hedgehog, instead of a green apple I should

103

put in an apple core only, or maybe an empty lighter? The porch isn't cozy or pretty. It's not even clean. Even so, when I think about my place in the family home, it's the porch that comes to mind, the glass eye of my youth, blind.

Exotic guests always visited my grandparents' house, exotic from the point of view of a child: at least the kind of child who is short and not very decisive. Women from the village, low and spread out like a potato mound. Covered in flowered shawls or shiny gold baubles. Men with dry and red skin, with mustaches and nails framed in dirt. Smelling of tobacco and shit. Some aunts, clean and willowy, always unhappy because they came from Warsaw.

The dressed-up aunts came from Warsaw. They came for the fresh air, though the yard smelled better in their memories than reality. They came because they knew they wouldn't leave without sausages, hams, mushrooms, eggs. Socio-engineers of communism knew how to create such a reality where family bonds flourished, family from the city retained close relations with relatives in the country: all one had to do is decree a lack of everything. The city loved the country, especially those who loved vegetables, like Juliusz Słowacki in *Ferdydurke*.

Among the aunts from Warsaw who haunted my grandparents' home one seemed extremely clean and willowy. I remember her well, or at least a fragment of her: I was the one who found and held the eye.

The scene must have taken place above my head, at the level of adults. I don't know what happened, but my aunt's eye fell directly at my feet and rolled under one of the dressers. My aunt screamed as if she'd gone blind. The eye was glass and blind itself, but she was screaming as if it was a fully functioning eye that had just stopped working.

I learned later that after amputation, phantom pains occur. I never read anything about phantom eyesight though.

My aunt was screaming, my grandparents and some other guests were trying to calm her down with their own yells, which was only successful in that my aunt's voice was drowned out by the others, which must have calmed her down. I reached, short and blind, under the chest of drawers, to pick up the glass ball. I held the eye in my hand, dusty and staring. I thought my aunt could see me. With one eye, the real one, blinded, she veers between relatives and guests, with the other, the sensible and real one, tickled by dust, she stares at me.

Someone (not my aunt) saw me and took my third eye. I had a third eye for so short a time, an eye perfectly revealed and plucked from the skull like a bean. "My third eye," I tell Kasia, who is stretched out beside me on the blanket, "is probably in a coffin somewhere now."

"Did that really happen?" she asked me, reaching for the tea. "Yes," I say, "give me a minute. I see . . ." "Darkness," Kasia interrupts me. "Darkness was already. Twice. First in *Seksmisja*, then after the creation of the world."

"You have a problem with chronology," I reply. "No," Kasia says after a sip of tea, "I watched *Seksmisja* before learning that God divided light and dark." I stay silent, so Kasia asks: "So what was first, tell me?" "At the very front was the back," I reply, annoyed.

Three cigarettes in the lungs, I return, my mother has finished with the vegetables which bubble in the pot. She sits in the dining room, I look at her: a cup of green tea and a finger on her left hand, thicker for the bandage. She's writing numbers into squares. Sudoku. After arriving I found booklets with puzzles everywhere, because it was one of the few distractions (and luxuries) of my mother. Perhaps it's thanks to those puzzles that she survived five years with only Cesar for company, a dog that didn't speak except for on Christmas Eve, but didn't drink either, which separated it from my father.

"What's for lunch?" I ask, because I don't want to argue. I've decided I'll bite my tongue off sooner than I'll argue with my mother. My decision will end with my tongue remaining intact and me angrily running outside. "Soup and a main dish," she replies, not even lifting her head.

"Would you like to be an adult?" I ask Kasia. She doesn't even think before replying. "No."

I turn the TV on. TVP Kultura is streaming old episodes of

Łossskot, a cultural program; which year could that have been? 2005? 2007? Or an even one? I met some TV hosts once, I was thirty and had already directed a play. I barely remember any of it.

"And you," she asks, finally calm, "Would you?" I consider this a moment, the sun is bothering me, tomorrow's history test is a thorn in my side. "An adult, no. I'd like to be an old man." "Why?" asks Kasia. "So that everything was behind me, and ahead only happiness and memory loss."

My mother leaves the puzzles in the dining room, she walks into the sitting room and sits down next to me. She looks at the screen and—I think—understands nothing. "I remember this program, son," she says. "That's when you were on TV the first time."

I never touched on such difficult topics as I did in high school. With Kasia. I didn't believe, though I probably sensed, that words were just words, and life just life. I still believed that the problem of describing reality could be brought down to the level of a problem whereby you assigned definitions to words. With time, my tongue got drier, it saved on words, I retreated from decorative adjectives, left behind synonyms, putting in commas pleases me. My interest in languages and life can be brought down to the level of punctuation: sentences write themselves and I only put in punctuation marks in the chosen places; I'm a believer of the unpopular school of thought known as emotional punctuation, often mistaken for laziness or dyslexia. I like question marks. I have ellipses. I have exclamation marks.

"Do you sometimes think," Kasia asks, "what you'll be like in a few years?" "I try not to," I reply. "I prefer to worry about my grades."

In high school I thought that with time, people get smarter, except for parents and teachers, who somehow fell outside of the rules that organized life. It turns out that isn't the case. Intelligence doesn't resemble fat, it doesn't grow on you with time. When I think of my high school self, I don't really differ from myself now: I was an adult already, I'd already made my first mistakes, those "basic" ones, I could already sense what I was capable of.

Eccentric aunts had husbands, some of them at least, some had more than one. From these husbands I can recall only Uncle Ignacy. He was the son of my great-grandmother, he lived in Warsaw, aunt Alina was his wife. Once a year I went to Warsaw with my grandmother—who for a fortnight or so ceased to be the mother-in-law in my mother's mind—to visit my great-grandmother, and so also the aunt and uncle. They lived in a modernist, prewar villa in Bielany. The villa was surrounded by an apricot orchard. They had as much money as ice and even more, because ice wasn't produced at all when the Communists ruled us. Objects that didn't melt in sunlight were preferred—tanks, for example.

Uncle Ignacy was good with engines, oils, and gears. In the garage, which was also a mechanic's workshop, he built luxury yachts, his private entrepreneurship: two yachts, launched first in the city, then on the lakes with a bottle of champagne, supplied a year's worth of a very comfortable lifestyle. Uncle Ignacy seems, in hindsight, to have been a man who commanded the luxury level of life, which was very un-socialist and, paradoxically, safe. Maybe that's why he never had any problems with the authorities—they had to swim on something and kayaks were too thin and easily capsized.

Uncle Ignacy also had a car in a fast color: red, yellow, orange. The car was from the West, and a sports car at that. Ford Capri, for instance. My brother's first car was a denial of my uncle's. First, it was cheap, second, long-lasting, third, slow. My brother's first car was a GAZ-67, olive-green, you didn't even have to lock it up because nobody in their right mind would want to steal it.

"Mom, do you remember the aunt who lost her glass eye?" I ask. "What are you talking about?!" she exclaims in surprise. "About the eye," I respond, "and the aunt." "Aunt Alina, the Warsaw one, son, you remember? She had a necklace with real coral beads . . ."

My mother's approach to Aunt Alina is well described by the adjective "ambivalent." On the one hand, aunt Alina led a big-city life, a life my mother wanted: a villa in Warsaw and Western cars, holidays abroad, no responsibilities. One the other hand, she lacked what my mother prized most: children.

Sometimes I think that we get exactly what we want, just concentrated more: like water in the form of powder and nothing to dissolve it in.

My brother, with whom we practice gestures on the side, has helped me a few times. After my second play, which was torn apart by the critics (I hadn't yet learned that critics must be made happy in a way that they won't even notice, but which will bring relief), I went back to Białystok. In debt, with no flat, a broken career, left by a certain actress whose talent remained a secret but whose cleavage was known to all. I don't think I'd ever been so close to Hobb: we didn't make friends.

My brother took me in for two months, he came to the train station in the new GAZ-67. He saved me, though maybe he doesn't know it. I always trusted in the good hearts of strangers.

CLAY

Hypochondria is best cured with amnesia, though even that doesn't always work. I've been suffering from some of the symptoms for years now, with no remedies for what my brother colorfully describes as the syndrome of having a pine cone up my ass. Something is stuck and will not be moved. It hurts least when not moved.

My grandmother had long, strong, gray hair that smelled of wax and a musty wardrobe. She liked it when I brushed it. She liked the comb scratching her skin. She liked it when I lay beside her on the couch while she dozed, and I wondered, for example, what was the point in this lying still when I could be practicing archery or going down to the stream with Teddy.

At the university, I struggled a lot, reading the antique philosophers, tripping over everyone and everything. I felt freer only in the twentieth century, when philosophy grew smaller and began to ask small questions, the answers to which were equally difficult though.

I remember my great-grandmothers only in fragments. One lived in Warsaw. The other in Bielewicze. One had an uncle Ignacy and an aunt Alina. The other two hands marked with liver spots. I remember those hands: one held a sweet, wanting to tempt me, the other—if I let myself be caught in this mousetrap—fell on my shoulder to capture me. My great-grandmother demanded attention, but I wanted to kiss her cheek as much as I wanted to face a speeding truck.

My body, nothing special, is composed of water, some carbon, calcium, all just enough to shape the vessel for water. When I was a child, I was charmed by a painting where God was molding—my grandmother's words—a man from clay, baking him in

an oven, and then breathing life into him. I regret that I'm not
made of clay, that my body doesn't crack at the point of impact,
that the cracks can't be filled with rain. No sand streams from
the cracks that could then be harmlessly swept under a doormat.

My great-grandmother had, apart from the spotty skin on
her hands, a friend in the next village. I only found out about
this recently, maybe three years ago, when my mother decided
to sell the ruin that used to be the house in Bielewicze. We were
visiting with my mother, looking at the house and barn, or rather
their shapes, sketches. It was September, or the end of August.
The house was at the edge of a wood. Instead of a fence on that
side there was a row of pines. Their branches were laden with
storks. They called to each other before leaving to Africa. Not
many sights seemed as absurd to me as the storks on the pines:
birds of warm climates on the needle-filled tree of the northern
and sandy earth.

My great-grandmother had a friend in the next village, possibly in Mieleszki. She was stubborn enough to go to see her, but
old enough that she couldn't get herself a driving license. The
family bought, or rather sorted out, because in the red reality the
verb "to buy" could only be applied to bread, milk, and vinegar,
possibly people, everything else was sorted out—two Melexes.
A driving license wasn't required, neither was petrol.

Three years ago we walked into the barn: between the walls
and roof full of holes we saw two small cars, affected by time
and animals. "One was charging," my mother said to me, "while
your great-grandmother drove the other one."

They make me think of papal mobiles. I imagine my great-
grandmother, the papal native of Bielewicze, a swallow of progress and ecological vehicles, flying close to the ground from
one village to the next. "She was crazy," my mother says, "totally
crazy. There wasn't a week that she didn't end up in the ditch."
"And she never hurt herself?" "No, son, not once. But she died
in the end anyway."

Zuza spent her teenage years in Africa. Her parents were
diplomats in some country that used to be a French colony.
That's where she got her driving license, or rather where she got

into a car and drove five hundred meters in a straight line, up to the table where a clerk gave her the document. Upon her return to Poland, she didn't drive. She bought a Fiat 126 late, possibly around the time we met. I don't remember where we were going, but I remember that when she made a turn, Zuza broke all the rules. There was a cop just past the intersection, and he waved us over. Zuza pulled over, rolled down the window, while the cop walked over, disbelieving that he was really seeing what he was witnessing. Before he asked any questions or asked for the documents, Zuza spoke, like an African princess: "I'm not drunk. I'm just this bad a driver." The policeman was speechless, eventually he choked: "Right, keep going then, I don't want to watch this."

Twenty-second, beauty paralyzes me. Along with sunsets, full moons, an arête on a navy background I cope with just fine, because these views are as beautiful as they are tacky. Tamed on postcards and electronic wallpapers, to some extent they are obvious. But the beauty that I see in people, thankfully rarely, is what paralyzes me, making me shy. It happens without warning, a stranger of either sex and any age: the first glance that haunts my brain after a flash of blue lightning that immediately makes me feel cleansed. I stare, on the brink of tears, as someone for a split second finds what they've lost and must give it up just as fast: someone got out of the bus a stop earlier, crossed the intersection, left the till. A strange situation to be in, a state that lasts for hours at a time, sometimes even into the next day. That's what paralyzes me: beauty which, slipping from body into word, slips into tackiness.

I met Zuza when she worked for one of the large media companies, first as a journalist, then in marketing. I don't remember the instance of our first meeting: mutual friends or some boring, stiff party at the Jan Sobieski III Hotel, four stars.

A month, sometimes more, for twenty years. That gives, altogether, more than a year and a half. Math: two plus two is always four, for twenty months I was happy, I'm not the best at addition. Happy in the house in the mountains, always with Zuza. I can't believe in the result. A year and a half of happiness and security, peace and ordinariness, and I only kept one, blurry, long memory, pale as if happiness could easily be rubbed out so as to not prod you with a sharp pain all the time.

I don't know what Zuza was made of: dough, meat, or clay. In the mountains she was composed of transparency. She stood by the table while I looked at her books, she didn't stand in the way of me seeing something, even a clean jar was not shadowed and lost by her presence. My great-grandmother said that an anemic couldn't even throw a proper shadow. Zuza could, but her shadow in the mountains was as transparent as her body.

I drove my mother to her first chemotherapy session yesterday. We were worried as much as before a first day at school or a wedding night. "Mom," I say, to calm us both down, "it's simple: you'll swallow the pills. Like communion. Instead of the bread you'll just taste something else. Just swallow it." My mother stares at me as if I had just grown horns. "Son, we're not Catholics, we don't take communion."

Sometimes I forget who I am and who I'm not. Name and surname, date of birth, address, profession—that, I remember. Polish nationality, if I had any doubts, I could just check my passport. But the rest—groups and gatherings, all that is fluid. I resemble an equation with a huge number of unknowns; I can't work myself out. I fall asleep an atheist, awake a devout Christian; on a Saturday morning I have Jewish roots, and in the afternoon I believe that antisemitism is imaginary; I sign a declaration for animal rights, just to buy a fur moments later, the animal depending on current fashion and trends as well as available funds.

"So you see," I say in the car on the way home, "there wasn't anything to be scared of." "You were right, son, like communion." She didn't even get to the porch door before throwing up, almost without any notice. I opened the door and gave her some tissues. She smiled palely. "I was always thorough. I'll have all the side effects. I promise," she joked.

My phone rings. I hate phones (eleventh). A private number. I pick up. I pick up only to walk away and not watch my mother cleaning up her own vomit.

"Hello," a voice says. "Hello." "Where did you get my

number? Who are you?" I ask. I hear a woman's laugh on the other end, tense, but familiar. "I got it from Paweł." My brain is working quickly, looking through old files and drawers that have been closed for years. Among all these mental activities I choke out an intelligent: "Oh." The laughter returns, a bit freer and longer. "You don't seem to have changed much." I stay silent, because the short retort I need is out of reach. "Don't you remember me?"

I lean against the wall of the house, I don't feel faint. I feel great, except for my memory, which is made of lead. My legs are like clay. A bad connection. From a constructivist point of view.

G 35

"Is something wrong, son? You look like you've been poisoned," my mother says. I wonder if she used the adjective "poisoned" with irony—her body is the one which has accepted a dose of poison. We sit at the table in the kitchen. I'm reading the newspaper and drinking coffee. The coffee is cold and dust will gather on the paper soon. My mother is filling in squares with numbers.

Sudoku: a single (doku) figure (su), from Japanese. The chart is a large square, nine by nine smaller squares, each divided into squares of three by three. The game consists of filling in the empty squares with figures between 1 and 9 so that in each row and each column all the numbers appear only once.

"Mom, do you remember . . ." I wanted to say "Kasia," but in the last moment I manage to not say the name. "Ka . . . Anna, I mean?" I finished. My mother looks over her squares at me: "What Anna?"

I'd like to know that myself. I feverishly try to dig up some kind of Anna from my memory. "Popławska," I choke out. "What's wrong with you?" my mother worries. In worry she is very convincing.

I tell her about the cemetery and Anna's grave, the one who died and then was born, "beloved." Only when I finished the sentence did I realize what an awkward topic I've chosen; my mother made me realize: she sighed, preparing to tackle another empty square with her pencil.

"Fill out the following with your strongest skills," I read in one of the applications: I was trying to get a job in a media company in the creative department, ten years ago, after the fiasco that my second play turned out to be. Truthfully, I should have written "doubting"; I can doubt anything and anyone, every step I take is punctuated with doubt. Cogito ergo sum. I can't be otherwise. I wrote: "Excellent communication skills," which wasn't entirely true; I am better at ending acquaintances than I am at keeping them up, which suggests poor communication—but I need to make those acquaintances first before I can break them, which involves communication.

"Five," my mother mutters.

It began with the drooping right eyelid—that could be the alternative beginning: once upon a time, in another time. That could be the beginning, why not: I don't know.

Kasia's eyesight was getting worse, not gradually, but in leaps and bounds. Of course I noticed the glasses, with the lenses getting thicker and thicker. I've been wearing glasses myself since primary school, so glasses worn by someone else didn't really surprise me or make me feel sorry for them, more their absence—in the reality of an elite high school and nerds—was what raised suspicions: either somebody doesn't read, or they didn't get enough iodine during the Chernobyl disaster; whichever way you look at it, suspicious.

Cramps in the appendages followed, pins and needles, lack of feeling, small and barely noticeable paresis, a longer reaction time to stimuli. Kasia was a master at camouflaging the weaknesses of her body. She used both loose and unfeminine clothes as well as ostentatiously tamed restlessness. When she stomped heavily, I never knew if it was to display her disgust at the world or because her feet were not fully under her control.

We were all unwell at some point: flus, tonsillitis, common colds. Twisted ankles, swollen joints, pulled tendons. Aching teeth, digestive problems, hangovers. All high school students get sick, but nobody hid that fact; on the contrary, everyone hoped to get sick and have an excuse to miss school. I'd get a coughing fit in the corridor and feel immediately surrounded by people hoping to be saved. My friends came like bees to honey. "Cough on me," they'd beg. "I have a Chemistry test next week and could really use a few days of peace." I coughed because I knew they'd do the same for me.

Kasia was sick much more frequently than most people. If I'd been the sort of person to notice details, I'd have noticed that her individual absences lasted at least a week, far longer than most common illnesses last. But the power of observation was never one of my stronger characteristics, especially when those close to me were concerned; closeness put to sleep my vigilance, chores took over.

"Three," my mother thinks aloud. Her "three" sounds like "tree."

Kasia's illness was characterized by an unwillingness to be diagnosed, but I only found out about this when at the university. First, this particular illness didn't usually show symptoms until the person in question was at least thirty, which is why Kasia's case was rather remarkable. Second, the illness was rather unpredictable. An attack was followed by remission, when all symptoms retreated. "It's like that game with hands, to see who's faster," Kasia said in high school. "You put out your hand and you don't know whether you'll snatch it back in time. To make things harder—you might also get hit on the head." Third, Kasia's illness was incurable. It was a death sentence, not very clear perhaps because nobody could determine the time or place.

What attracted me to Kasia was a sense of mystery, I knew from our first meeting in class that under her words was hidden a different, secret world. Everything she said cast a shadow and had a deeper meaning: "I have to spend my summer in Germany at my aunt's, and I hate her," she said. I didn't know where the "have" came from; I knew she wouldn't tell me.

We spent only one summer together, after the third year of high school, three weeks on a cycling trip in Mazury, camping in a tent. There were two other couples, Alicja, who was in our year, and her boyfriend Arthur, Alicja's senior by ten years; Maciek, a student of Polish at the university in Białystok (very stressed) and Agnieszka, his girlfriend, also at the university.

I don't remember many situations of three against five: odd numbers, sad, there was always one without a pair.

The first situation: we had to ("had to," Kasia would say) go through a sandy path in the woods. The wheels kept getting stuck in the sand, we pushed the bicycles that were laden with tents and food instead. It was boiling hot. A bottle of water fell out of Kasia's basket. She pushed it back in. After a few meters, the bottle fell out again. After the fifth time Kasia, who never swears, instead of placing the bottle back in its place, walked over to the nearest tree with it (a pine) and began to hit the trunk as if the bottle were an axe, each time yelling: "Fuck, fuck, fuck." We left our bicycles, Alicja, Artur, Agnieszka, and myself, rolling around laughing.

The second situation: we put up the tent by the lake. We got there dirty and tired and went straight to sleep. The weather in the morning was terrible. We all needed a wash. One stinks in rain as much as in sunshine. I ran out of the tent and straight into the lake. I hate water, I soaped myself, I can't swim. I took a step backward and began to drown. The sky closed above me in bubbles of water and soap along with slimy weeds. I couldn't call for help; water is not my environment, it has no syntax, punctuation, or even mistakes that might be corrected with a red pen. Drowning, I thought that it's a shame. A shame. I woke up on dry ground, convinced that I was dreaming. A wet dream. Not really.

The third situation: we cycled about forty kilometers on asphalt roads, and the passing trucks were more tiring than the conquered kilometers. A shop. I barely had any money. Kasia bought herself a Snickers (because it had nuts) and a Mars for me (because that's what I preferred and she loved me even if I had no money). We were eating the chocolate bars when Kasia said: "They cost the same but Snickers has nuts. I don't understand how you can prefer Mars."

"This sudoku is really hard," my mother complains. "Or maybe my head's just tired?"

The fourth situation: we're lying in the tent, it's still light outside, summer, we're kissing and touching, probably even without knowing that what we're doing has a name; I'm looking at her breasts, I've spent three years wondering what they would look like, how the nipples would turn out to be: resembling those from philatelic stamps or the calendar: small and dark, large and light? Between her breasts I can feel tiny light hairs; this I hadn't expected, this wasn't on the pictures.

The fifth situation: morning, the tent stank of burned rubber, Kasia got up probably to go to the toilet, nobody gets up unless they must, I can hear the zipper being opened and then a shout. A cow pushed its head into the tent, and Kasia pushed her hand into cow shit.

"How do you assess your resilience to stress? Put an 'x' next to one of the numbers, where 1 means no resilience whatsoever, and 10 indicates a high resilience," I put an 'x' next to the 10, I always liked to exaggerate.

But it wasn't during our only summer together that I found out that the mystery about Kasia is simply her illness. At the start of our final year Kasia was taken ill again, and she missed two weeks of school. I called her house. Magda picked up. She didn't like me. "My sister's in the hospital again, stupid," she told me and hung up.

I got scared, not that Kasia was in the hospital; the hospital was there to go to when the need arose. I got scared because Magda said "again." I'd never heard anything about Kasia going to the hospital at any point in the past. The "again" threw me off balance.

Then, I felt rage; I'd been lied to. This was followed by the high school question that sounded like it came straight from Dostoyevsky: did Kasia's lie throw a shadow of doubt on everything that was between us? Later, I learned I hadn't been lied to, Kasia just didn't tell me everything just as I kept some things to myself too, if anyone was lying it was me—to myself.

I went to the hospital. Kasia's mother was a doctor and I assumed she'd have taken Kasia to the hospital at which she worked. I wasn't wrong, the receptionist gave me a room number. I took the stairs, the elevator didn't work. I met Kasia's mother in the corridor. "How is she?" I asked. She looked tired, had two teenage daughters, no husband, night shifts, Kasia's mother always looked tired. "Not too bad," she said. "What wrong with her?" I asked. "She'll tell you," she said as she walked away.

"There's low pressure today," my mother informs me, putting

the puzzles aside. "I'm going to go and lie down. For a bit."

I walked into the hospital room. Kasia was in the bed by the window. She was reading something, a huge book in red binding, *The Newest History of Poland* by Roszkowski, our final exams were drawing near. There's no break even if you're an invalid. Kasia looked absolutely fine, but the "again" that I'd heard from Magda eliminated an ordinary disease. We said our hellos, she was surprised to see me, embarrassed and confused, like someone who has just been asked a question in class.

"Magda has told me everything," I lie, sitting on the chair beside the bed. Kasia's lips tighten in anger. She says nothing, probably contemplating revenge on her younger sister, possibly trying to decide between simple suffocation or defenestration. "There's just one thing I don't know," I continue. "What's the disease?"

She says nothing. I wasn't expecting an answer. I sit by her and I feel almost everything at once: anger, bitterness, fear for her, I want to hug her and humiliate her all at once—almost everything, almost all at once.

"I knew it would be like this," Kasia says. "I knew it." I don't say anything, something bad is happening inside me. Like after the bicycle incident with Iwona. Something is breaking, hurting. Something again for the first time. "Why didn't you tell me?" I ask, and her hand finds mine, this isn't pleasant.

"I was afraid," she says. "I was hoping I'd die before having to talk to you about this. I was hoping I wouldn't die. You know me, I'm a humanist."

"You haven't died," I point out drily and tear my hand from hers to cover my mouth. I didn't think I'd say something like that. I'm terrified. For the first time in my adult life I'm terrified and I see no way out.

Only now do we look at each other. I look at Kasia: I love her, I have no doubts about that, but in that particular moment I really didn't like her either. She looks at me. I surprise myself, and the other patients in the room, and Kasia: I begin to cry, to sob, as if Iwona had just stolen my bike again and I could only watch with a bloody calf.

"Below list your skill(s) that are your strongest attributes," I stare at the form, not enough space, I think. I wonder, first about the form: should I be listing nouns, forming sentences? I decide on the noun. I wonder about the answer and without really knowing why, I write: "tomato soup." Then I cross that out and throw the paper away. I walk out. I didn't get that job. I went back to Białystok. My brother picked me up in his car.

Twenty-third, I can't cry. I only ever cried as a child; in primary school I was stubborn and barely cried at all. In high school, the only time was in that hospital room with Kasia. I haven't cried since; my father's funeral, the humiliations of my adult life, breakups, defeats. I gave up crying as one might give up smoking, for instance. Step by step, year by year and—nothing. Sometimes, rarely, my body doesn't hold tears, just as it might sometimes be unable to stop excretion. The mechanism the same, even if different muscles are used.

There are questions that I return to (seventh), questions that are as worn as the pages of a men's magazine: Why did I start crying then? is one of them. I have provided myself with a number of answers. Some seemed quite amusing, traditional as Freud with a top hat and cane, straight from a Viennese cafe with Elfriede Jelinek in the background. But, really, I don't know, I can't break through the years and memories, I can't.

I stopped crying as suddenly as I'd begun. Kasia was hugging me. "I'm sorry," I choked out, sniffing. One of the patients was looking at us, clearly moved, like we were a holy picture or a scene from a telenovela. I looked at Kasia, all puffy-eyed and sniffly, and I didn't even have to ask the question. "She has a brain tumor," Kasia whispered in my ear.

My mother lies on her side on the couch in the living room. She breathes in with difficulty, almost snores, sleeps. Her hands are crossed before her face as if protecting it from a blow: like a boxer, though she's missing gloves. I stare at my mother and for the umpteenth time I wonder: What am I really doing here?

Before I left the hospital, Kasia said: "G thirty-five." I was trying to figure out what she meant the whole way home. It sounded like a chess move: an impossible move, there was no such place. It sounded like the number of a gun perhaps, something I was sure she wouldn't know.

It sounded like an answer given by a supercomputer in Douglas Adams's work, *The Hitchhiker's Guide to the Galaxy*. The computer answered Fundamental Questions: Why are we alive, what is the point of life, the universe, and everything else? After millions of years of working things out he decided: "Forty-two." Kasia said: "G thirty-five." That was, I have to admit in all irony that is left me, an answer far more precise.

GUARD

My mother is lying on the couch in the living room, she sleeps during the day more and more frequently, she's even taken out a blanket: folded into a neat square, it's waiting on the armchair for "low pressure," for an "I need to lie down for a bit." My mother always loved cleanliness and neatness. My brother used to say she was a Nazi hygienist. My mother once told him to fold the blanket, and only after the seventh or eighth attempt when she was satisfied did she go to the kitchen to torture us with tomato soup. My brother and I stood over the blanket that was folded in a square. My brother said: "This is a Nazi square." "Make a swastika out of it," I answered, and began to laugh hysterically.

Forty-second, I avoid Fundamental Questions. I can't provide the answers, I've been raised on the philosophy of the twentieth century, not very antique, focused on the problem of language and its relation to the world. I was allergic, I remember, to the French school, for instance Derrida and Deleuze, a lot of words and contents not unlike those of the stomach; French philosophy made me think of Genet's stories: sweet farts, too many adjectives and commas to cover up the lack of words that held any meaning. The only twentieth-century philosopher I like apart from Gadamer is Wittgenstein. Really, though, neither of them are philosophers. They are writers. They wrote treatises that differ from stories only in their lack of anthropomorphic characters.

Forty-second (thirty-fifth??), I avoid Fundamental Questions. At the university I was taught to think that questions to which one might find answers are questions asked in the wrong way. But you still can't run away from them, even when they're leaning on crutches or against the wall. Even such a simple question as: What do I believe in?

God? Out of the question, I'm sorry. I'd like to, but I can't. None of the Messiahs, Jesus or Muhammad, for instance, convince me. Maybe if their replicas survived until today something in their bearded faces would charm me: shiny skin, sadness, full lips. I can't believe in a person without seeing them first, in God—I can't.

Good? I don't know, honestly, what that means. All that I understand is: "What goes around comes around." But that has nothing to do with goodness, it's only a certain rule that should be respected for one's own good. Like with the Rules of the Road, the rule to trust, but not fully, other members of road traffic. It's the only rule that has a chance to be understood by everyone. A rule which wipes out the stone tablets like acid. Strong enough to have society build on it. Enough for a big family to become a nation, if a small one.

Forty-second, what do I believe? That with some ease I can show that I believe nothing. But I live on Earth, I breathe air, nothing is a vacuum and I must believe in something, even if the external world could get used to the stump if Fundamental Questions were amputated.

When I try to imagine a perfect, happy society, all I see—my imagination is not that vivid—is the society I am part of. All that should be eradicated are the Fundamental Questions. It's not difficult, you could distract someone with product information, about ten different washing liquids, for instance, as many softeners as cheese for breakfast, cars and insurance, there's not time to waste contemplating details such as: Why am I alive and what is important? The more important question is: How much? This is an approach I do not criticize. I count myself among those who use it.

I attended logical semiotics classes at university. The professor's initials were three *J*'s: Jacek Juliusz Jadacki. Students would say: "Call me jay jay jay." Logical semiotics was meant to take my mind and teach it some logical culture, elegant thinking, something that on paper would be the equivalent of good table manners. I passed a difficult exam with a B: I never mix up my cutlery.

I'm trying to modify the Fundamental Questions, for instance like this: What would I defend? What? I think of those I love, places, maybe some things, important, but not irreplaceable. Throwing away the useless nouns, this would be my answer: I'd stand up for ownership.

For instance like this: What did I defend? What?

In answer there comes a word that has lost all meaning, a word used to clean floors, to fill holes, to excuse silly things: I'd defend freedom. The right to make one's own decisions; not just decisions, but the right to make them. The right to privacy and the rights of the individual that has nothing to do with independence or other people. The right to make mistakes.

If I connected my answers, it would seem that freedom is connected to ownership. At first this may seem absurd, like an oxymoron.

Since my mother has come back home, I've stopped drinking, with no regrets, merely with some relief: to sleep, I swallow pills. After an hour that is still and stiff as if I've just been beaten, when the tick-tock of the clock follows the rhythm of my heart, only to—then—replace the blood in my veins with liquid time, the flat ceiling isn't so flat; four corners begin to fall like the corners of a tissue, to enclose me within them like an igloo. Before the chemistry pushes away my consciousness fully, I feel a squeeze in my chest, a last attack of breathlessness, after which I will open my eyes in the morning, many hours later.

I study this uneven connection: freedom and ownership. The longer I think, the more I find in myself the conviction that there's something there. Freedom doesn't exist outside of the material world, it becomes abstract, nothing. Because what is freedom? Not needing anything, feeling anything, not depending on anyone, and not allowing anyone to depend on you? That's not freedom, that's death, and perhaps it is attractive because it occurs in a living organism.

The last attack of breathlessness, but the lead soldier sits on my chest, I try to breathe in but I taste metal in my mouth, the remnants of blood that's pushed by the seconds now in my veins, the seconds marching to the pendulum of the clock that ticks inside my ribcage.

I wake as suddenly as I fall asleep. My legs and arms are heavy, my head lifts with difficulty; somewhere my headache has lain an egg and now it's heavy, something in the eggshells is moving and trying to break free, trying to break through my skull—I twist in pain, there is a glass of water and some Cetanol on the bedside table, prepared ahead of time. Only this helps, it's addictive and dangerous, sold on prescription (thank you, Paweł Drenasz), but it's the only thing that works on the parasite that has made its nest in the branches, or at the foot of—maybe in the crown of—my nervous system. If reincarnation is possible, which I doubt, then in the next life I'd like to be called Cetanol.

Mr. Cetanol, forty years old since birth, so I wouldn't have to live through my childhood, youth, and teenage years again. Mr. Cetanol, a citizen of Great Britain, for instance. I don't want to be born into a walled in country again, which plays without a shadow of talent but with huge determination the Messiah of Nations. I don't want to be the Antemurale Christianitatis, I don't want to be the Shield against communism, I don't want to be the Courage sentenced to death in the Warsaw Uprising. I'd prefer something common: an ordinary citizen of an ordinary country, without complexes among the history of megalomania. British works perfectly. Or Dutch. Or Portuguese. I don't want to be Polish: once is enough.

I swallow the pills and wait for them to take effect, to tear away the pain as autumn tears leaves from trees, I wait for about fifteen minutes. Then I can get up. The inhabitant of the egg in my head has just had his wings clipped by chemistry, at least for a few hours.

I try not to give my mother reason to complain. That's why I take a shower before and after bed. I always shave in the morning, even when I don't want to I brush my teeth. I use wax to make my hair look acceptable and fashionable, resilient against the wind for twenty-four hours, according to the producer. I put on clean clothes. I turn on my phone to see if anyone has called. My lips twist in disgust of their own volition: I turn the phone off.

I go downstairs. My mother's up. She's waiting in all breakfast preparation. She waits for the noun: for instance "scrambled eggs" or "sandwich": slices of ham perfectly fitting the slices of bread, with a thin slice of tomato and some salt and pepper. On Sunday my mother lets herself (and me) taste some luxury: mayonnaise.

I eat breakfast, my mother makes coffee. She's learned how to use the machine that I can't use, bought a few years ago for a ridiculous amount of money. It's connected to the internet, like almost everything that costs a lot, and can order coffees by itself, filters. I wonder if it could call an ambulance?

I dream of having a cigarette, my body needs the poison to begin another day: Cetanol is just right for entering the world, it opens the door like a guard who has no neck.

Mornings are the best. My mother and I both fulfill our needs: her need to be useful and irreplaceable, mine—for someone to show me some tenderness, dressed in anything, even sandwiches. I eat breakfast and go out onto the porch. My mother mutters something about the evils of smoking and my lifestyle choices, and how the smoking—along with my grandmother—was the death of my father.

A chair on the porch. Uncomfortable, it's strange that it hasn't been burned yet. The porch: an aquarium with glass on three sides; side one: a cemented yard, with flowers of oil from crappy cars that my father drove; side two: Victory Street, the name has been changed multiple times, I don't know what it is now, probably John Paul II Street, or Piłsudski; side three: a view of the garden, the two bare walnuts and—if you lean out—the chestnut, saved from disease.

First, I was born, in Białystok, in the seventies children were born in large birthing rooms in a rebellion against tradition, grandmothers, and warm water. First, I was born and I know that I had no control over it, what's more, I wanted to get out. As if I'd been in a hurry. In pain and the smell of Lysol and pharmaceuticals; in the artificial light and sterilized tools, needles, painkillers, swear words, and spells.

Second, I learned to talk, twice. Everybody learns to talk.

First "Mom" and "Dad," the basic cells of society in the first words. The first words are similar in all European languages, filtered through a child's mouth and ability to articulate they sound as if the Indo-European roots were once again taking over the European lands, like boughs—or twigs, the brittle sticks of a bird's nest.

Second, I learned to talk, twice. I feel like a fillet, forty years after my first word, an orthodox fillet, white and of the best quality, raised with vitamins and in fresh air, with no backbone. In the past people were scalped, now they're made into fillets. It's what you call the progress of civilization.

If I'd forgotten what nationality I am, I might look into my passport. The hard binding has a purple color, luxurious like a Bishop's robes, and it even smells like incense, with golden letters, just like on my parents' tombstone (no date of death though); one can read: The Republic of Poland, European Union. Those who can't read can see the golden outline of a crowned eagle: wings, beak, and talons.

Though in Podlasie the most frequently observed bird is—apart from the common pigeons, sparrows, and rooks—the stork, the eagle has been my companion since I was young. In school I learned to associate its image, though I saw the real bird only once and in the zoo, chained to a tree like Teddy was in front of her doghouse, with the fatherland, identity, and language. My younger brother accurately summarized the concept of the fatherland and community over a bowl of tomato soup: "If you don't understand what someone is saying, just hit them," he said. My brother used, I guess, stronger words than my memory.

This axiom of my brother's, though accurate and inductive, did not sit well with me. I'd be the one getting hit. Because—second—I learned to talk, twice. First I talked like grandfathers, like my hated-by-my-mother grandmother and her husband of the bees-that-nearly-killed-me. I spoke in a tongue that has not been denoted in any Atlas, because in the time of communism the matter of language was of the highest importance, connected to the Polish People's Army and security.

But it's not my beloved Polish language that has turned out

to be my first. My first was my grandparents', which my parents named, with some embarrassment, simple, and any language experts, as soon as science stopped depending on atomic bombs and friendships between nations were put off for later, the dialect of Belarus.

I must have forgotten what I'd learned. My parents moved to Białystok, a town more Polish than Kraków precisely because its multiculturalism, as the Polish minority was called, in a politically correct manner on the Eastern Borderlands at the time of the second Republic, had been burned out during the Second World War. The Polish burned, so did the Germans and Russians, everyone who could start a fire: in Białystok people had to settle down and rebuild (the order of this being significant). Afterward there was a new order, theoretically open to "smaller brothers," and practically pushing them away to the margins, even—if this was possible in the shadow of atomic bombs and mobilizing strategies—beyond the margins.

And I'm one of those, I'm about a centimeter to the right of the page, enough to be noticed but not enough to fall away from the text completely. I—Grzegorz, a person-fillet or a fillet of a person—am the proof of the successful politics of the Polish Republic. Proof that the limits imposed on members by the European Union haven't been breached: I'm breathing and I'm safe, after all.

Second, I learned to talk, "Mom" and "Dad" are not the basis for discrimination, they sound similar in many languages. The first words were accepted by the Polish Republic, it was more difficult with the words that composed sentences. Poland agreed to serve suppliants as long as their vocabulary and syntax resembled that of Mickiewicz, a real Pole, as everyone knows. Poland stood for "soft polonization," rightly so.

Soft polonization—hard perhaps in comparison to my parents' generation—was based on the appearance of accepting differences. For instance, a child from Belarus is born, takes its first steps, goes to school; for it to be able to learn its language, the parents have to articulate their desire for their child to learn it. It may look sweet written down, but in practice no parent is going to bother to leave the field and go to school to sign a paper.

I was born in Podlasie, I speak the language I love, which is my second language. The first has been wrung out of me by my parents, because they cared for me. I don't know if I can feel the loss because I'm not quite sure what it is I lost. A lack of awareness of the extent of the damage affects an evaluation of it, though it doesn't make the crime any less significant.

Maybe I shouldn't dismiss such a possibility, nothing bad has happened to me? Maybe I'm trying to explain to myself out of cowardice my own defeats, to blame others for my mistakes? I don't know. Really, I don't.

My mother asked for me to wake her so she can watch a TV show. "Mom," I say, "wake up. Wake up." She opens her eyes and sees her own hands, crossed in front of her face in a protective gesture. I think it's called a guard, I'm not sure. My mother lowers her arms, explains herself as if I were a judge who caught her doing something illegal. "I had to cover my eyes. The light was bothering me."

SUIT

"Hello," a voice says. "Hello." "Where did you get my number? Who are you?" I ask. I hear a woman's laugh on the other end, tense, but familiar. "I got it from Paweł." My brain is working quickly, looking through old files and drawers that have been closed for years. Among all these mental activities I choke out an intelligent: "Oh." The laughter returns, a bit freer and longer. "You don't seem to have changed much." I stay silent, because the short retort I need is out of reach. "Don't you remember me?"

I lean against the wall of the house, I don't feel faint. I feel great, except for my memory, which is made of lead. My legs are like clay. A bad connection. From a constructivist point of view.

"I remember," I say. I sit down on the cement with my back against the wall. "Wouldn't you like to see me?" I can't say anything. I don't know the answer. "Hello, are you there? Hello?"

"Yes," I choke. She's silent for a moment. "Paweł has my number. If you'd like . . ." she pauses, then hangs up. I put the phone down next to me. Only now do I realize that I'm sweating, in a matter of seconds my shirt is soaking, my feet sliding around in the plastic socks like soap in a wet hand, my hands have fallen to my sides of their own volition; the coolness and moistness coming from the cement calm my trembling. I sit like that for a few minutes, but I must get up, my mother is waiting.

I get to the steps which lead to the porch. The vomit has been cleaned up. I sit on one of the stairs. I try to breathe evenly. Nothing bad has happened, I repeat to myself, I just don't like surprises. I really don't. Of any kind.

The door opens and my mother speaks to my back: "Don't just sit there, you'll get a bladder infection." I seriously doubted that.

"I'll smoke my cigarette and come in," I say, trying to make my voice sound as normal as possible. It doesn't, that's probably why my mother doesn't insist, holds back the quips about nicotine, carbon dioxide, and my father. She falls silent and disappears back inside the house.

A few days have passed since the conversation in the hospital, and I only saw Kasia in school, once her body had repaired itself somewhat. Seemingly nothing had changed, I loved her the same, richer with the knowledge that this is a terminal illness and should bring us together. On some level it probably did: I was the only one in the school who knew the truth (and the Chemistry teacher, which is why Kasia always got special treatment from her); secrets bring people closer. And tear them apart.

We didn't talk about my visit at the hospital, or her disease; here was the first subject we didn't want to discuss. Something important happened at the hospital then, though I might not have been aware of it. I felt heavy minded, "smarter but slower," Kasia joked.

Something stood between us like a screen, first; then it became a wall over which we could no longer see each other.

I don't remember what I felt. If my emotions could resemble toys, I'd ask my mother and receive a precise answer: with a price (before and after redenomination), a detailed description and flawless dating and various digressions on top of that. But I don't remember. Sometimes I manage to reconstruct a part of myself from high school: I throw the forty-year-old me into the body of my eighteen-year-old self, assuming that we don't differ too much. The pillar of emotion which supports me, the me that's over twenty years younger, I now fill with sense, straw and echoes, holding on to something that might be called psychological probability. The result of such emotional archeology, of digging out fragments of old sentences, merging the lines on the windows into pictures, the result is highly unsatisfactory and doubtful, from a methodological point of view.

I was raised in constantly present insecurity. Everything that I was used to—disappeared. My grandparents and Teddy, and with them even my first language—even the "woof-woof" sounded different in Polish. My parents threw themselves at each other's throats, so I expected them to disappear as well, that I'd become an orphan, I even packed a suitcase once with all my toys. Insecurity and temporariness made it difficult to decide whether what happened to me was a reward or punishment.

I was polite and got sweets, ate all of them at once and then suffered stomach pains, sometimes vomiting. So were those sweets a reward or punishment?

I fought with a neighbor, overcoming my own disgust of physical violence. My father praised me while my mother forbade me—for the whole week, which for a child is forever—to play out in the yard. She also told me to apologize, which I refused—another week.

I got a reward at a theater festival and lost a friend, who was also a director, and who was enraged at this result.

And so on. And on.

Third, I learned to read and write, with a huge effort, testing the patience and perseverance of my parents and teachers. There was no bad will in it on my part. In the world of numbers I could move with ease, numbers were clear and transparent, each one had a meaning to it that was exempt from a mathematical sentence, letters though—baaing and stupid like a flock of sheep—needed the neighborhood of other letters to gain meaning. Numbers were beautiful and slow, and letters were uneven and always needed company. I still learned to read and write, my third.

Gradually the world of letters began to fascinate me more, it engrossed me. I realized that letters, the poor—I thought then—imitation of numbers, describe the world far better and more accurately than numbers; this chaos and mess, insecurity and temporality. The unchanging change and necessity of light and which leg one got out of bed with first in the morning.

After many years the world of letters and—to a lesser extent—the world of theater began to be one in which I felt safe.

I calm myself enough to light a cigarette, I'm afraid that the moistness from my hands will permeate the tobacco and put the cigarette out.

A gypsy caught me once somewhere near the main train

station, I showed a complete lack of assertiveness and before I knew it she was holding my hand, looking through my genetic suit like a scanner set to the function: palmistry. You'll have a long, good life, two children, and you'll die of a heart attack. I'm over forty, I need to get a move on to make that prediction come true.

There's so little that I remember from the past, as little as what I remember from the future. Sometimes I imagine and dream. The future takes up less space in my head than the past and is characterized by a similar probability and lack of clarity.

I learned that some people are forever, and some only occasional (my fourth). For instance my brother, it seemed, was forever, but we don't keep in touch and he has disappeared within the walls of his home, with his wife, in his son's bedroom, on the way to work which he traveled to in his old green car. For instance my mother, after my father's death, became less real than dust, and now she's back and is probably brewing more green tea in the kitchen, despairing at my life so she won't have to take care of her own. For instance Kasia, she was supposed to be gone, but she just called.

I learned that I have no control over who stays and who goes. I'm afraid this isn't entirely true, that I do have some power over this; it's easier to go through life pretending that important decisions are made without my part in them.

I crush the butt against the stair and put it back in the packet. My mother would have spasms at the sight of butts lying by the door. Though—in the current situation—that might as well be a reaction to the chemo.

My final year at school might be defined by the word "stress." I don't remember it, so it's another assumption. Highly probable though. Exams of maturity and exams to get into college are sources of pain. In terms of dates, these were the first months of taking full responsibility for one's actions and country (characterized as the Army Recruiting Command, dividing up boys into military categories; what's interesting, those who would die first in a potential war would be those in category A, as if the Command wanted to get rid of the most genetically valuable citizens, and only afterward reach for other alphabetical letters: B6, for instance, me). In terms of physiology, this was a time of hormones, sperm which poisoned the brain, as one of our teachers of physical education liked to joke, about a hands-on approach to life. "What poisons girls' brains then?" one of my classmates asked. The teacher thought deeply before responding jovially: "Sperm, too!"

Each of us was in his own world, and none of these worlds was free from stress. I must have resembled a human fragment, I guess. I don't remember, but I found an old photo from high school, this house tends to be cruel. I didn't recognize myself: a thin member of the male sex with a five o'clock shadow, a loose jumper, and with bags under my eyes: that's me?

We were meant to go to prom together. My parents got a suit, with a velvet vest, and cherry Doc Martens. Kasia's dress rustled with taffeta, flowing meters of it, square, blue, a slippery material. "Don't I look like a box of chocolates?" Kasia asked, showing me the dress. Magda was eavesdropping, there was decaf coffee cooling on the table. "No," I answered. "Chocolates aren't usually wrapped in blue." "Pig," she replied, but laughed anyway.

I got up off the step. I got onto the porch. Addiction, or fear, so addiction, kept me from going back inside the house, so I sat on the chair. I lit another cigarette.

Kasia and I didn't go together. She got sick again a few days before. I saw her at the hospital again. For the first time she looked really ill. One eye, the right, the one with the lid and the laughter, was covered by a bandage. Something with her cornea or nerve, I don't remember. Her left hand lay on the hospital bedsheets, squeezing a green tennis ball. I remember that tennis ball well, I couldn't have come up with something more absurd. "What's that for?" I asked. "When I get a cramp . . ." she paused; it was raining outside. "So my fingers don't squeeze together too tight." "Oh," I managed. I never learned to play tennis.

I went to prom alone, I don't remember anything, I woke up the next day in a friend's house, where we went in a small group to finish ourselves off with alcohol. My pants were filthy.

It wasn't long after that our relationship, or what we called our relationship, began to be an issue. I don't think we loved each other any less. I was absolutely sure, this I remember, that I never met anybody who complemented me so well. Later years showed me that—unusually—I'd been right.

The smoke bites my throat. I know what my Tarot card would be: a Smokehouse. Everything all right on the outside, but everything rotting on the inside. Advice: "Try to breathe in more fresh air."

In the final year, Kasia was more absent than present at school. It wasn't that noticeable, because in the second term people only attended those classes they were going to sit exams in, so we didn't even have to attend Physical Education.

We didn't see each other often, sometimes at school, we had History together. I didn't walk her home, we finished classes at different hours. We barely ever met up outside of school, we had a good excuse: not enough time and so much to learn—that was the excuse for our separation. Sometimes we saw each other at birthday parties, and we held hands, out of habit, three years of learned gestures.

Sporadically I would visit her at the hospital, always announcing myself beforehand though: I would call her house and talk to her mother or sister, asking them to pass on that I would visit on such and such a day, such and such a time. In the final year Kasia regularly ended up at the hospital where they would fix small issues and run endless tests.

I almost forgot the Kasia I fell in love with. A new Kasia appeared: thinner, drawn with pain, tart as a gooseberry, and covering her: thin skin, transparent as watercolors with red and blue landscapes where needles had poked her, as if the needles pumped color into her; her eyes lost their shine, Kasia looked at me with new eyes, the eyes of an old woman, I'd get goosebumps and preferred that she only lay still and stare at the ceiling. Her smell changed, she began to smell like her mother: medicine and the hospital, sleepless nights and unsolved problems.

In single sentences, small gestures, sudden and momentary, the Kasia I knew would return: one of the doctors would ask: "How are you doing, dear?" and she'd reply after a long look at her own body: "Lighter, about a kilogram less each day." Lighter, lesser, it almost rhymed. I tend to get rather embarrassed when reality rhymes. Rhymed objects with events, a cause identical in the last syllable with effect—it plants doubts in my mind about how real I am myself: I'm brought down to the level of an ordinary event, I can be analyzed and mistakes might be made in me.

I don't know if anyone understood "Forty-two," the answer of the computer to the Fundamental Question from *The Hitchhiker's Guide to the Galaxy*, I know that the meaning of the more precise version, "G thirty-five," was revealed to me by accident not long before exams. I don't remember: an article in a newspaper, a program on TV or radio, maybe a scrap of a conversation?

Guests.

Guests, friends of my parents, temporary but intensive. I remember them because they had a cool son, younger then me by a few years and as admiring of me as he might be of an older brother had he had one, but he, Michał, didn't, because he'd been born too early. His approach was very different to my brother's. "Watch and learn," I'd tell my brother. My brother would show me his middle finger: he picked it up from the movies, he wasn't really such a bad kid.

Guests: she was a doctor, he the main guy running the National Sanitary Inspection or something, I don't remember. She had a face that was the shape of a heart, sometimes we exchanged a few sentences, her nails were red. I don't remember my question, if I asked it at all. I remember the answer. G 35 in the International Statistical Classification of Diseases (ICD-10) indicates multiple sclerosis, I learned, which is incurable, unpredictable, she said, and cruel.

I ran the name of the disease over in my head. It sounded like an oxymoron. Multiple sclerosis, almost like single remembrance, if you want the negative of it. A name that had no meaning, only death, and simultaneously—I realized—a name that brilliantly depicted the meaning of the illness: there is no meaning to illness, after all.

After the guests left I helped clear the table and wash the

dishes, then I went upstairs to my room, I couldn't sleep, I didn't fall asleep for the first time in my life. I didn't have to wake up to go to school the next day because I was never asleep in the first place: I lay in bed for some hours. My first sleepless night, it's not a pleasant memory, maybe that's why it's kept so well. I remember that I convinced myself that Kasia was already gone, that she was not really there anymore, that the disease took her; it's only taking her now, but it already took her.

Kasia didn't sit the exams with us. The oxymoron attacked her body and made it helpless, it attacked with the same ferocity as something that sounds sensible might—I found out about this from our mutual friends, we were no longer seeing each other.

I light another cigarette; after forty, I shouldn't smoke so much. I shouldn't, but why not? What's really keeping me alive? Only my mother. My fear for her. Nothing else is left. I lost any illusions that my job is of any importance, or that I have something important to convey: work shouldn't be a reason to stay alive, it shouldn't be the meaning of a life, at its highest value it only shows an excessive pride on the one hand, and on the other—serious psychological imbalances.

What keeps me alive? My mother and my fear for her? I wonder, why not complete this list with living people: my brother, friends, Kasia who has risen from the dead, or at least her voice?

Everything that I've written and directed has referred, directly or indirectly, to happiness. Like a scientist I've kept a distance between my subject and myself, not identifying with it, bearing the casualties myself and a meager gain in the form of hope. I was being eaten away by the inflation of meanings for the so-called culture and arts.

Did I find out over these years, doggedly creating adaptations and fighting with actors and directors, with my own shortcomings, did I learn anything about happiness? It's time to answer honestly: did I learn anything?

First, from a purely practical and technical perspective: happiness is boring, trivial, the audience is restless in their seats as if there was a spoonful of pinworms that accompanied each ticket: the chairs squeak, the less patient audience members leave, more often to get their coats than to use the toilets. The tickets are nonrefundable.

Second, happiness appears for a moment, sometimes in the plural, it resembles, as one of our teachers (that uncomplicated specialist of hormones and Physical Education) once said, a stretched out orgasm: less intense, but long enough that you can time it, sometimes lasting as long as hours or days.

Third, the house of happiness is the past. Happiness builds its nest in the past, which is more pliant to the manipulations of the present or future. Happiness appears like a forgotten relative, a guest from the past who brings peace, slightly musty herbs, elegant old objects, and unfashionable suits.

Fourth, happiness doesn't exist by itself, it can only play on the floorboards of the world, it needs heroes, objects, events; without a background or frame it vanishes, or doesn't appear at all.

Fifth, I could count a sixth and seventh. I'd count maybe ten, maybe more, but nothing comes of such counting, nothing can.

Nothing tires me more than myself; no one. My thoughts, dry and fruitless as the desert sands: dunes change shape and blend into each other, changing positions like the sand in an hourglass.

Sometimes I play at questions with no answers, tailoring: a suit from my parents, similar to theirs, genetic. How many changes can I make? Where should the holes be made, threads taken out without the threat of destroying it all? How to die and keep the seams in place? If I'd been born a woman, would I think about this genetic suit?

I sit and smoke another cigarette on the porch, inside the dirty aquarium, the walls of which haven't been touched by a cloth in months, I sit and smoke, goldfish. Goldfish, I think I'm losing my balance, I'm being flipped upside down, the air isn't so bad, I sit normally, my brain works, somehow, but works, I'm staying afloat for now. Goldfish, if you were a Christian saint, everything would be all right. In my culture you can address monologues to saints. Fish are caught and eaten, I don't remember any wishes.

DECEMBER

CHRISTMAS, A HAPPY REMNANT of pagan gods, incorporated years ago into the body of Christ (and the Church) with the arbitrary decisions of hierarchy. Christmas in my house was always double. This doubleness didn't really fit in with the Holy Trinity, but it's a step, possibly a step forward, in relation to singleness.

The first Christmas Eve is in December, according to the calendar that affects the Catholic majority. Fish swim out onto the table, long plates of herring and carp, sometimes some fillets and a pike floating in jelly, an eel if I bought one, my mother is disgusted by them being too expensive, feeding on dead things. The Christmas tree is decorated with baubles like pinecones, glittering in the artificial lights that have probably been produced in China. Shadows dance on the wooden floor, then in one's head before falling asleep. Nobody works. My father, mother, and brother are at home. On TV everybody has beards, prophets and actors, sportsmen and presenters, Jesus and Santa, only the Pope and one of the female presenters, the blonde one from the culture department, are beardless: I probably mix them up at times, sometimes the blonde makes sense and sometimes the Pope looks like an old woman.

In January (so December in the Julian calendar) is the second Christmas Eve, more elegant and orthodox, usually in the country with grandmothers and aunts; all that is gone now, the grandmothers have followed their husbands down the badly lit road, it's easy to get lost. I'd like to think that the grandmothers are waiting, with sandwiches and lard, with grimaces and gestures that I remember well, or: that I might remember well. The house has rotted and fallen in on itself after the last owners left: the roof has bent itself into the shape of a bow, a mirror image of a cat's back, the line of the roof and the cat's back's form, if you'd join them, make a circle. The roof shingles have scattered around the building and grow into the ground, just like Antonovka's around the apple tree in the orchard.

In January (Julian's December) is the second Christmas Eve. First we were at one of the grandmothers' in Gródek, then we went to the other one in the white house. I don't remember the topics of conversation, I assume they were the same every year, only present details would be changed in the matrices of these conversations, to make more precise the world where novelty has not been anticipated: someone else died for another reason, the hay is bad or not, harvest is good but let's not exaggerate, the pigs are sick but not terminally, the meat is edible, the cow has had another calf, though five years ago.

It always snowed, as long as the grandmothers lived global warming hasn't had the courage to peek around the clouds. I like snow (twenty-fourth), when it's snowing and when it has already fallen, reminding one of the world of old TVs, when news and movies all depended on the weather: a gale that tore at the antenna could blow apart any progress in building a social-ist order, snow in the "bloody dwarves' beginnings of a reac-tion." The snowstorm fell onto the bulky rectangles of Brazilian plantations, where the evil Leon wanted the beautiful, more by definition than appearance, Isaura. The snowstorm settled on the pixels of the clothes of members of the *Dynasty*, winds pulled at the silhouettes of the heroes of *Return to Eden* like a deforming mirror in a house of mirth, like bodies looking at themselves in glass surfaces.

Snow hugged the world and squeaked under shoes, glittered in sunlight, covered dog shit and created new paths. Among the inedible things I thought snow was the best: snowdrifts kept my father in the house, for a few hours we were a complete family, we couldn't go to school so we made snowballs and built snowmen instead, went for sleigh rides, began an igloo. Among the edible things I liked mayonnaise the best: yellowed from egg yolks (and later paints), with the consistency of melted jelly and an indescrib-able taste. Snow made me think of mayonnaise, and vice versa.

Christmas meetings made me think of presents at first, with rarely seen aunts and uncles who would stagger like candlelight in the wind. They staggered because they were drinking, my grandmother told me once. I didn't understand, I drank too, compote, for instance, and I staggered only on ice, usually when my brother pushed me.

Gradually I grew up like all children do, the presents stopped being my only source of happiness during Christmas. I was happy to see my grandmother, aunts and uncles, the dogs tied to the doghouse, immortal clones of patchy and short-legged uglies, happy to see the pines under the snow, for the conversations at the table, the hay under the tablecloth, the starch that broke off at the edge of the table like paper. I grew until I grew up enough to stagger on the floorboards like my aunts and uncles.

The more pleasure I gleaned from our Christmas gatherings, the fewer family members sat down at the Round Table. Aunts and uncles were getting old, breaking legs, feeling offended, dying, out of boredom or spite. The Christmas dishes survived longer than the people, my grandmother took more care it seemed with that than she did of her family, and so the number of plates far exceeded that of the guests.

I was fascinated by the extra setting for a surprise guest. A guest who never came to eat with us; he or she changed every year. First he looked like Tomek Wilmowski, then Winnetou, then Pan Samochodzik, or the brave Atreyu from *The Neverending Story*: the friends I didn't have. Then there were the women who were madly in love with me, with curly hair and perfect manners, long looks and a cough indicating a noble and terminal illness, women from the novels I read. Then the extra plate was just an extra place. And then came the ghosts of those absent.

Today is the first day of December, and for the fortieth time in my life the transhistorical countdown has begun, that resembles the countdown at Cape Canaveral before the launch of a shuttle. We count days and hours since the birth of Jesus, the tension grows, though the risk of failing isn't large; he's been born at the same time every year for two thousand years. After birth, in the next few months, symbolically Jesus will live thirty something years, to then forgive our sins, also mine, at Golgotha, to rise from the dead at Easter. Sometimes I think that quantum physics, which cautiously deals with our ontological habits, couldn't possibly rise in a different culture; other cultures treated time with respect, Christianity has allowed itself fireworks and the breaking of common sense and logic. The sky looks beautiful when fireworks, flashes, and multicolored explosions of light push the stars down to the role of understudy actors in our civilization, hanging up there like a huge microscopic lens.

Today is the first day of December, the computer informed me, I was checking my emails, horrible, the snow hasn't fallen, the temperature is stuck around zero, shop windows are decorated with fake snowflakes and Santas in red suits. "How are you?" I ask. "We have no more eggs or potato flour."

She's better than anticipated. That, obviously, makes me happy, but it also worries me, which has nothing to do with the health of my mother. In December sudokus, even the hardest puzzles, won't manage to push Christmas away, at most we might wait until December, the one from the other calendar, the second December.

I'm afraid that we will spend Christmas Eve alone: my mother and myself, as for guests—an empty third plate. Our close family is either dead or in different cities and countries, and other relatives we only ever see at weddings and funerals. I doubt that my mother will want to see her sister in Kraków or her husband's brother, who lives in the country in the white, now gray, home. I doubt that any of my mother's friends will invite her. I doubt she has any friends at all. I doubt that my mother will want to make the Last Supper. "Son, it's only a few months until Easter now," she'd say.

Nobody in the family knows of my mother's condition. She's forbidden me to tell anyone about the cancer, as if she's decided to disappear from those lives altogether, to use her death to punish relatives, those only by blood and name, she's decided to die quietly and vengefully: she has baked herself into a shell with all her loneliness, pride, hurt, and betrayal. I understand her, I understand her desire to punish others, especially my brother and his wife. I understand, but I also understand that she won't persevere in her decision. She'll want to say goodbye, even beg for pity. Or maybe I'm mistaken? Maybe she hasn't really accepted that the end is near, and she won't want to tie up any loose ends? I don't know, I really don't.

I'm afraid of Christmas Eve: the preparations, cooking, I'm afraid of the TV program, the same movies played over and over, especially the so-called family comedies, I'm afraid of memories, the first commercial for paper towels will make me cry: to dry the tears I'll need a paper towel myself. I'm afraid of a phone call to my brother, or from him. If something calms me it's Cesar: he's dead and will not want to speak.

Twenty-fifth and for the hundredth time, I'm a coward. I could be a hero only in a novel, as much as jelly might be when faced with a sword. If I have any intuition at all it's probably only useful to avoid any dangers that might come my way, turning away my head at the right moment, like the bishop of Berkeley, and when the worst happens, the worst will come face to face with—an unresponsive consciousness.

Forty Decembers, correction: eighty Decembers, pressed into my memory like a particle board; the bones and skin of my skull make me think of autumn-colored covers on the couch I slept on, where under the shiny paint bits of wood stuck out: memories and paintings in which a borer has eaten out corridors.

Today is the first day of December, the first of two, from the Gregorian calendar, I drove my mother to the hospital and back, another dose of chemo. I forgot why the radiotherapy has been rescheduled for later, though Paweł explained. "Probably because of Hiroshima (Nagasaki?)," my mother joked in the car: she held a tissue at her mouth, one decorated with red flowers. Paweł explained in detail and professionally, thrombocyte, erythrocyte, bone marrow, I don't remember anything: his words flew into my ear like a paper document into a shredder.

Diagnosis projections, postponed. They are hopeful about the diagnosis, radiotherapy has been postponed, these strange words make me think of time. Is it time, presented as a code in words? Decision of the physiological tribunal, after which we might appeal to Judgment Day?

The third month, the first of the Decembers; I spent three months in Białystok with my mother. That's how quickly this time has gone by, simultaneously stretching beyond the boundaries of my patience: I've become so flexible, spread out like butter on the slices of days, that I don't find energy within me for anything other than what is absolutely necessary.

Three months, a quarter, time for a report. A report from a city, or just a floor really (my mother barely ever goes upstairs). I left to burn Cesar's body, and came, it seems, to bury my mother. When I pronounce the words "bury" and "my mother," something strange and unsuitable begins to happen to my body: I get goosebumps, my throat goes dry, my gums begin to itch, and my teeth move: if I coughed my teeth would fall out and shatter, all of them with their expensive fillings.

I'm in a worse condition than on the day I arrived, which might be easily missed, because my worsening condition is deteriorating much more slowly than the background, by which I mean my mother, which in turn might suggest that I'm fine, which is untrue.

I've barely read anything, I haven't written anything, watched anything. That worries me least: in my profession one almost is obliged to have writer's block and depression. The constant inspiration might harm my reputation, and would put a question mark over my artistic aspirations. I don't know why the audience and critics demand that an artist leads a difficult life. I do know that this absurd way of living does seem to bring in more money.

Over these three months I've barely kept in touch with other people. My mother, Paweł, otherwise nameless people, shopkeepers and workers in the garden, a few phone calls: the phone screen assures me I'm talking to a real person, giving me a name and surname, possibly a pseudonym.

This excess of time and simultaneously its lack. I stuck a stick into my own brain, some memories come back, I've mixed the water and it's fogged up, the spinal fluid is moving around like wine in an open bottle. The cork (cap?) lies on the top shelf, where I can't reach it.

My memories refuse to arrange themselves in any kind of pattern, a broken kaleidoscope. Pictures don't bring any answers, tied up in ribbons and smells, covered with decorative paper made of a student's charms and disappointments. I blame no one but myself. Once, with a friend, Michał, we decided to go for a beer in Fort Mokotowski. We were looking for a place called Blame, but we didn't find it. We ended up in a rock club, narrow as a one-way street. The place we wanted to find had a different name, Prudence, a noun which appears only, as an archaic term, in quotation marks.

Five minutes ago I was sitting at my desk, in my room on the first floor, on the first day of the first December, staring at the keyboard, the screen with its bitten apple, the view outside my window: low roofs, a field with a dirty stream that looked like a scar, on the horizon a gathering of apartment blocks with a white bell tower of a Catholic church, painted on the sky with the condensation of planes.

Now I'm lying on a neatly made bed. The top cover my mother found last week, it's gorgeous, white and cherry red, it must have been in the wardrobe for about thirty years. "Here," my mother said. "They don't sell these anymore. Your grandmother got it." My mother used the word "grandmother," which meant her mother; about my other grandmother she always said "mother-in-law."

For three months, I look through past years, months, hours, I don't find anything that could be used as a foothold on the wall of the past. I don't know whether this should make me happy or sad. Because, really, what was I expecting? That I would dig out individual memories, embarrassing and hidden—straight out of a textbook for psychoanalysis—that I might then arrange events in a straight sequence of consequential happenings?

That what? My father molested me, my mother pushed my head toward her vagina, my brother gave me pleasure, or I gave him that, perhaps?

I'd like that. I mean, I really wouldn't, but at the same time I would, because nothing would be so good for a forty-year-old as a curtain that was raised and a trauma from the past that was provided as an explanation for the present. If I might call my mother's dying something trivial. I can't.

With the greatest self-satisfaction and deepest pain I must conclude that the bowl in which my character was mixed has no pathological cracks. My father never bothered to molest me, he was too busy working; my mother's hands forgot to try to give me pleasure, maybe she didn't like me that way; sodomy never occurred to my brother, though we slept in one bed for a few years. I could tartly observe that my loved ones, behaving in the most ordinary fashion, ruined my life.

After three months of navigating between pills, the hospital, and the photographs that kept falling from the house walls, I am forced to face reality: my reality has been glued together from events that are too ordinary to describe, those whose owner is often difficult to identify, from chosen tastes, musty smells, and mistaken touches.

I must face commonness and ordinariness. I didn't think it would be such a difficult adversary. Difficult to catch, hard because spread out in numerous places—multiple places.

After three months I'm no wiser about myself. I can congratulate myself for trying: I haven't argued with my mother once, I pay without a word, I drive the car (the oil pressure indicator is driving me up the wall), I do the shopping, read the papers, drink coffee, smoke cigarettes, I haven't touched upon the difficult subject once, I haven't called my brother, but I picked up the call from Kasia, I was in the pub Attic thrice where amid the smoke Paweł's face loomed, gleaming with the golden rims of his glasses, my classmate and friend now again, considering the circumstances.

The material is slippery, the white and cherry-red cover has geometrical designs on it, they don't look very complex: you just have to substitute the right values to get the right answers. The Carpet Factory Agnella Białystok SA.

I go down to the kitchen. My mother is sitting at the table. To her right is the device that measures her blood pressure, which is almost a hobby of hers now. The book with sudokus is a bit further away. And a pen. An ordinary, yellow pen with a blue top, the cheapest. To her left is the device to measure her blood sugar, we got it no later than last month, and next to it another note-book in a hard binding with a picture of a beach and palm trees on it, like a wallpaper, maybe that's where my mother records her blood sugar levels. My mother's diary would be a strange thing to behold, mere numbers, like a code, instead of emotions. In the notebook, I looked once, is a column titled "Observations," and in it: "I ate white bread" or "I had no appetite" or "a stressful week." In front of her is the TV program, on it a cup of tea. If my mother was a saint, these would be her attributes: devices to measure pressure and blood sugar, information about the TV, sudoku puzzles.

I don't sit at the table or begin a conversation: my mother, or rather her body, revealed, paradoxically, by the items in front of her, embarrasses me. I look at the woman, surprisingly thin, and if not for the power of habit I would swear I didn't know her. I don't know this skin, the crow's feet by her eyes, the muscles that have unstuck themselves from bone and now hang idly in her clothes, the neck with a necklace of wrinkles and marks: warts and liver spots—a stranger, sitting at the table in a strange place that used to be my home. I haven't learned my mother yet, her body, aging and mistreated by chemo. It happens that I don't connect the shadow in the chair, clutching the remote, with the energetic and fat woman who sent kisses as I left and handed me money. If anything links these two people, it would be the gestures: unique gestures.

Sometimes I think that my mother is played by an actor. I stand still, surprised, for instance in the kitchen, because the physical conditions are not what they ought to be but the act-ing is good: an unfamiliar figure drinks her tea in a familiar way, twists her lips in a known grimace, corrects her fake teeth as my mother would had she had them. This actress, I'd like to say, should get a raise. And then she should be fired: I want my mother back, the real one.

I don't sit at the table, my mother embarrasses me, this actress who's copied her gestures, stands by the sink as if to check if there are any dishes that need to be washed. There aren't. Thankfully, her bag is on the countertop, and things that my mother (this actress) has bought. I take out two kinds of cheese, slices of skilandis, cream for the coffee, and then hair dye, L'Oréal. I take it out, a little box. A blonde beauty smiles at me. Her teeth are perfect, it seems she has an infinite amount of them, like a shark.

For some absurd, I don't know if ever planned, reason, there's a mirror above the sink with a gilded frame, wooden angels hug the surface just as they have for decades, with rubbed miniature noses out of which my mother has dug out dust for years: in the surface are reflected the figures sitting at the table. There aren't many. Ghosts, apparently, don't have a reflection, just my mother: hunched and in a dark sweater, studying the TV program and warming her twisted fingers on a cup of tea—as if her ostracism could be turned back around and reformed. The first December.

I see the back of her skull and the combed hair, less thick than the beard of an eighteen-year-old, cut above the back of her neck, and I hold the dye in my hand: L'Oréal, because you're worth it.

I don't know why, but I find it unfair, the whole box of hair dye and only remnants of hair, it's really unfair and squeezes the heart, a disproportion and uneven chances: I'm on the side of the underdogs, so my mother's (this actress that is only temporarily hired), and so my own. In the mirror I can also see Grzegorz: slightly curly hair over a bowl of tomato soup; so is this the way my mother, washing dishes for decades, learned my grimaces and table gestures, over the bowl of tomato soup with noodles (rice?)? I can see my faces, the one years past, chubby and feeling sorry for itself, the dimples into which so many women fell later (and the director of one of the theaters), a pale pink line of lips with a hoof upside down; only later, when lead filled the body, did the corners begin to droop, looking like a Greek letter. I see the shadow of the future face, shaven and tired, this face gives rise to—perhaps my ego is too big—a certain kind of lust; it asks for a soft gesture that would fall on the temple like a pill of Cetanol, it requires soft arrangement in the vale between breasts, with a nose in shiny photographs; this face, my face, might be easily broken, it shouldn't tire itself so, a delicate picture of gatherings

and galaxies, of stars and blue nests that are easily rubbed off a
porcelain surface, this dish, this face, won't be of any use for long.
I feel relief. December has come.

HEAT

THE SQUARES OF MY MOTHER'S sudoku resemble a chessboard, instead of pieces—towers and bishops—there is a less literal denotation: numbers, one to nine, nine squares, each with nine squares.

The squares of my mother's sudoku resemble a chessboard on which numbers are moved instead of pieces, pure powers that cannot be held; a move can be taken back, as I learned, the storm may recede.

The squares of my mother's sudoku resemble a chessboard, a version for professionals, the squares aren't divided into white and black, all the figures, nine numbers repeated, play on the same team, on one side; white and black never play against each other, that would be too simple, a game against the board itself, and even so they are rarely successful. A mistake occurs at times, made by the printer for instance, that makes winning impossible. A draw is not anticipated.

I rarely commit a faux pas. Blunders are not my strong suit, not because I pay so much attention to the societal norm. I don't usually say much, trivial comments about the weather or traffic, coughs: I try to eat all the time to avoid talking. On this basis they think that I'm interesting and intelligent. Which is amusing, really, because I, looking at myself, would reach an entirely different conclusion; that I'm hungry, for instance.

I rarely commit a faux pas. Not by any fault of my own. Michał, my friend, the one from the club Blame, came up with a great synonym for faux pas: "I committed a foyer again." It amused me greatly. It's in the theatrical foyer that the blunders would occur.

My mother always paid attention to form, she always thought

about what others might think, more so than what she might think, as if believing that others are right instead of her.

My mother hated the country, her mother-in-law, and gossip, but she never found it in herself to stop caring about what others said. It was like opium or heroin, the strongest kind of addiction: she could cry for nights because someone in the neighborhood had said, for instance, that my brother had been kicked out of the Border Patrol. "Mom," my brother would rage, "for fuck's sake, I'm still working there, stop listening to those cunts from the village. How the fuck old are you?!" My mother wouldn't reply to my brother's question, she'd nod her head sadly, even the swearing didn't wake up the attack in her. Or defense.

My mother believed words, even if they turned out to be lies; she was afraid that the person who spoke last was right, whatever they were saying. It was no revelation, but I managed to successfully weed out the characteristics in myself that I hated seeing in my parents, at least some of them. For instance, twenty-sixth, I don't care what others might say about me. My lack of responsiveness has achieved even pathological levels. I hated so much my mother's reliance on the words of the villagers that I can't understand what people might say about me now, it bores me so; I just wait for the person talking to me to close their mouth, as the sign that they have stopped talking about whatever it was that they were saying about me.

Twenty-seventh, I managed to successfully weed out the characteristics in myself that I hated seeing in my parents. I don't know if that was a smart thing to do, but it's too late now. For instance, I've never met anybody more difficult than my father. He was petty, always unhappy, pointing out the details in the background and unable to see the bigger picture, always twisting your words—what an objective characteristic, I should congratulate myself on my powers of observation and tolerance for the flaws of others. My father was difficult, I love him, because he was my father and he died. I love him because he died. I never liked him much while he lived.

At my father's funeral, five years ago, I don't remember what I felt. I was happy he was gone, for one. Sound the trumpets, angels sing, the fucker's gone: no offense, Gran, I always loved you; and that dog, Teddy, remember? And Iwona, and Oleg . . . I triumphed over my father's coffin, I kissed his cold lips, a heroic kiss, the first one given with delight, maybe I had a boner that resembled more that which occurs after death than pleasure, I don't remember, I whispered in his ear, as if he could hear me: "What took you so long?" I triumphed over his coffin, but it was a meager victory. I didn't win, not in my name was the victory taken. I fought with my father, and I won with an old man. Second, I felt sad that he was gone. I didn't think about myself but my mother, I cried though I never noticed the tears: "You fucking dick," I prayed with the other mourners, "why did you leave her alone?!" My father didn't reply, though he was lying there in his finest clothes, and usually when he was dressed so he didn't ruin the atmosphere and answered any questions people directed at him.

I remember my conversation with my mother at the funeral, highly unsuitable; really, my family feels far too comfortable at cemeteries. The coffin was in the grave already. My mother, standing beside me, began to complain in a whisper: she didn't like the place they picked, she wanted another, closer to the chapel or farther, just elsewhere. She'd been complaining ever since I got home. I interrupted her mid-sentence: "And where would you like to bury him? In the Holy Land?!" she fell silent, then replied: "No, son. Not there. They have the largest recorded number of people who rose from the dead."

Twenty-seventh, I managed to successfully weed out the characteristics in myself that I hated seeing in my parents. I'm not an antonym of them, just a mirror image, a power with the opposite sign. I'm more like a bare tree. My father paid attention to details, I never do. But not paying attention to details isn't the characteristic that defines me, it's just a lack, a bareness, a scar. I'm composed mainly of scars.

Twenty-eighth, and this is my greatest achievement, I try not to judge others. Of course, the judgments come of their own volition; the happy face of Paweł D., the veins that slip from skin on a clutching hand; the judgments come of their own volition, but I don't acknowledge them. I try not to judge, because I can sense, intuitively, that judgments passed on others really shed light on my own person.

Twenty-ninth, I try to live by one rule: "Don't hurt others." It's a difficult and ungrateful rule, but—if obeyed—with time becomes something natural, obvious, like a cigarette in its pack. It's not really a good rule, it probably comes from my twenty-fifth, I'm a coward, and hundredth, at your service.

Thirtieth, I always wanted to talk about the things that hurt me, within the bounds of retaining basic psychological hygiene, such as washing hands before a meal: instead of water there are words, instead of soap, a period, it disinfects just as well. It didn't work, at first there were no words, not the right words, and when they appeared I had no one to talk to. I never woke up with a scream, if it wasn't for movies I wouldn't know that that happens at all.

I'd wake up sometimes, I remember, knowing that I dreamt something, I remembered that the dream made no sense. I'd wake up sweating, always in an embryonic position, with a ready mind, not even thinking about a cigarette or coffee, or newspapers. And suddenly, for no reason and with no warning, for a few seconds that took my breath away, I'd be paralyzed with pain, a terrible pain in the purest form, separate from external people and events, terrifying. Even now, at the mere memory of it, my hands moisten. I would put my arms around what I had: my legs, myself. I can't describe it and I don't think I would like to. I was like the touch of the absolute, for a few seconds, or truth, or emptiness, I don't know.

After such an attack I would feel as one reborn, I would suck in air as if it were the first time and I'd know I would be born many times, many times, always for the first time, until I died, when, finally?

I learned, twentieth, that time is something private, intimate, like unuttered thoughts, like unclear, glimmering emotions that push dust off wings. Time is brittle but not blind: an old imaginary image of a grandfather with a long beard, combed and shiny, imagines time better than an electric watch. With a grandfather I could sit down and talk, play a game; with a watch this would be mad, unless the watch had a dictaphone.

The body collects time, time is put aside in cells, it circulates, present in blood and lymph nodes, measured by the cramping of the heart. Time moves unevenly, feet that grow cold slow down the flow, a heat wave speeds them up as the seconds speed together to the same gate.

Layers, from time to time, are put aside in the body unevenly, like residue carried on the currents of the river. In primary school our teacher showed us the cross section of a tree, teaching us to count the rings. "Each ring is one year," she said. So you can count how long a particular tree has lived? A cross section is like a tombstone, counting is far easier than in the case of the dead, you don't need a sheet of paper which—I think—is made out of trees. With some imagination some of the rings become numbers, or just one number really, which is repeated until the axe falls, a number bigger and bigger and increasingly irregular, written in a trembling hand: 0. "I don't know how old your aunt is," my mother said to my father. "Mom," I joined the adult conversation, "it's simple. You should just cut her in half and count the rings." My mother dropped her fork. "You see," she said to my father. "Pathological. This is your fault." My father smiled, a rare thing for him, he didn't like this aunt. "Son, it's a great idea," he said. "Now, go upstairs!" my mother barked. They were going to start arguing.

The only difference between my parents was their sex: enough for them to create a child, but not enough to give that child a shape. My parents also used language differently. My mother always called me "son," in the nominative case, as if accepting my shape without question, the shape that was borne by her and learned to breathe independently so as not to choke. My father always, rarely, referred to me in the vocative, "son," as if trying to correct me, discipline me. There is something about the vocative that demands an answer, like an order, a suit, "Yes, sir!", while the nominative never does. I loved my mother more, I have no doubt—children don't love their parents equally, and the same can be said of parents and their relationship to their children, it's sad. My mother seemed better, less interfering, she didn't wait for answers and an echo of my words was enough. Only later did I find out that my father was the one who was grammatically correct. My mother is alive while my father isn't; custom has won again, which I conclude with pity, more than it might seem, really.

My father is, I must regretfully admit, a fascinating figure: I would gladly put him in the position where a chess power would sweep him away, a queen or an l-shaped knight, even a normal pawn. My father's main characteristic was his absence, he worked and worked outside of the family while still being a part of it. My father, my absent father, was the first lesson in absence, or even nothingness, that I had; a lesson well learned.

My father worked hard, morning until night, seven days a week, for decades, dividing the fruit of his labors between two homes: ours in Białystok and the other one in the country with white walls. According to my mother this division was unequal, though my brother and I didn't complain: during this Round Table Agreement we could eat bananas. Bananas were the fall of the Berlin Wall—nothing but dust from construction, an interruption of the news, then a western; our world was westernizing itself, but the familiar deficit of heroes (and voiceovers) remained; prairie landscapes were poor too; generally it was good but there was always something missing—that we remembered; totalitarianisms, like governesses, are effective.

My father resembled God from pendants: always present but hidden. An unidentifiable something could pull him out, on a necklace, from under my mother's shirts, like a little devil. We didn't understand much, my brother and myself over bowls of tomato soup, then time stood still, my father was reflected in the mirror over the sink, my father, though beardless, brought to mind biblical heroes, the silver profile on the pendant that is kissed so it acts in the name of the Holy Trinity. In the forest of daily gestures, serial actions and thoughts, my father's position, more in an idea than physical presence, was firm. Not even a drunken stutter could change that.

My father was absent, working and working, and when he

wasn't working, I was in my room, praying for a higher power to send him to work again. So that he might get lost at work and disappear. His absence hurt on a daily basis, but that pain was nothing compared to his condensed presence. If you took the truth out of that—the world would be arranged in a rather amusing manner: what you lack hurts, but what you have hurts more.

If I risked a generalization, with my father in the background, I might say that my father: the God of the Seventh Case (son!) blurred the categories of being and nonbeing, wanting and not wanting.

My therapist—maybe I should sue him?—told me once to visualize my own soul. "And what do you see?" he asked in a low voice. "A slice of Swiss cheese with holes," I answered, because I was hungry.

My father, God of Seven Pains, tried to be a good father. He worked simultaneously so many shifts that I, putting all the shifts of my own forty years together, wouldn't reach his weekly norm. He worked for us, we consumed the labors of his fruit, but we saw him rarely. My father was absent, this absence was omnipresent, it changed the signs in my head: a plus is an equals sign, like two arms crossed in a guard position. My father, always absent, sometimes was around. He wasn't very convincing in his material form, petty and irritable, he was much better at being away from home, his body, our thoughts, in the corners of our eyes.

I don't remember the last conversation I had with Kasia, we broke up three months before exams. I assume there must have been some conversation. I remember where: her room on the seventh floor. Was Magda, the younger sister, eavesdropping?

I remember only that the doors closed behind me; I remember not the gesture but the sound, the bang and then click of the lock in the door like a swallow. I stood on top of the staircase, an elevator painted in gray with tattoos of light like a light side of henna, bright horrors and fortunes from St. Andrew's day, composed of a sunny wax and frozen on the surface of the gray paint. What did they predict? The door closed behind me and I felt a wave of heat; I didn't really understand what had just happened. A high temperature causes the egg to coagulate, it doesn't serve a precise forming of thoughts. I don't remember the conversation, we must have talked, must have: I don't remember the words, only the wave of heat, barely material, and sunny patterns on the doors of the elevators, as if someone had emptied a bucket of cold water over me.

GUESTS

REPORT: NOBODY HAS COME to visit me in three months, I haven't visited anyone, unless you count hospital visits. I told my friends from Warsaw, when they wanted to drop by, on their way to Poznań, they were driving through Białystok, I said: "No. Better not. I need to be alone." But maybe I lied?

Report: for three months now my brain has been busy with images from the past, guests dug out of the corners of my brain, between lumps of naphthalene and dry saliva, broken toys lost on the way, paintings over which sentences trip and hit in all their force, losing commas, colons, teeth, a red-and-yellow bus.

A red-and-yellow bus, a "jelcz," made of plastic of poor quality, correction: when my mother bought the bus, it was probably built from plastic of poor quality, but now, after a few decades, the material has gotten better: my bus is made of letters, three letters, and colors are made of twelve.

My parents bought me toys, cars, guns, devils, helicopters, once even a boomerang (a boomerang that didn't come back, it got lost the first time I threw it); toys for boys. I never got a toy that was nice to the touch, a soft teddy bear, no animals, even wanting Pinocchio didn't melt my parents' hearts: "You'll lose an eye on that nose," my mother cut the discussion short.

My mother will happily tell the anecdote, I don't know if it really happened or if it just happened in language, it doesn't matter: "It was quiet, I went to see, son, why. You were sitting on the carpet, the green one with leaves, that your father . . . You were sitting there and nursing something wrapped in a towel. That's where the holes in the towels come from . . . You were nursing and singing. It was a bus."

My mother shares this anecdote in its many various forms,

depending on the audience and atmosphere she puts the emphasis in a different place: humorously, to point to my weirdness / something else, it's the anger at the dirty towel ("Son, you never use a towel like it's meant to be used!").

"Mom," I asked once, "what was I singing, do you remember?" She puts on a thoughtful face, says she doesn't, only to say after a few days: "Jelczu, tiny jelczuniu, that's what you sang." Hours pass before I can attach this answer to a question that I might have asked a long time ago or that I haven't yet asked. Maybe in the world of my mother's memory the past and the future are the same, both cutting off at an edge but leading to the same point on a circle.

On one side of the equation, three months, on the other? A pile of broken toys, black-and-white stories on TV, vibovit and visolvit? Plays that I'm still to direct, the Kasia I will win back, a mother I will lead through the River to take back to the world?

Nobody visits me, so I will start paying the visits.

Visit one: my brother, sister-in-law, and Mikołajek: I'll buy some flowers, wine, chocolates, and a toy for the child, I'll hesitate before making the choice, something contemporary and expensive, or something from the past, a jelcz of good quality with better details than on the original, made of metal, Miś Uszatek or Willy the bee drone? We sit in the living room with my brother, he showed me around their house, it's big and functional, like his wife, but this is not the time for petty cruelty. I asked if he sold that old green car. He says no, "Still going strong," he adds with pride. "Like our mother," I'd say. We burst out laughing. My sister-in-law brings glasses. 'I'm driving," I say. "You can stay the night," she offers. I pretend to hesitate, then say: "I'd like that." We drink vodka, my brother and I, talk carefully at first, about my mother and the miracle (that she's still alive," then about the present, plans for the nearest future, and finally we go back into the past. Careful explorations into memories, like spoons in tomato soup, we try to take only a little bit at a time so as not to choke. I go out for a cigarette in the middle of our conversation, onto their terrace: the play has about ten breaks so the legs don't even cramp. We get drunk, "Have you christened Mikołajek yet?" I ask. "No," my brother replies, "we were waiting for you." I feel moved, tenderness squeezes my throat, my brother also tears up. Vodka needs to be washed out. Or pissed out.

Visit two: Paweł Drenasz, his wife and children, absent, visiting his wife's family. I hand over the flowers and wine, and something else, I don't know what: something personal, a small thing, a few old and valuable editions of a men's magazine or a technical one, for instance. We talk lazily, culturally, remember old times, at the end I thank him for saving my mother. We promise each other to meet up again as soon as possible. I go to the taxi thinking this is such a good house, a family that works well, good people. What a good thing I was leaving.

Visit three: I overcome my fear and call Kasia. We talk as if the last twenty years haven't grown into an impassable distance between us, as if we had just seen each other the previous week: we are divided at most by a thin, clear layer, like two coffee beans snuggled against each other in one fruit. Kasia invites me over and I feel a heat wave: she might have picked a less private place, she texts me her address. I spend a long time thinking about a gift. Eventually I make my way to the accessories shop and buy a belt. I press the doorbell. Kasia opens. She lets me in. I don't dare kiss her cheek. I take my coat off, we go to the living room, she makes decaf coffee, she remembers, I think. We begin to exchange our life stories: the trains with ourselves in them go off the rails at times, but "We're here," Kasia says, "at the same station." I remember the belt. I hand over the little package. "What's this?" she asks. "A ring?" We burst out laughing. Her right eyelid droops a bit. She opens the package and takes out the belt, looks at it with surprise: she is looking at a leather belt, but is remembering our conversation from decades ago. She answers: "Have they closed the shop down?"

Visit four: I've just turned fifty and I've been to the States, where I was collecting an award, the climate has become fully unpredictable, flowers bloom in winter, apple trees blossom, the Chinese are everywhere and in June there are snowfalls. I'm stuck at an airport in New York, it's a miracle I made it for Christmas

Eve of the Julian December back to Białystok. I get out of the taxi, there's even some snow on the streets, I open the gate carrying as much as the three wise men must have in their day, the gate opens (without a squeak) and I walk to the porch; there's a green car parked in front of the house. I walk in. I take in the smells: carp, sweet grain pudding and prosphora, herring, mushrooms and—my mother's specialty—borscht with dumplings. A brightly lit home, preparations and welcomes in the kitchen, everybody is congratulating me on my prize, I congratulate my brother and his wife on having another child, she's already showing though she's only three-months pregnant, "You look great, Mom," I say. She kisses my forehead, she has to set aside the plate with the herring and lean on my shoulders to do so, I have to bend my head. "I love you, son," she says.

FLAT TIRE

I GOT UP AFTER ELEVEN, thirty-first, I don't like the moment of waking up, you can't pretend you're still asleep, I got up late but I went to sleep late too, I began to write. I forgot that in writing words let me stop thinking: from period to period, other signs along the way to take a breath and pause, a relief. I had a dream: my nose was itching until I finally sneezed and all my teeth fell out. I got up and checked online for the meaning of dreams: teeth falling out was meant to symbolize the death of a loved one. "Stupid," I said out loud, shutting down the laptop. I went downstairs angry at myself: first, I got up, I'm always angry at myself then, at my body, second, I read a stupid piece of information online.

I didn't find my mother in the kitchen, I got scared, checked the bedroom, bathroom, and living room but she wasn't in any of those. My fear grew, I went out onto the porch: she was sweeping. "Mom," I almost shouted, "what are you doing?!" My mother straightened her back. "What will you eat?" she replied. "Scrambled eggs," I growled.

My mother put aside the brush and we went back to the kitchen. "Have you eaten?" she asked. "You brother called," she replied.

I was weirdest when in primary school. I had female friends, no boys. I wore glasses and a bag that was too heavy; my back would bend so that I had to lie down a lot; I could lie down and read. I was always borrowing something from the school library: Szklarski's Tomek books, Panów Samochodzików, Astrid Lindgren, in desert and wilderness, and from the most spectacular items—even the librarians gave me strange looks—*The Trilogy* and *Pharaoh*.

I liked Sienkiewicz most of all: I don't know who I loved more, the sweet Nel Rawlison, with dimples and curls, suffering from malaria, or the fourteen-year-old Staś Tarkowski. I definitely imagined myself walking into the world of fiction and African baobab with a box of quinine and bag full of goods. We lived happily ever after, I imagined before falling asleep, the three of us, until we were divided by sleep. My Nel was like Iwona, Staś like Oleg, and the baobab like a pear. Our elephant was called Teddy and it wagged its tail.

I like Prus most of all. Ramses VIII, an unlucky number, a young pharaoh who risked his life to save his country and himself. I felt sorry for him, I admired him, I drew the right conclusions. For instance this: Whoever wants to die a natural death can't have too strong opinions (thirty-second) and proclaim them too energetically.

"With tomatoes?" my mother asks.

In primary school I had female friends, no boys. I differed from the boys, a skinny body and glasses, the hair on my legs only appeared in the last class of primary school, that was enough to spend lunch break hiding in the toilets. But, the funny thing is, though the primary school world didn't save me from humiliations, I had no major physical tortures directed at me. I was a good student and a teacher's pet. It wasn't fear of the teachers that stopped my classmates from beating me up regularly. It was rather a feeling of deep alienation and an impossibility of reaching an understanding. They respected me because they were busy with themselves, they sensed I came from somewhere else: on the one hand more intelligent than them, on the other—really bad at sports; someone harmless, even funny, and if they changed their minds, I was right there anyway. This balance, thankfully for me, kept up for eight years. If someone had given the word to make all boys the same, I would be the first victim: I'd be the first to burn in the barn of the primary school, or rather in the toilet as we had no barn.

"More peppers?" my mother asks.

In primary school I stuck with the girls. Girls were different from boys. The differences include the obvious: they were clean, they didn't fall over unless someone intentionally tripped them up, they could read and count, construct sentences that didn't only express their wants, articulating themselves above the boyish "eee" and "yeah." Most importantly, girls didn't use physical violence as a weapon, which impressed me, though they cried often: the eraser left a mark on the paper and a sob was at the ready. Despite this flaw that was, I thought, a hydraulic defect, I preferred girls to boys.

"Decaf or normal coffee, son?" my mother asks, she asks every day, though she knows the answer so I don't even have to respond.

In primary school I had three friends. Kasia and Basia (like the squirrel, just spelt with a capital letter and she always reacted to her name). I can't remember the third name. Ula? Or maybe Agnieszka? A bet: if my mother puts the mug of coffee before me, not spilling a drop, it will be Ula. I wait.

Ula it is. Kasia, Basia, Ula, and I. A few words have been saved from those years, but no images. I remember they existed, that we found a treasure once, that we played—almost like boys might—on Commodore or Atari, which meant Kasia, Basia, or Ula had rich parents. Kasia, Basia, or Ula had gold earrings, which characterized girls from poor families. Kasia, Basia, or Ula had a set of twenty-four felt-tipped pens called the "rose of the desert," which in turn meant that she had a father working in Libya (her mother was in Poland, someone had to take care of the children). That's how my memory works, pitiful, no pictures but deduction, everything assumed, the connections and how the brain works are the clearest because the final result—doubtful.

Agnieszka it is. Kasia, Basia, Agnieszka, and I. After classes we would stay at school, the four of us, for an hour or two. We went behind the school to a small yard between the boiler room and the big hall where we had Physical Education to play. We played jump rope, boys played football, for instance. I don't remember the rules. We needed a skipping rope, a few meters. But the elastic from underwear worked too. The best was long and springy. Two people acted as pillars and between them stretched the elastic. We called the game "one-two-three" and one could always chant too. I remember that I liked the jumping. Nothing more.

My mother staggered and dropped the cup (Agnieszka, after all). The cup fell onto the rubber carpet and I don't think it shattered, the characteristic sound of breaking ceramics was missing. My mother bent over as if she'd been punched. She caught the edge of the table. I got up, dropped a fork, upset the container with salt (scattered salt means a fight): "Mom?!"

I took her by the shoulders, I was silent now, I stood with my mother in a strange position, an unfinished gesture, neither hugging her nor holding her up. An unfinished gesture, a strange position, because both are pointless, with barely a drawn vector to point the direction.

It's been years since I held my mother. Her body is like a sponge, I could squeeze, squeeze out the blood and fluids, all the time that she has left, and at the end the characteristic sound that accompanies the breaking of a person, like a bunch of dry grass used to burn fires in winter, a dry twig.

I help my mother, slowly, to get to the armchair in the living room. It's been years since I held my mother, I haven't touched her so deeply and literally: I feel a sudden physical closeness and embarrassment, because I can't pretend that my mother is just an abstract concept, a social rather than material being—it's not the abstract mother I'm helping now, but the material (practical) body; the quantifier is undeniably detailed, also called the existential quantifier, as unsuitable as that may sound.

In this sudden explosion of physical closeness there is also space, which only increases embarrassment, for gender. My mother is a woman, old and used, but a woman, and her body resembles the bodies of other women her age, a vehicle that my mother has chosen, the social and emotional (general quantifier) mother, to live and move from place to place in, for instance to the arm chair, now, with my help.

I'm terrified, this shouldn't be happening, I help her sit down. Before I run to the phone to call for an ambulance, I look at her face, a split second, the corner of an eye, crow's feet, her eyelid fluttering as fast as butterfly wings.

Calling, I can't erase my mother's face from my mind. She has her mouth open and her lower lip seems limp, hanging from the corners of her mouth, revealing her lower teeth. "Victory Street 43!" Her skin shines like freshly whitened walls. "Fuck! Sorry. Please check what this street is called now, the number should show on your phone!" Her eyes are huge, as if some force was trying to push them out, the pupils have almost taken over the iris. "Fuck!" I throw the receiver away and run for the mobile. I call Paweł, I speak quickly, swallowing up every other word. "I'll send an ambulance in a moment," he says calmly. Her hair, a single thin strand, has stuck itself to the white wall of her forehead like a spider leg, a few thin lines painted, like a "frozen chestnut" or "northern walnut."

I walk over to her, first stroking her, wasting seconds and an entire gesture, the hand rests on the armchair, then I touch my mother's cheek, moist, the skin of my hand sticks to hers. "In a moment, Mom," I tell myself. "Hold on. I promise." I don't know what I might have been promising. Nothing important, I don't think.

My mother's face is suddenly lit up by two suns, blue and red, it looks horrific. The ambulance has stopped outside the house, and the light, blue and red, is spinning around like those on police cars. I get a grotesque feeling that my mother has broken the law and will be arrested, that in the European Union one isn't allowed to be dying, it's an illness, and even if—only in protest of . . . (please fill in the blank with the appropriate word(s)).

"In a moment, Mom," I repeat, tearing my hand away from her cheek, an unnecessary and unpredicted explosion of emotion, or maybe fear, I don't know. I run out onto the porch, for the first time not thinking about a cigarette, I trip over the brush and run out into the yard, I open the gate. A paramedic gets out of the ambulance, followed by the driver. They ask me for the NIM (number of medical identification) and in response I give them a bunch of swear words. They don't seem surprised. They take out a stretcher and we go into the house: "In a moment, Mom," I mutter; maybe I've gone crazy?

I help them put her on the stretcher. I'm enraged by their professional and dry touches. The house is old and the doors wide, there's no problem with the stretcher (I had to move the table, I kicked the cup with a still puddle of coffee, like blood), it fits through the doors easily, then the porch, we lift it high, my mother weighs nothing, and into the ambulance.

My mother's in the ambulance, an oxygen mask and injection. "What's that for?" I ask. "A sedative and muscle relaxant," the paramedic answers. I find it very difficult to stop myself from tearing out his aorta. I can see he wants to ask me how we're related, because that's the procedure. "And your wife . . ." he begins. It's a close call, I almost hit a stranger. The stranger realizes in time and waves his hand. We drive, I don't even lock up the house.

We go with the sirens blaring, other members of the road traffic obediently move aside, as far as they can. I look at my mother, I swear everything on everything, I even offer my life for hers, like Abraham pressing his knife to Isaac's neck, an echo of two thousand years. Around the Church of St. Roch, the patron of plague victims, when we're over the bridge, something happens that has no right to happen, the ambulance is pushed off balance to the right; a split second later it leans over, my mother's body, other objects fly at me, I hit the wall. "Flat tire!" I hear the driver—maybe he doesn't shout that at all. Something explodes in my head.

BORDERS

I WAKE UP IN THE HOSPITAL; I say I wake up, but that's not the right word. I haven't lost consciousness, at most my consciousness has been muted and pushed out of my body, hit by various objects from an unknown fate, paid for, each one, by insurance, I suspect.

I wake up in the hospital; I have no problem with the noun (hospital), just the verb: I wake up, though I never fell asleep. The ambulance turned over, caught a flat tire at a high speed, these things don't happen, they shouldn't, not to ambulances.

I wake up: first, I see the ceiling, the crisscrossing on the lampshade bothers my eyes. They could consider such details, I think. Only after a moment do the most recent events come back to me: I worry about my mother, again; worrying too much weakens the body, but I keep my thoughts moving.

I wake up, blink, trying to get rid of the lights in front of my eyes with the blinking, which is as effective as trying to wave away smoke with my eyelids.

I've gotten used to the ceiling, my shoulder hurts, I can't turn over. The walls, those close to the ceiling, seem dangerous, slowly my peripheral vision returns. I allow further square meters to pass and be processed in my brain: the walls are smooth, no chipped paint can be seen; thankfully, a private room.

I work my way from the ceiling and along the walls to the hospital beds. The room, for a hospital, is very comfortable: I see a TV and computer, doors leading to the bathroom, and a parody of a living room: a table and three chairs, red, with flowers. I wonder why this color was chosen; maybe patients bleed while having coffee? This bit of ordinariness, I think and know, I can't be wrong, must cost a fortune.

171

Ceiling, walls, and my bed. Only then do I realize that I'm
not the only guest in this luxurious chamber. On the other side
there's another bed. There, though I can't see, is my mother.
Relief is the first thing I feel. But then there comes the pain in
my head, stubborn and delicate, like crystal bells, as if someone
was using a feather to tickle an exposed bone. Tickle and tickle.

I can't express . . . I don't know . . . Being with my mother in
one room seems unsuitable, embarrassing. I don't want to cross
another boundary, the one of embarrassment. What now? Are we
going to be changed in the same room, use the same bathroom?
Will I masturbate in the toilet (if I get there) and she'll pretend
she's gone deaf? The nurses will wash our bodies with only a
screen between us—will there be a screen?

We've been through this, once is enough. I was swimming
inside her, I kicked her uterus to get into this world. The only
time my body was in my mother's vagina, or rather, it came out
of it, I don't remember any of it, the first breath, scream, response
to a tap on the back, overcoming the boundary of water and air,
nothing. I don't even remember peeing into nappies.

I'm not fully aware of the boundaries of my own body. I have
a head and neck, my right side and left arm—I know, because
a slight pain frames these body parts in a light outline, a low
electric current. It's not much for a person, unless I now resemble one of Picasso's creations, posing each body part separately.
I focus on the missing parts. The right hand comes back first,
the skin touching a hard mattress: cast. I can forget about mas-
turbating. I can only hope for wet dreams. Or a nurse's touch,
potentially; I hope I don't get a male nurse.

Then I feel my feet, after the pins and needles: two feet, two
lines of pins and needles going from my big toe through my
knee and into my groin. Only my left side is missing. I'll find it:
I breathe a sigh of relief.

I don't like to travel, because I don't like crossing boundaries,
thirty-third. I hand over my passport and wait for the stamp, I
feel—for those twenty-four seconds—bared, pinned like a butterfly; I'm smuggling nothing, I haven't broken any laws, but
I feel guilty; an undefined guilt; I carry it in me like a mother

carries a child, but my guilt, undefined and unspecified, will never be born, will never scream, I have no right to abort, my life is not in danger, my life is not the consequence of rape.

I don't like to travel, thirty-third, every journey seems to be extravagant and unnecessary, almost a rape in itself. I don't like to cross borders, I prefer my own dominion, boring and tamed, the walls of the apartment in Stary Mokotów, where perhaps I'm not the happiest, but the range of unhappiness has been set: a broken vase, cigarette ash burning a hole in a favorite book, a wine stain on a white and black shirt, nothing worse can reach me. Larger unhappiness has been eradicated. Larger happiness has too, but that's a price I readily pay. Paid.

Thirty-fourth, I wondered how to divide people. I looked for a deeper category than sex, race, skin color, beliefs. I looked and found only one: dream, or rather the first moments after waking up. Dreams leave changes in the bodies, a stamp of amnesia. Some wake up swollen, as if they'd been having nightmares, as if they were at parties with no self-control or faced endless interrogations, as if the dream was imprisoning the body. My mother is one of those in this category, I've inherited the tendency to swell in the mornings. Some people wake up pink, with brilliantly stretched skin, as if dreams took them to some beautifying places, renewed them.

I couldn't look enough at Kasia's face. The orange rubber of the tent put carrot shadows on her skin. The shadows painted the outline of a gate that I didn't know how to walk through. I waited for her eyes to move under her eyelids, following the sleepy illusions, until the corner of her mouth might be raised almost imperceptibly, until her lips, dry and slightly open, would let out a bubble of air—enclosed in saliva, a reflection of a sleepy dream drifting toward the top of the tent: it usually shattered when it was about halfway there, and if I was lucky it would fall back on me.

The doors open with a squeak, very unprofessional and homey. Paweł D. walks in, the one responsible for our luxurious room, my classmate, a forty-year-old I don't particularly like, with golden frames on an elegant nose, clean shaven, smelling too strongly of expensive aftershave.

I wonder how to greet him. I can only think of a dry threat: "I'll sue you for that flat tire," but without an exclamation mark.

He clears his throat, as if to calm me, I bet they are taught that specific way of clearing their throats at medical school. Subjects for fourth-years: "Universal Ways of Clearing One's Throat." A seminar for first-years: "How to Write Prescriptions Illegibly."

Paweł takes hold of a chair and picks it up so as not to drag it across the floor with that unpleasant sound: my mother, the passenger in the other bed, is asleep, I think. Paweł sits down heavily, I have to hear how his butt cheeks find their place in the chair, he's looking at me and knows I'm conscious, he doesn't know I'd send him straight to hell, the seventh or something, I won't be that specific, he can pick.

"Grześ," he starts, "we have to talk." The first answer that flows to my tongue resembles a simple no, a lack of acceptance of the terms on which a conversation might take place; the second response, easily choked down, is a swear word; only the third one makes its way through my throat: "I need a cigarette." Paweł D., to my surprise, doesn't protest. "Let's go outside," he says. His hand reaches across my body, it's not a pleasant feeling, I get up with his help, I can see that one of my legs is in a cast too.

Rather clumsily do we make our way down the corridor. My legs and lungs commit the journey to memory. Doctor Paweł Drenasz and I, a director in a hospital gown, who can't even remember how he got dressed in it. Paweł says: "Wait." I lean on the wall and he opens the wide door, we go out onto the balcony, only two chairs and an ashtray on a silver leg that grows out of the terra-cotta, springing from it like a mushroom.

I sit down, broken and irritated, the touch of Paweł's hand, now gone, burns like a metal ring. "Wait," he repeats. The trees in the park are bare, they should plant some evergreens. It drizzles. Tiny drops blur the lines of objects, pushed by the wind they settle on skin and cast alike. Cold. Paweł comes back with a blanket. He covers me tenderly. I'm worried that he actually likes me.

My left hand—the right one is uselessly stuck in a cast— searches my body under the blanket. Paweł smiles lightly, with his eyes, golden glimmers run along his glass frames. "Wait," he says for a third time. He pulls out a new packet of cigarettes from his pocket, hands me a cigarette and lights it. I breathe in, I say nothing, I've decided to say nothing. I press my lips together. I'm the one who is suffering—the little egoist within me speaks— and he, Paweł, is paid for taking care of those who suffer.

Paweł is also silent, I didn't know he could be, that he can allow himself to waste his precious and well-paid time.

"Yesterday on Theater Television," he begins, "they were playing your play, the third one, I think, *Why Am I Absent?*" "The second," I reply.

"The second," he repeats, playing with the pack of cigarettes. "It was really good." I don't deny it, I don't thank him.

"I don't have the best news," he says. "Priests are the ones who cheer others up," I say.

He nods, as if in agreement. "You were unconscious. We were worried there might have been brain damage. That's why we ran some tests. Your mother agreed . . ."

"How is she?"

Paweł breathes in, deeply, like someone does before a dive. "Everything is all right, if one can say that about her," he pauses. "A few bruises, nothing more . . ."

"So her cancer is fine?"

"It's fine," Paweł agrees unhappily, I don't think he's used to such conversations. I put out the cigarette and ask for another. "I bought them for you," he says, handing it over with a lighter.

Is he not crossing a boundary, I wonder, between doctor and patient? If my memory serves, patients shouldn't accept gifts from doctors and vice versa. O tempora! O mores!

My entire body hurts, I never liked moving or exercise. It's not good for the body. Not good.

"You wanted to tell me something," I say. "So tell me."

"Grześ, I'm not sure how to say this . . ." he spreads his hands in a gesture of helplessness, then closes his hands into fists which fall onto his thighs, symmetrically. "Maybe like this: Grześ, smoking isn't going to cause you any harm anymore."

TUMOR

"I DIDN'T LOCK UP THE HOUSE," I tell my mother. She's silent; if the ceiling were a mirror I might have been able to see her face, a white sheet, a shroud. "A stupid idea," my mother decides. "What?" "To put us in one room," she clarifies.

Paweł walked me back to my room, greeted and said goodbye to my mother. "How are you feeling?" I asked her after he left. The question seems impertinent, but it slipped out by itself, like a weatherfish. My mother responds with a short, dry laugh.

Very often, I feel like one of the antagonists of a boring play. A play that, surprisingly, is put on over and over, though it's full of mistakes and awkwardness. First, the characters are badly written, their motivations are dull, nobody known is performing. Second, the drama is bad, the first interesting thing occurs after forty years and immediately gets stuck in bad dialogue, left there, its potential not met.

I cheer myself up by thinking that I can't act well, I can't create a character of flesh and blood, because I haven't read the script until the end: the director only throws us our current lines.

I know that the curtain will fall at the end. I doubt there will be applause, doubt anyone will want an encore.

"I talked to your brother," my mother informs me. "He'll lock up the house and bring over some things."

I don't remember how old Mikołaj is, my mother's only grandchild, probably a few. I remember how, typically for my brother, he told my mother about his wife being pregnant: "Mom," he said, "we had an accident."

Not much happened until the evening: the audience fell asleep, chairs creaked, dinner was served, my mother went to the bathroom four times and ran the tap to drown out other noises, the nurse looked in three times (once with batteries for the remote). Then the TV was on. Sometimes my mother turned off the sound, sometimes the picture: like a seamstress trying on the TV material against silhouettes cut out of the hospital linen.

I was in the bathroom five times before evening, I also turned on the tap, and waited. I smoked six cigarettes. The way to the balcony, braved alone, would take ages, the way back—millennia.

The silence grew thicker, made big balls of thick, unfinished sentences that got stuck on the rubber floor: when going to the bathroom, one had to very carefully choose where to put down the healthy foot and crutches. At home the silence was spread over two hundred square meters, like cold air, it stuck to the ground floor, escaped into the garden. Here and now—one room, my mother was right, a stupid idea.

I try to tame the bed and make a nest out of the covers and pillows, in which I can hatch something or even just myself.

I try not to think of anything, to forget the conversation I had with Paweł, to keep my brother's visit away from my consciousness, and so step-by-step. Another. As long as another step follows, and the next day after that step.

I try and try. I only manage one thing well, but I learn: I go to the bathroom, lean on the wall, slide down to an uncomfortable position in which I can hug the toilet. I put a finger in my throat. I wait for the spasms. I've thrown up everything, but it's not for the contents of my stomach that I'm waiting. I'd like to throw up the egg that the pain has lain in my head. I throw up tears.

CAST

MOST OF ALL, I LIE HERE. My current occupation doesn't differ that much from my previous ones. The differences are less horizontal, more vertical. First, my lying down costs the insurance company a fair amount. Second, I smoke less, because to smoke—it turns out—one also needs legs, the assistants of nicotine, pillars of addiction. Third, I lie with my mother, who does everything she can to not be lying here too. She's had the chance to make friends with other patients on the ward. It's easier than making friends with your son.

I lie, unprepared for this lying. I said no to Paweł a few times: no more tests. I went as far as the colloquialism: "I'm sick to death of tests." Paweł claims this is unreasonable. I got angry, answered that the unreasonable thing was me getting into the ambulance, or coming to Białystok in the first place. We both knew I was lying.

In two or three days we're going home. I'd have gone home by now, but I need to get some strength to be able to jump up the stairs to the first floor, it requires some mobility. The cast is in the way. The worst is when it itches: if my teeth and jaws could be taken out of their place, I would have torn the white shell to pieces. If.

I'm very irritated, that's why I barely speak: I wouldn't want to hear what I have to say.

When the itching is unbearable, I start to think about what I'll do. I think of the works and dreams. My dreams aren't that big, maybe that's why they're indestructible, because they fit in the palm of your hand.

I imagine a small house somewhere in the mountains, always summer, I live alone, once a year someone might visit me, having left the trail and gotten lost. When the itching gets unbearable, I imagine that I'm scraping soot off the bottoms of the pots. Or I use a scrubbing brush to wash the floors. Or I brush the hair of a wolf-dog. Or I scratch off old paint from the walls. There are many things to do in a country house when the skin itches at the hospital.

My brother came twice. For a bit. I pretended I was asleep. I don't even know what he looks like. He sounds like he used to. The second time he came, he brought my laptop. I never asked.

My mother got up and went out to the corridor with him. Or somewhere even further. I don't know, I never asked. Once she came back with a tacky alabaster tree. She bought it in the shop downstairs, or got it as a gift. I'm not asking. A tree for luck.

I've never broken anything before. I didn't know a cast could be so annoying. A white case for a human.

I've lost interest in myself. I focus on anything, my mother's illness, I try. "Luck in unhappiness," my mother said, summing up the cuts and bruises, she didn't suffer any other wounds. After the accident she hung like a moth, stuck to the stretcher. I didn't buckle a seatbelt. I didn't think ambulances could have accidents like other vehicles.

Thirty-fifth (forty-second?), no Fundamental Questions. The answer I will take on faith, "Forty-two," and I don't understand it, but it can stay that way.

Not only Jesus was born on December twenty-fourth. I'm a Capricorn. My mother committed a foyer, following in the footsteps of the Virgin. I was always irritated by my mother's aspirations. Is it possible to aim higher than the Star of Bethlehem?

In three weeks I will begin the forty-first winter of my life. The year XLI was not rich in events, I checked: Caligula was murdered, Seneca chased away, the younger one, from *Oedipus*.

Paweł comes in. We go for a cigarette. I smoke. "I'm going home tomorrow," I say. For the first time, Paweł's face isn't shining with optimism. He's unhappy. He shakes his head, twists his fingers: the joints click.

But whatever I think and say, Paweł is intelligent. He doesn't try to convince me to stay at the hospital, to show me how nearsighted I'm being. It wouldn't change anything. I'm far-sighted anyway.

Paweł understands, though, that sometimes words aren't necessary, they can't change anything, or save it. The fact that he accepts my decision, though he disagrees with it, I see as a compliment. Paweł, for a moment, the moment in which this silence lasts, stops being a doctor who saves lives, and becomes a friend.

I wanted to call a cab, but Paweł stubbornly set his mind on sending an ambulance. "I've lost my faith in ambulances," I say. "Then I can drive you, in my car," he suggests. I decide to make a joke: "You know what, I think I'll take the ambulance."

My mother stayed in the hospital another two days. She could have come back with me, really, but she stayed. I didn't even have to ask Paweł for anything. "You're probably likely to stay by yourself for a bit, get used to it," he might have said. He didn't, there was no need.

Once at home—nothing changed—I realize the laptop stayed at the hospital. I call Paweł. He promises to drive it over in the evening, personally. I don't want to agree, he insists, I give in.

It's not dirty, but I begin to clean, as much as a body with two limbs useless can clean. I get rid of the coffee stain on the floor. After two or three hours of moving around the smell of sweat overcomes the hospital, antiseptic smell. Washing myself is harder than cleaning. I miss the two hands of the nurse.

I don't watch TV, thirty-sixth, unless I have to. I watch TV instead of: a person, situation, decision. Instead of thinking, work, conversation. Against myself. Out of fear. Of lack.

I jump from channel to channel, this jumping reminds me of me, up and down the stairs and floor, hop-hobble-hop-hobble. I finally find Cartoon Network. Nothing like watching programs for children. I decide to nurture the idiot in me. It's going well, I'm even amused by the cake thrown at someone's face and a world saved by a thinking pizza, and then the doorbell rings.

Hop-hobble-hop-hobble, Paweł with the laptop and a paper bag. Behind him, he stands in the doorway, small tornadoes of like form, golden ones made of drizzle pulled along by the light of the street lamp. It's drizzling.

"Thank you," I say as a greeting. I guess I should invite him in. The elephantine tornadoes of drizzle tie themselves into knots, untie themselves, the wind hits and is broken on the walls of the house where the paint has chipped in some places.

"You'll come in," I sort of ask. Intentionally I avoid the question mark at the end. I don't want Paweł to reply: "Gladly." Suddenly I realize that my question that's not a question sounds like a command instead. "Thanks," he says to my greeting. I clumsily swing my arm in an arch, wanting (and not wanting) to invite him inside: my cast hits against the wall.

I was charmed by the image of God from my grandmother's stories, molding and burning a man from clay, honorable and strong: either he will withstand the impact, or he'll break, nothing in between. I was charmed by this image, I always wanted to be formed from light clay and—it turns out—I've been made of plaster instead: a white shell that gives the inner parts some shape, a sarcophagus of a mummy. They will take my cast off in two weeks. I'll lose my shape. I've lost my form already: I'm out of breath by the seventh step.

GLENTURRET SINGLE CASK

PawEł closes the door to the porch, the gesture is similar to the one my mother makes, only this is internal, inside out. Hop-hobble-hop-hobble along the long corridor, the kitchen and dining room, and the living room at the end, the echo is muted by the ugly wallpapers.

Paweł gently puts the bag with the laptop on the table. I fall into a chair. He takes out two bottles of whiskey from the bag. Unknown brand.

"Don't get up," he says. "I'll get them myself." I give him the coordinates of the right cupboard in the kitchen (mirror, angels in a gold frame, turn right, two steps, fourth door from the left, hallelujah). He comes back after a moment. He opens the first bottle and pours out the golden liquid into the glasses. "I forgot," he says as he slaps his forehead like a slapstick actor. From a pocket of his jacket he draws a packet of cigarettes. Cuban with black tobacco. "My lungs are touched," I say, accepting the gift.

I light a cigarette. "I'm sorry, but could you open a window?" He doesn't answer, he gets up and opens one. He sits back down. We lift our glasses. "Toast," I say, "to what?" For a split second Paweł's face looks normal. "You're not the only one with problems," he answers. We clink glasses, and swallow.

I know my whiskey. I don't know this one, but it tastes good, older than me, for sure. A bottle must have cost a fortune. Maybe more, I don't know. I'll piss it out like a cheap Johnnie Walker.

"Delicious," I say. "I don't know what occasion might explain such extravagance."

"You've skipped over the question: Doctor, may I drink?" Paweł replies.

"I know the answer, doctor. Since you brought the cigarettes

183

and alcohol, I conclude that they can't harm me. Unless you're a murderer. Or . . ."

Paweł swallows the alcohol, all that was in his glass. He pours himself more. We drink.

"I wasn't sure I should come," he says. "I don't know if it's right. I can't help either you or your mother. Besides, you know the statistics," he swallows, sets the glass aside. "Maybe it's a good thing that the odds aren't in your favor."

Thoughts swim within me, golden, like an electric current, like a ball of lightning that lights up hidden places, the G-spot, traced in a feather on a bared bone.

"What's not right?" I ask.

"I can't help you, but maybe you can help me . . ."

My turn, I pour the whiskey, clumsily, the left hand always supported the right, now—pushed into the foreground—it trembles in the light and clinks the neck of the bottle against the glass. Stage fright.

"Why me?" I ask. Paweł looks at me with a hurt expression, like a teacher who has taught his pupil the answers and cannot now understand the mistakes.

But his eyes light up; in the same moment he looks calmer, as he understands that his answer is supposed to help me.

"Because if you want to play this way, Grześ, you're the most trustworthy person. Like a Swiss bank."

"I don't think," I say slowly, I feel heated from the inside, "that medical etiquette allows you to take away hope."

"Please," Paweł scoffs, "save me. I hear enough of that at work."

He waves a hand, waving away a winter fly. We say nothing, I light another cigarette. These smell of cigarillos, I'm going to have to air out everything tomorrow. My mother will complain anyway. Paweł pours, I don't know if I'll manage this speed. Before this sentence even finishes voicing itself in my head, I burst out laughing. Paweł, though he's not a part of my thoughts, smiles too.

"I know your brain better than you," he says. 'I saw the test results."

"Yes?" I sound as surprised as an old maid. "And what did you see?"

I can see that this question has surprised him. He regains composure quickly, however: "Patches," he replies.

"If you ever decide to have a lapse," I say, "you'd get patches. With nuts as big as tumors."

We pour out another round, the butter is becoming more buttery. I don't like to get drunk with men. There's less frivolity with it, less happiness, just the hangover that's the same.

"You know," says Paweł, "I married into a rich family before graduating from the university, doctors going back as far as they knew, maybe even back to healers."

I can easily imagine a situation of the pariah at dinner parties. I've experienced that myself. But in my profession surprising successes are allowed.

"I'm sorry," I say, "and on the other hand, you have my admiration. What is she like?"

"You'll laugh. Her profession says it all: she's a dentist."

I do indeed burst out laughing. A short one, in my defense. Paweł laughs too, he has nice teeth.

"I think I know what you mean," I say.

"Yes?"

"I think," I think, "it's like this: you have a wife and two daughters, you have their pictures in your wallet. I saw them. You probably have a big house and two or three cars, a full bank account. Am I right?"

"And? What else was I trying to say?"

"You take night shifts so you don't have to be home, one after another, or whatever it is you doctors can take that keeps you away from your homes."

Paweł is silent. I take my role as host seriously and pour out another round of the amber liquid. Paweł's face looks pleasant for the first time. He's handsome, well kept. Alcohol and slight worry, maybe embarrassment, can be seen in the drawn corners of his mouth and eyes, they make me think that if I were an actor, I would like to cast him in difficult roles. It's not easy to play an ordinary man. It's easy to overdo it.

"That sounds like the plot of a bad movie," he decides.

"Precisely," I reply.

We sit in silence. It doesn't embarrass us. It's healthy.

"Remember, twenty-two or twenty-three years ago," Paweł changes the topic, "Agnieszka's eighteenth?"

I don't remember.

"We were playing spin the bottle. We drank a lot. Remember?"

I remember only, though I would prefer not to, the salty, restless tongue in my mouth. But that wasn't Paweł, but a boy from my year.

"That was you?! Impossible," I say.

Paweł nods his head like a figure of Buddha.

Paweł pours out the rest of the first bottle into our glasses.

His confidence slams into my lack of it. It's impossible, I tell myself, but looking at Paweł I can see that it's likely. My memory gives in to his. I don't remember, but I give in.

"What do you want from me?" I ask in a slight panic, before realizing that the panic, at least from my side, is out of place. I'm not the one baring my soul.

"Nothing," he says with a smile. "From where I sit, from those test results, Grześ, you're no longer here. How can I want anything from someone who doesn't exist?"

Paweł finishes the whiskey. He twists his features in a grimace. For the first time. This grimace doesn't encompass the past, it comments on recent events.

"You see," Paweł says, opening the second bottle, "we're playing with bottles again."

A very strange conversation. I try to control the general flow, but I don't understand that much. I don't know the destination. Not long ago, a lack of a destination didn't stop me from following the flow of conversation. People change.

I'm not surprised that my memory has failed me again, I'm used to it, that my memory gives in to other memories. Paweł is what surprises me. I don't know where he's going, if he's going anywhere. It's not really Paweł who surprises me, but my own blindness.

Paweł isn't wearing his gold frames (contact lenses?). His face doesn't shine with optimism, it's not happy and satisfied. He's rather thin. And definitely lonely. And—strangely—definitely intelligent. He used to like football and biology, we sat at the same desk.

"You took it easy," I say, indicating the cast.

He smiles, the corners of his mouth and eyes slip upward.

"Unintentionally," he replies.

Paweł is opaque. As if I were seeing him for the first time, as if I understood him and simultaneously was wrong in every detail. How can I believe in the right answer when the equation leading to it has been solved incorrectly?

"What do you intend?" he asks.

A few answers come to mind, ambitious and not, I hesitate. I pick the most honest one, unexpectedly: "To bury my mother."

Paweł's forehead creases, he rubs his chin with the inside of his palm. I didn't notice this gesture before. "It would be rude, unsuitable," I clarify, "to die before her!"

He looks at me.

I realize what I've just said. Honestly and stupidly. It was some consolation though: honesty is often stupid. I begin to laugh. Paweł tries to stop himself, but faced with a situation so comical, the border between life and death, it's not possible. He joins me, it's been a while since I laughed with somebody. I forgot how enjoyable it is.

"That's exactly what I envy you. That," he repeats.

"And you?" I ask. "What's wrong with you?"

Paweł turns the glass around in his hands. He has deft fingers. He could be a juggler or surgeon, maybe he is? I never asked if he performs surgeries.

"I'm happy. Except that sometimes I don't have anyone to tell how much I miss something, something that's missing, an emptiness inside, none of my friends would understand."

"And your wife?"

"Is a dentist!" he says, enraged.

"So she's an expert at fillings," I say.

We burst out laughing. The second bottle continues.

HEAD

I HAVEN'T SUFFERED FROM a hangover in a long time. It's just as I remembered. No change, I'm healthy, or at least the signs of a hangover are no different in a healthy head than in a diseased one. Banging and air putting pressure on my temples. An uneven step, thirst, nausea at the sight of food as last night's dinner tries to cross the fence made of my teeth.

Paweł left after midnight. I walked him to the front door myself. The talk with him was good for me.

I don't know Paweł and I don't know if I'd like to get to know him better. But our conversation helped, him as well, according to his assurances. We did each other a mutual favor. He realized that the kind of life that seemed so attractive, my lifestyle: without financial or family commitments, in the capital, the world of stars and smog, carries the same destruction with it as the kind of life he has chosen, which—sometimes—has seemed to me to be the more sensible and happy one: wife, children, home, peace, stability.

"We've taken different paths to the same place," Paweł said, with relief. "Maybe our year wasn't the best, unlike the whiskey you brought," I replied, with relief.

It was reassuring, that conclusion of a drunken conversation, trivial perhaps: the choices you make won't bring happiness or a permanent satisfaction, and that's because there's an alternative version of you in your own head, less concrete, and so more attractive, an uninvited guest. Consolation? Only in others, it's impossible to find it alone, the source has closed up along with the belly button.

I put my head under a stream of freezing water. The water begins to burn the skin, a small relief: one pain covered up by another, and this second one—in a few hours—will be covered by a third, fourth, until the Cetanol stop rolls around.

I don't know why I need a complete head. I'd keep my eyes, perhaps the lips too. I don't need the inside, that inside can't help. An embarrassing situation: I'm intelligent enough, I flatter myself, to search for questions, stir the water, but not intelligent enough to find the answers, to see the blurry shape. It's a stalemate, the only dynamic resolution is: selfmate.

I crawl to the couch. I try not to think about anything. I focus on the pain that's exploding in series in my skull. Red dwarves and blue giants push around, multiply, explode, but my head is bulletproof, at least inside. Caput, as the Romans said.

HOURS

I OPEN MY EYES. It's dark outside, it's dark in the room. I must have fallen asleep or lost consciousness, same thing. The pain is lighter. Hop-hobble-etcetera to the phone. It's after four in the afternoon, two missed calls, Paweł and a private number. If it wasn't for the fact that I'm already stressed out, I'd stress out: I hate it when someone calls from a private number.

I can't remember the details of the evening's meeting. We were sitting for hours and we drank a river. I'm afraid that we spoke honestly, whatever that means.

How could Paweł let me drink so much?! It's unprofessional and irresponsible. He's a doctor, after all. I'm a patient. Patients are allowed to act stupidly. They're not paid for bearing responsibilities. They should listen to doctors. The exam for being a patient, I aced it, or rather drank to it until the last glass.

The script from last night's conversation is full of holes, the immune system of my brain is working, sending out antibodies to the virus of idiocy, but I still remember more than I'd like. Paweł and I shared wise theories about life, like those found in Chinese biscuits. I'm allergic to those, just like anything else that is produced in China, including mementos sold to tourists in Białystok.

I don't like reasoning. I don't believe in wisdom fitting into a single phrase. "The apple tree, like a snowflake, brightens the face and cools emotions," or: "It's not the sun's fault that the bat is blind in the morning," or: "Give in half as much to wisdom as you do to temptations, and you'll be on the right path." They are of even worse quality than Chinese toys.

I used to believe that after forty, people didn't think at all, or think clearly, in paragraphs, or—aware of the limits of

191

language—they limit themselves to saying only what can be said: "Buy me a pack of cigarettes, please," for instance.

I was wrong.

The twenty-fifth hour of each day is the one that I miss, the one I need to organize this world and to remember it, the fragment that I could learn to know.

STOCK MARKET

SHARES PLUNGED ON THE STOCK market. Values plummeted down by three percent. The truth has reached the bottom conversion rate in relation to the Euro since introducing the currency to the stock market. Beauty is not worth investing in, according to financial advisors. Return on investment has been spread into infinity, minus infinity. Honesty, experts have discovered, is not a precious metal that might stop opportunism in a proportion of eighty to twenty, like tombac.

Shares plunged on the stock market, but there's no reason to panic, according to worldly authorities. Deflation, paradoxically, is increasing our purchasing power. We can buy, for the same value, twice as many goods or ten times the amount of truth than we could twenty years ago, for instance.

Live and let live, the value of the world keeps growing. We're richer. If it's the end, it's a happy one.

WARRANTY

MY MOTHER CAME HOME after three days. Paweł drove her himself because I asked him to, afraid she wouldn't want to get into an ambulance and would ask my younger brother instead.

My mother is acting unpredictably. She can lie still for hours, or bend her head over a sudoku. She can be lively in the kitchen cooking dinner, baking—we throw out most of it. She complains that I don't eat anything, that I don't appreciate her work, or respect the family. I don't ask: "What family?" I smoke out on the porch. The standard of this glass aquarium, in terms of comfort, has risen: the armchair is there, Paweł helped me, my mother didn't protest.

The cast, cementing shape in place, has revealed a truth about me, the surface truth: I'm clumsy, I always have been, banging into walls and objects, dropping cutlery and cups. My clumsiness is especially obvious when eating soup. The left hand spills more than what finds its way into my mouth.

"Who will you invite for your birthday?" my mother asks. We are sitting at the table, eating a sauerkraut-and-meat stew with mushrooms. The question about my birthday is also a question about Christmas guests. In the first December the emphasis was usually on my birthday, because the "real" Christmas Eve was waiting in the second December, but in practice the double birthday was tied into an irreversible knot, which didn't bother anybody.

My mother in quick, short sentences goes to the supermarket to do some Christmas shopping. She understands that as long as I have the cast, I'm useless.

My mother checks her blood pressure and blood sugar levels. She has recorded the results in her diaries in neat numbers, like a child. She looks at the numbers and asks: "Son, do we still have warranties for these?" "Why do you ask?" I answer, a pretty poor response. "Well, because," she begins, skittish, "I have such good results, but I feel so poorly."

WHEN

When my brother had to walk over my stretched out legs, he'd say: "Move those wooden sticks."

When my mother was afraid of something, she would start to eat. She was more afraid for others than herself. She weighed almost a hundred kilograms before my father died.

When my father was in a good mood, he gave me piggyback rides.

When I was in a good mood, I'd imagine I was with my family and friends.

When Zuza began to like someone, she was rude to them: just in case.

When I visited my grandmother as a student, she'd cry for joy. She died of dehydration. I didn't go to the funeral, I was abroad. My mother didn't think it was necessary to inform me.

When my brother saw his own blood, he fainted.

When my mother saw somebody else's blood, she'd start acting, no panic. She carried out one action after another, like a cut made by a scalpel is followed by another, cutting the skin of reality.

When I realized that I'm not very gifted, and only at times hardworking, I wanted to finish working altogether.

When my father died, I thought that my friends had begun to leave me. I was embarrassed: my father wasn't my friend. You can choose your friends.

When I saw Kasia at the hospital for the first time, I think she already knew.

When I look into the future, I see only my parents' tombstone.

When I look into the past, I see the future.

LYMPH NODES

SWEAT, SUET, AND MILK, saliva, fluids, and bile. Nothing that a human body, complete and closed, can't bring up. And sounds. Sometimes blood from the nose, lungs, urine; the chosen ones have stigmas. And then there are tears.

"Who will you invite for your birthday?" my mother asks the next day again. I don't know how I should understand this question. Is it automatic (a December stroke)? Unthoughtful (my mother forgot I have no friends in Białystok)? Or bitchy ("My brother" would be the answer to garner the most points)?

"Paweł," I say.

"Paweł," my mother repeats, like an echo. A dry echo.

It was at the hospital when I decided I would think small, no more than required. I won't let myself be taken away by sentences, kidnapped by words: I will be faithful to my first love, forced—myself. Afterward, I don't know when, soon, I will force myself to come to a summary. I know what this summary will say. I still need to see what conclusions are reached. I don't know those. It's too late for conclusions.

A person can be undressed in many ways. The shortest was limited to clothing (a game of spin the bottle, for instance). A slightly more complicated one was brought into the division: body and soul. An older and more noble form of undressing, too complicated in a commercial world, designed (for its own destruction) by the Roman Catholics, has been eliminated, because it required a flexible and scholarly mind. I think about the three-way division of man: body, soul, and ghost.

The ghost is the most mysterious, it's obvious and a necessity that seeps into every body. The ghost is bigger than a person, but formed in a singular way. It can't be seen. It resembles air, omnipresent. Its absence leads to breathlessness, a painful death, and a lack of rights to judgment: the Holy Tribunal will not convene.

In the twentieth century the undressing of a person continued: first to a bikini, then out of skin, totalitarianisms got rid of souls in millions. The masters of intellectual puddings won, the men of simplicity. The soul was chased out of the body. It survives in sentences, as a subject, for instance, an archaic noun. The soul isn't used, not even the visible one made of iron, it's in museums and attics.

Next to my hypochondriac tendencies, I was inclined toward solipsism. Solipsism, verified by people and events, by bills and bank accounts, couldn't develop in a way to bring relief. Solipsism remains a tempting vision, unattainable and—sometimes—leaning toward melancholy.

Possibly the only remnant of solipsism is the conviction, rather absurd, that human bodies produce not only electrical energy like batteries—a thought cannot exist without electricity: complete blackouts are the ideal wastelands, deserts on which there are no ideas—but also time. In a human body there must be an organ, thirty-seventh, an organ that is still waiting to be discovered, a lymph node that produces time. Bodies produce time. The more bodies, the more time. The more time, the smaller the chance of consuming time.

This temporal lymph node in my body had stopped working as it should a while ago now. I hadn't noticed the moment, if it occurred at all, when something began to go wrong with time. It flows in leaps, from event to event, it stops like an operating system for weeks at a time: I can see the blue screen of death when this happens, there are no chances to retrieve any files from the RAM: what's funny is that this acronym stands for random-access memory. The world should be reset. "Reset" is a word that has pushed out the older one—"reincarnation."

GEOMETRIES

I'VE GROWN USED TO THE CAST on my leg and arm, as if I was born in a plaster sarcophagus. I've come to terms with my mother's death. I'm just waiting and, on one hand, hope I won't live long enough to witness it, and on the other—I'm afraid to leave her alone.

There is still enough space to ensure we don't bump into each other, the diagonal movement of the pawn is easy to stop. We sit in front of the TV, my mother and I, like an old married couple; the sitcom actors speak the lines instead of us, they love and hate instead of us, they arrive at a certain hour on TV like the closet family, of which the head is the button on the remote. The commonness of the heroes, their theatrical ability to make shallow what should be insightful is reassuring, like a warning, a riverbed: "Mom, if we start to really talk, we'll fall to the level of sitcoms, do you really think it's worth spending our last weeks like that?" I could ask.

Though we talk more than we have to, the subtle changes happen outside of words or in spite of them, they bounce off the body like a body that is reflected in the mirror. First, I look increasingly worse, I barely recognized myself in the bathroom yesterday, I wiped the glass with a towel but that changed nothing: huge eyes deep in the dark circle of the holes in my skull, colorless hair, too much skin. Second, my mother is disappearing, not inside her body, outside of it, the body that has grown thinner over the last few months by tens of kilograms, she's vanishing in actions—or the actions disappear in her, like lines that join up the dots. She doesn't tidy the cups away, not straight away. She's also vanishing in the words, she's not even enraged by my smoking on the porch.

Or maybe she's saving her strength for another round, which is why she only performs those actions that are absolutely necessary, she rests in her corner as often as possible, just so she doesn't get disqualified?

Every other day, Paweł pays me a visit. My mother usually goes to the bedroom, we sit in the living room. We went upstairs twice: I was showing Paweł some things on my laptop, for instance. I wasn't expecting this sudden closeness, it makes movement more difficult than a cast does.

We were sitting in the living room, my mother was preparing decaf coffee, for me, and green tea for the guest, very healthily. I asked Paweł not to come again. He grew still, and a long silence followed. "Do you think I'm doing this for you?" he asked. I nodded. He smiled bitterly, I rarely saw such a sad face, such a helpless one, drawn in despair, too sad a word. "I have enough of dying at work," he said. "I come here not because . . ." He hesitated, reset the sentence: "I visit you because I need to." I was silent.

"I'll go now," he said. "Come tomorrow," my throat asked him. He smiled, left, and came the following day with a chocolate cake, for no reason. He told my mother that he got the cake from a patient. He was lying. I found the receipt in the bag, with a date and timestamp: it was paid for fifteen minutes before he got to our house, with a credit card, the owner's name was Drenasz; I doubt that Paweł is his own patient. I heard the creak of the door, and then the new gate. For no reason at all I was attacked by sadness. Strong sadness. I began to cry. I'm changing.

The mirror is not the only proof of my condition, but also what makes me cry. Tragedy still leaves me unmoved, like the story of Romeo and Juliet, written in a space of details: the shape of a mouth, motionless hands, a tragedy won on a disparity of minutes and misunderstandings. I'm touched by details: four sugar crystals on the table that my mother missed and didn't wipe away, the paused gesture over a cup—my mother can't remember whether you pour in hot water first, or put in the teabag.

I'm the child of my parents, which is obvious, and of deficit.

The basic products were missing: meat, sugar, yeast, toilet paper, but also authorities and examples. The world of good and evil burned down with the crematoriums, communism cynically switched around the moral values, good became bad, though bad didn't necessarily become good, more like justice, if I can remember. I'm the child of value deficits, the inflation of heroes, a campaign of picking potato beetles in the fields and cleaning woods: On guard!

What—this is a rhetorical question—can you expect of one whose heroes included Hans Kloss, the child born after his father's—Konrad Wallenrod—death? What can you expect of a generation who should honor Colonel Kukliński? The majority of the not-so-bronze heroes of the most recent decades have been marred by reality; they are more real, but also more attractive. The shopkeeper who turns away the chance to earn more money, keeping his income at twenty percent, say, is as heroic as (the so-called) cautious opponent of communism, who signed a document to cooperate with the Security Service, though he never did anyone any harm, according to the archives.

I didn't think that the geometry of my face would change so much in three months. The web of delicate wrinkles, which is clearest around my eyes and mouth. My facial muscles are weaker, as if someone had slipped me some Pavulon. A stranger's face. I must learn to recognize my own reflection again, like a child.

We're watching a rerun of *Dynasty*. "Who'd have thought it," my mother says. "Who'd have thought it?" At first I think she's referring to the show, which she's seen many times and—I think—even the first time around showed no surprise. But my mother isn't commenting on the televised reality. She's referring to the other reality: two bodies on the couch. She's right.

We watch films with a French gendarme. They are comedies, we don't laugh though, my mother even cries at times. My father really liked such movies.

We watch *Clan, L for Love*, we watch a lot. I've never watched so much in my life; maybe sometimes, when I was really ill.

We don't watch the news. We've eliminated sports. Artistic programs are banned. The same happens with ambitious movies.

My mother and I have struck a TV deal: we will die in tacky surroundings, nothing deep.

Euclid gave geometry its shape, five axioms that are the measurement of the earth. I'd like to do something similar, a new branch of anthropometry: a few axioms describing everything that can happen, carrying-over point, figure, surface, size, depth into the world of the body and emotions.

THROAT

I HAVE TWO HOURS FOR MYSELF, at least. My mother has gone to the supermarket with Paweł. I asked him, it's Christmas Eve next week, my mother hasn't stopped talking about shopping, at breakfast and dinner. I asked Paweł with some embarrassment, but also with surprising spite: if you want to make friends, then suffer, take my mother shopping, that's what friendship is, I thought and was embarrassed at my own thoughts.

I sit at the kitchen table. The phone lies in front of me. I used to think that dying meant pain, suffering with a capital letter, that's what I thought because I didn't draw any conclusions from my father's death, for instance. Dying is accompanied by surprise most of all, it seems. And a lot of unfinished business.

When I have to do something that I really don't want to, I try to push it away from myself as far as possible, to be able to observe my actions from a safe distance. Then I see some actor, more or less similar to me, who says the lines I couldn't speak.

The actor picks out a number on his phone. A new model of the iPhone, an African family might have food for a year. The actor pulls his facial muscles into a grimace of pain. He's pretty good, I must admit, convincing: I believed him. For a few seconds nothing happens, the audience member could get bored, the cameraman has made a brave decision by not cutting this scene short. Finally some voice sounds across the stage—I reach this conclusion based on the actor's face: the muscles fall into the shape of fear, blood colors the skin (too much red light). The actor pretends he can't say a word, he pretends very well, and it's only the first take.

"Hi, little brother," the actor says, controlling his voice perfectly. "I'd like to invite you over for my birthday," the actor continues. Now the cameraman is charging straight ahead: the actor listens, concentrating hard, to the words uttered on the other end of the line, for a few seconds. I can't describe his expression. "Thanks," the actor replies. "See you on Christmas Eve. Thanks," the actor says.

The actor puts the phone back down on the table. With the tips of the fingers of his left hand (the right one rests in a cast) he strokes the glass surface of the phone. This gesture is one I would also cut out, it's unnecessary, redundant, unexplained by the past.

The actor closes his eyes, the makeup artists and designers have done their job: it's difficult to not like him. He seems tired and, not a very fitting word, noble. The audience member is on his side, even if he's rather bored. He does have Coke and popcorn.

Before the emotions that are stretched across the palette of his face play out, the character chooses another number. "Hi," says the face, "I have your number from Paweł." The words make their way through his throat with difficulty, this actor is really good. "I'd like to invite you for my birthday," he says.

I wouldn't be able to act that out so well. I sit at the kitchen table. I wait for my mother and Paweł. I can't believe that I've just called my brother and Kasia. I'll have to check my bills. Happiness is choking my throat.

GRZEGORZ

Paweł carries in countless bags with shopping that he arranges in a pyramid on the table, and then on the floor of the kitchen. My mother emanates happiness, I haven't seen her like this in a long time, she's almost flirting with Paweł, she even has a good word for me: she calls me by my name: "Grześ," she says, "I bought the shrimp you like so much."

Paweł also seems happy, really happy. It must be some December disease. I mutter something and hop-hobble to the living room. I turn on the Discovery channel: Americans are bombarding Tokyo. TVP shows a crisis in government. I pick Tokyo.

My mother unpacks all the things, the bags rustle, cupboard doors shut with a click, objects move. Paweł comes over to me with two bottles of beer. He gives me one and sits down next to me. He really is acting like an old family friend, more at home than even I am.

I stare at the black and white explosions. Paweł is silent, I turn the TV off. "Thank you for taking my mother shopping," I say. Paweł looks at me carefully, recently he's stopped wearing his glasses, he wears contacts, barely resembling himself at all, I could like him, I don't want to.

"You probably won't be able to . . ." I start, "but it's my birthday on Christmas Eve and I'd like to invite you. My brother and his wife and son will come. And Kasia with her daughter."

"Thank you," Paweł says. "I'll be here."

I wasn't expecting this response. "And your family?" I ask.

"I moved out this morning," he replies.

"I'm sorry," I say.

My mother comes into the room to ask if Paweł will stay for

dinner. Paweł glances at me questioningly. "Paweł will stay," I tell my mother. She leaves, and Paweł smiles at me. That smile is irritating. "Shouldn't you be devastated now?" I ask. He bursts out laughing. Then he says: "I am."

"Where will you live?" I ask.

"I'll stay at a hotel," he replies.

"This house is big," I say, and feel the hairs on my head standing on end, "you can stay with us. For a while."

It must look comical, two very surprised faces are studying each other. Paweł is taken aback by my suggestion. I'm taken aback by my suggestion. We stare at each other.

"Are you kidding?!" he finally exclaims.

"I'd like to be," I reply bitterly.

Paweł covers his face with his hands.

I get up, "I'll talk to my mother," I tell him. I go to the kitchen. I explain the situation to my mother, I ask if Paweł can stay with us. My mother listens closely, it seems she understands everything. "Son," she replies, "of course. He's your friend. And in my condition it will be good to have a doctor around. I'll sleep better."

Paweł got my brother's old room, upstairs, next to mine. He's just carried two suitcases upstairs. My mother is happy. She's making us coffee. My mother's full of energy. Suddenly she has exactly what she's been dreaming of: a full house. Perhaps there are only two of us, but that's already an improvement on the last five years and Cesar. And in a week the house will be even fuller: son, daughter-in-law, and grandson, Kasia and her daughter. Maybe someone else. Christmas Eve.

My life seems meaningless. That's why I'm trying to give it some form. I'm forty and I've decided to clothe those years in words, a word for every year, forty words, on the twenty-fourth of December there'll be a forty-first. I was trying to come up with a key, the key isn't really that important, but I've started anyway: from a name, Grzegorz, my name, or rather my parents started with the name. The name decided the form, the words came of their own volition, like objects, almost tangible, the seventh letter of the alphabet. Seventh, there are questions that I return to. For instance this: Why do I find it so difficult to accept the love and devotion of others?

The seventh letter turned out to be the most important, determining—perhaps—my life, giving it shape. *G.* A good letter, like any other.

We had dinner together. My mother prepared dinner. Cutlets, fried and jugged potatoes, pickled cucumbers. I ate the soup without protest, with rice, that must mean I'm really not well.

My mother went to bed early. As happy as ever. That will pass, I thought.

It wasn't even ten. Paweł and I were sitting in front of the TV. I chose, provocatively, TV Romantica. We drank beer. Paweł changed into pajamas. I didn't think I'd ever see him in pajamas. "Thank you. Really. I never thought . . ." at first I think these words come from the lighthearted show we were watching. But no, Paweł said them. He made me feel rather shy.

Suddenly I find it hard to believe that today happened not just in my head, but also in the real world. That I spoke with my brother and Kasia. That Paweł has moved in. I can't believe it. I tense up, a lot.

"Grześ," Paweł says, "take it easy, relax. I'm the one taking a risk, not you."

"How?" I ask.

"You know how," he says,

"Tell me," I say.

"You don't want to hear it," he says.

The TV shows some greasy makeup streaming down Juanita's face, Juan just left her.

"All right," Paweł says. "You asked for it," he says, and falls silent.

"You're taking a risk," I say, "Because you're making friends with, beginning to love, someone who will soon be gone," I say.

Paweł doesn't answer. I want to cry, I've really changed.

"I couldn't have said that better myself," Paweł says.

"I'm sorry," I say. "I'm really sorry. I didn't mean to."

Paweł sits beside me, tense. I put my arm around him, the one in the cast. His head rests on my chest. Paweł begins to cry.

Midlife crisis.

I stroke his hair with my left hand. I have no experience in such situations.

"I'm sorry," I keep repeating. "I'm sorry."

WE PLAY

THE CAST CAME OFF YESTERDAY. I'm lighter. The preparations for Christmas Eve / my birthday have begun for real now. My mother bubbles with energy, just as she used to years ago. She's cleaning, varnishing, pickling. Dusting, moving, baking. I'm happy to see her in such good form, but it also terrifies me: this is exactly what I was running from when I left Białystok, one of the things anyway. Paweł also looks good. He tries to act with some reserve, he looks sad at times though, but he looks happy too. The situation in my home resembles the plot of a family movie. We all act well. I got the role of the villain. I will follow the rules and eventually break and pass over to the light side.

I have no appetite. "Eat," my mother says. "You have to eat," Paweł repeats, though, I admit, this is the first time that the prospect of Christmas brings me some joy. I'm calmed by familiar objects. I'm calmed by the thought of seeing my brother and Kasia. I will be good. A new beginning. Another.

Thirty-eighth, I believe in spelling. Higher orders, religious or ethical, have turned out to be too stiff. I could only believe in something smaller, a group of rules that my mind could get around, rules possible to obey. A group of clear rules, allowing exceptions and leaving some space for neologisms. God-got. Spelling gives words shape, and shape specifies meaning.

I barely take any part in the birthday preparations. Paweł takes my place. My mother doesn't protest. I sit by myself on the first floor. I write, the right hand is useful. Sometimes I go downstairs, we drink tea or decaf coffee together, Paweł goes out for a cigarette with me. He's started to smoke: he still can't inhale, chokes, coughs. "You're hopeless. No good," I say when he turns green yet again.

I've begun to believe it will all be all right. I have my mother back, my brother, Kasia. I've made a friend. It will be all right, I'm beginning to believe. I've started to eat, I don't want to though. I read once that the soul weighs twenty-one grams: the difference in weight between a living man and his just-expired corpse.

I don't think I have a soul anymore. After death I will be heavier by my twenty-one grams. After death, my soul will come back to me. I've suffered a defeat. A pretentious defeat. Defeat has been written into the network of my veins, and the network itself into the tangle of my sentences. But I'm not embarrassed, I believe that I'll get further than my forty words. It's embarrassing. This will to live.

GLOSS

THERE WERE A LOT OF PEOPLE at the cemetery. An unfortunate date—just after Christmas, just before New Year's Eve. Snow had fallen. People in mourning, trees and tombstones in snow. Barely anybody spoke.

I knew a few mourners. Grzegorz's brother, his mother, Paweł. Some actors came too. I knew those from the screen. The ceremony went smoothly and routinely. Some people cried. I didn't. It was cold in the church. I might have gotten a cold. Paweł kissed his lips. Then they nailed the coffin shut.

I threw a handful of earth, so I didn't stand out. I put down the flowers, a bunch of carnations. He liked those. Grześ's mother took me under the arm. We walked along a snowy path. Mrs. Anna stopped by one of the tombstones.

"Look, child," she said. "The doctors already set a date of birth, but she died before she was born. It was a car crash. Poor Ania. Grześ liked coming here."

Paweł dropped me off in Białystok. He didn't look good. He shouldn't have left his wife. I know what I'm saying.

At the end of March someone from the publisher called. They got my number from Paweł. I agreed to read the text.

"His final text," the voice on the other end told me.

I read it. I didn't know what to write. An introduction or an afterword—they gave me a free rein. First I prepared the contents page. Then I prepared another. I'm not an editor. I don't know how to edit my own life or the city in which I live. My daughter is often sick, crying.

In Grześ's writing I'm struck by the tackiness of it all. I could say that he plagiarized his own life.

I read an essay by Maria Janion when I was at the university.

I remembered one sentence, unfortunately out of context, that tackiness is an irreplaceable desire to achieve harmony, an apologia of "simple" moral values, giving everything a happy end, something like that.

I saw Grześ's mother. I saw Paweł. I saw Artur, Grześ's brother. These meetings didn't erase the difficulties. I don't have any literary qualifications. I'm an expert in developmental psychology.

Maybe I should write that Grześ was the best person I've ever known. That he was the love of my life. That I'll miss him. That's what one writes. It's a polite formula. But it's not true.

I missed him before he died. In high school. When he left me before exams. I had as much of him during life as I do after death. We didn't get the chance to meet again on the day of his forty-first birthday. He died a day earlier.

He wasn't the best person I've ever known. Maybe in a few years he would be. I know what I'm saying.

I chose the title for the last chapter. I have the chance to comment and conclude his life. I haven't asked for this distinction.

When someone receives a prize, they say: "I didn't expect it." When someone receives punishment, they often say nothing at all.

A List of Forty Titles

1. BOUGHS
2. PORCH
3. NEWSPAPERS
4. GRAVES
5. GAMES
6. GATHERINGS
7. BUTTON
8. CLOSET
9. GEOGRAPHY
10. IF I HAD
11. GENETIVUS
12. GONG
13. WILLY
14. ELSEWHERE
15. ACCESSORIES
16. MOUNTAINS
17. GAZ-67
18. CLAY
19. G 35
20. GUARD
21. SUIT
22. DECEMBER
23. HEAT
24. GUESTS
25. FLAT TIRE
26. BORDERS
27. TUMOR
28. CAST
29. GLENTURRET SINGLE CASK
30. HEAD
31. HOURS
32. STOCK MARKET
33. WARRANTY
34. WHEN
35. LYMPH NODES
36. GEOMETRIES
37. THROAT
38. GRZEGORZ
39. WE PLAY
40. GLOSS

A List of Forty Numerals

1.	First	Boughs
2.	Second	Boughs
3.	Third	Boughs
4.	Fourth	Boughs
5.	Fifth	Boughs
6.	Sixth	Boughs
7.	Seventh	Boughs
8.	Eighth	Boughs
9.	Ninth	Porch
10.	Tenth	Newspapers
11.	Eleventh	Newspapers
12.	Twelfth	Graves
13.	Twelfth	Games
14.	Thirteenth	Button
15.	Fourteenth	Closet
16.	Fifteenth	Geography
17.	Sixteenth	If I Had
18.	Seventeenth	If I Had
19.	Eighteenth	Genetivus
20.	Nineteenth	Elsewhere
21.	Twentieth	Heat
22.	Twenty-first	Mountains
23.	Twenty-second	Clay
24.	Twenty-third	G 35
25.	Twenty-fourth	December
26.	Twenty-fifth	December
27.	Twenty-sixth	Heat
28.	Twenty-seventh	Heat
29.	Twenty-eighth	Heat
30.	Twenty-ninth	Heat
31.	Thirtieth	Heat
32.	Thirty-first	Flat Tire
33.	Thirty-second	Flat Tire
34.	Thirty-third	Borders
35.	Thirty-fourth	Borders
36.	Thirty-fifth	Cast
37.	Thirty-sixth	Cast
38.	Thirty-seventh	Lymph Nodes
39.	Thirty-eighth	We Play
40.	Fortieth	Porch

Acknowledgments

The author of this books thanks the Society of Villa Decjusza and the Book Institute for the possibility of participating in the Homines Urbani Program.

Note on the Text

matka w krześle drewnianym (the mother in the wooden chair) and *rozkład jazdy* (timetable), the poems quoted on pages 38 and 40, were both written by Tymoteusz Karpowicz and published in *Słoje zadrzewne* (Tree rings), 1999, Wrocław, Wydawnictwo Dolnośląskie.

Ignacy Karpowicz is a Polish writer and translator. His fifth work, *Balladyny i romanse*, won him the Polityka Passport prize in 2010. He was previously nominated for this award for his debut novel *Niehalo* (2006) and has since been nominated for the Nike Literary Award for *Gesty* (*Gestures*), *Balladyny i romanse*, *osci*, and *Sońka*.

Karpowicz translates literature from English, Spanish, and Amharic, a Semitic language spoken in Ethiopia, and he has lived in Costa Rica and Ethiopia. He now lives in Poland.

Maya Zakrzewska-Pim is a Polish-British translator. She grew up in Warsaw before studying English at Trinity College, Dublin. She completed an MPhil in Education at the University of Cambridge and began a PhD there in late 2016.

Author Interview

What do you think is more important when it comes to reading: the author's intentions, or the reader's interpretation? Or are these equally significant?

I think that the book is 'finished' only after it has been read. Before that, it is an outline of something, a meal that still needs to be prepared for one to eat it. The author's intentions are of course important during the book's creation, however after that, the reader's interpretation is of greater import.

In writing Gestures, is there something specific that you were hoping to communicate to your readers?

Every book that has had an emotional effect on me was a complete and whole world in itself, even if the fundamental building block of this world was fragmentation or a lack of something. Whilst writing Gestures, I wanted to create such a complete and whole literary world, organized around a single hero who observes his private world in 39 short chapters. I find it difficult to encompass the novel's essence—perhaps: find the time to study reality, and yourself in it. Perhaps this touches upon corny sententiousness, but sometimes this is the best way to describe the world.

What effect were you trying to achieve with the novel's ending, an ending which gives rise to so many contrasting emotions— disappointment, bitterness, but also a sense of peace . . . ?

I thought a long time about the ending with my editors. Eventually we decided on the more controversial option. It's a natural progression from the earlier chapters. The preceding chapters and the ending together lead me to conclude that people have the tendency to make plans and organize their realities (internal and external ones), without taking into consideration those chance events which turn everything upside down. On the other hand, it is precisely this unplanned occurrence at the end of the novel that completes the hero's intentions and plans.

To what extent do you share Grzegorz's views of the world, love, family relations, etc?

While writing the novel, I probably shared the same views. Now, however, I view the world differently, with less passivity, though the essence remains the same—experience the world with sensitivity as well as ruthlessness.

Where did you find the ideas for Gestures, did you have any specific inspirations?

I was writing Sonka at the time, and I realized that I didn't understand one of the characters. I thought that I'd write about him, to learn more of him and so—unexpectedly—Gestures was born.

What words do you think are most accurate to describe Gestures?

I will answer in a Borges manner—Gestures is best described by Gestures.

SELECTED DALKEY ARCHIVE TITLES

MICHAL AJVAZ, *The Golden Age.*
The Other City.

PIERRE ALBERT-BIROT, *Grabinoulor.*

YUZ ALESHKOVSKY, *Kangaroo.*

FELIPE ALFAU, *Chromos.*
Locos.

JOE AMATO, *Samuel Taylor's Last Night.*

IVAN ÂNGELO, *The Celebration.*
The Tower of Glass.

ANTÓNIO LOBO ANTUNES, *Knowledge of Hell.*
The Splendor of Portugal.

ALAIN ARIAS-MISSON, *Theatre of Incest.*

JOHN ASHBERY & JAMES SCHUYLER, *A Nest of Ninnies.*

ROBERT ASHLEY, *Perfect Lives.*

GABRIELA AVIGUR-ROTEM, *Heatwave and Crazy Birds.*

DJUNA BARNES, *Ladies Almanack.*
Ryder.

JOHN BARTH, *Letters.*
Sabbatical.

DONALD BARTHELME, *The King.*
Paradise.

SVETISLAV BASARA, *Chinese Letter.*

MIQUEL BAUÇÀ, *The Siege in the Room.*

RENÉ BELLETTO, *Dying.*

MAREK BIENCZYK, *Transparency.*

ANDREI BITOV, *Pushkin House.*

ANDREJ BLATNIK, *You Do Understand.*
Law of Desire.

LOUIS PAUL BOON, *Chapel Road.*
My Little War.
Summer in Termuren.

ROGER BOYLAN, *Killoyle.*

IGNÁCIO DE LOYOLA BRANDÃO, *Anonymous Celebrity.*
Zero.

BONNIE BREMSER, *Troia: Mexican Memoirs.*

CHRISTINE BROOKE-ROSE, *Amalgamemnon.*

BRIGID BROPHY, *In Transit.*
The Prancing Novelist.

GERALD L. BRUNS, *Modern Poetry and the Idea of Language.*

GABRIELLE BURTON, *Heartbreak Hotel.*

MICHEL BUTOR, *Degrees.*
Mobile.

G. CABRERA INFANTE, *Infante's Inferno.*
Three Trapped Tigers.

JULIETA CAMPOS, *The Fear of Losing Eurydice.*

ANNE CARSON, *Eros the Bittersweet.*

ORLY CASTEL-BLOOM, *Dolly City.*

LOUIS-FERDINAND CÉLINE, *North.*
Conversations with Professor Y.
London Bridge.

MARIE CHAIX, *The Laurels of Lake Constance.*

HUGO CHARTERIS, *The Tide Is Right.*

ERIC CHEVILLARD, *Demolishing Nisard.*
The Author and Me.

MARC CHOLODENKO, *Mordechai Schamz.*

JOSHUA COHEN, *Witz.*

EMILY HOLMES COLEMAN, *The Shutter of Snow.*

ERIC CHEVILLARD, *The Author and Me.*

ROBERT COOVER, *A Night at the Movies.*

STANLEY CRAWFORD, *Log of the S.S.*
The Mrs Unguentine.
Some Instructions to My Wife.

RENÉ CREVEL, *Putting My Foot in It.*

RALPH CUSACK, *Cadenza.*

NICHOLAS DELBANCO, *Sherbrookes.*
The Count of Concord.

NIGEL DENNIS, *Cards of Identity.*

PETER DIMOCK, *A Short Rhetoric for Leaving the Family.*

ARIEL DORFMAN, *Konfidenz.*

COLEMAN DOWELL, *Island People.*
Too Much Flesh and Jabez.

ARKADII DRAGOMOSHCHENKO, *Dust.*

RIKKI DUCORNET, *Phosphor in Dreamland.*
The Complete Butcher's Tales.

RIKKI DUCORNET (cont.), *The Jade Cabinet.*
The Fountains of Neptune.

WILLIAM EASTLAKE, *The Bamboo Bed.*
Castle Keep.
Lyric of the Circle Heart.

JEAN ECHENOZ, *Chopin's Move.*

STANLEY ELKIN, *A Bad Man.*
Criers and Kibitzers, Kibitzers and Criers.
The Dick Gibson Show.
The Franchiser.
The Living End.
Mrs. Ted Bliss.

FRANÇOIS EMMANUEL, *Invitation to a Voyage.*

PAUL EMOND, *The Dance of a Sham.*

SALVADOR ESPRIU, *Ariadne in the Grotesque Labyrinth.*

LESLIE A. FIEDLER, *Love and Death in the American Novel.*

JUAN FILLOY, *Op Oloop.*

ANDY FITCH, *Pop Poetics.*

GUSTAVE FLAUBERT, *Bouvard and Pécuchet.*

KASS FLEISHER, *Talking out of School.*

JON FOSSE, *Aliss at the Fire.*
Melancholy.

FORD MADOX FORD, *The March of Literature.*

MAX FRISCH, *I'm Not Stiller.*
Man in the Holocene.

CARLOS FUENTES, *Christopher Unborn.*
Distant Relations.
Terra Nostra.
Where the Air Is Clear.

TAKEHIKO FUKUNAGA, *Flowers of Grass.*

WILLIAM GADDIS, JR., *The Recognitions.*

JANICE GALLOWAY, *Foreign Parts.*
The Trick Is to Keep Breathing.

WILLIAM H. GASS, *Life Sentences.*
The Tunnel.
The World Within the Word.
Willie Masters' Lonesome Wife.

GÉRARD GAVARRY, *Hoppla! 1 2 3.*

ETIENNE GILSON, *The Arts of the Beautiful.*
Forms and Substances in the Arts.

C. S. GISCOMBE, *Giscome Road.*
Here.

DOUGLAS GLOVER, *Bad News of the Heart.*

WITOLD GOMBROWICZ, *A Kind of Testament.*

PAULO EMÍLIO SALES GOMES, *P's Three Women.*

GEORGI GOSPODINOV, *Natural Novel.*

JUAN GOYTISOLO, *Count Julian.*
Juan the Landless.
Makbara.
Marks of Identity.

HENRY GREEN, *Blindness.*
Concluding.
Doting.
Nothing.

JACK GREEN, *Fire the Bastards!*

JIŘÍ GRUŠA, *The Questionnaire.*

MELA HARTWIG, *Am I a Redundant Human Being?*

JOHN HAWKES, *The Passion Artist.*
Whistlejacket.

ELIZABETH HEIGHWAY, ED., *Contemporary Georgian Fiction.*

AIDAN HIGGINS, *Balcony of Europe.*
Blind Man's Bluff.
Bornholm Night-Ferry.
Langrishe, Go Down.
Scenes from a Receding Past.

KEIZO HINO, *Isle of Dreams.*

KAZUSHI HOSAKA, *Plainsong.*

ALDOUS HUXLEY, *Antic Hay.*
Point Counter Point.
Those Barren Leaves.
Time Must Have a Stop.

NAOYUKI II, *The Shadow of a Blue Cat.*

DRAGO JANČAR, *The Tree with No Name.*

MIKHEIL JAVAKHISHVILI, *Kvachi.*

GERT JONKE, *The Distant Sound.*
Homage to Czerny.
The System of Vienna.

JACQUES JOUET, *Mountain R.*
Savage.
Upstaged.

MIEKO KANAI, *The Word Book.*

YORAM KANIUK, *Life on Sandpaper.*

ZURAB KARUMIDZE, *Dagny.*

JOHN KELLY, *From Out of the City.*

HUGH KENNER, *Flaubert, Joyce
and Beckett: The Stoic Comedians.*
Joyce's Voices.

DANILO KIŠ, *The Attic.*
The Lute and the Scars.
Psalm 44.
A Tomb for Boris Davidovich.

ANITA KONKKA, *A Fool's Paradise.*

GEORGE KONRÁD, *The City Builder.*

TADEUSZ KONWICKI, *A Minor
Apocalypse.*
The Polish Complex.

ANNA KORDZAIA-SAMADASHVILI,
Me, Margarita.

MENIS KOUMANDAREAS, *Koula.*

ELAINE KRAF, *The Princess of 72nd Street.*

JIM KRUSOE, *Iceland.*

AYSE KULIN, *Farewell: A Mansion in
Occupied Istanbul.*

EMILIO LASCANO TEGUI, *On Elegance
While Sleeping.*

ERIC LAURRENT, *Do Not Touch.*

VIOLETTE LEDUC, *La Bâtarde.*

EDOUARD LEVÉ, *Autoportrait.*
Newspaper.
Suicide.
Works.

MARIO LEVI, *Istanbul Was a Fairy Tale.*

DEBORAH LEVY, *Billy and Girl.*

JOSÉ LEZAMA LIMA, *Paradiso.*

ROSA LIKSOM, *Dark Paradise.*

OSMAN LINS, *Avalovara.*
The Queen of the Prisons of Greece.

FLORIAN LIPUŠ, *The Errors of Young Tjaž.*

GORDON LISH, *Peru.*

ALF MACLOCHLAINN, *Out of Focus.*
Past Habitual.

The Corpus in the Library.

RON LOEWINSOHN, *Magnetic Field(s).*

YURI LOTMAN, *Non-Memoirs.*

D. KEITH MANO, *Take Five.*

MINA LOY, *Stories and Essays of Mina Loy.*

MICHELINE AHARONIAN MARCOM,
A Brief History of Yes.
The Mirror in the Well.

BEN MARCUS, *The Age of Wire and String.*

WALLACE MARKFIELD, *Teitlebaum's
Window.*

DAVID MARKSON, *Reader's Block.*
Wittgenstein's Mistress.

CAROLE MASO, *AVA.*

HISAKI MATSUURA, *Triangle.*

LADISLAV MATEJKA & KRYSTYNA
POMORSKA, EDS., *Readings in Russian
Poetics: Formalist & Structuralist Views.*

HARRY MATHEWS, *Cigarettes.*
The Conversions.
The Human Country.
The Journalist.
My Life in CIA.
Singular Pleasures.
The Sinking of the Odradek.
Stadium.
Tlooth.

HISAKI MATSUURA, *Triangle.*

DONAL MCLAUGHLIN, *beheading the
virgin mary, and other stories.*

JOSEPH MCELROY, *Night Soul and
Other Stories.*

ABDELWAHAB MEDDEB, *Talismano.*

GERHARD MEIER, *Isle of the Dead.*

HERMAN MELVILLE, *The Confidence-
Man.*

AMANDA MICHALOPOULOU, *I'd Like.*

STEVEN MILLHAUSER, *The Barnum
Museum.*
In the Penny Arcade.

RALPH J. MILLS, JR., *Essays on Poetry.*

MOMUS, *The Book of Jokes.*

CHRISTINE MONTALBETTI, *The Origin
of Man.*
Western.

NICHOLAS MOSLEY, *Accident.*
Assassins.
Catastrophe Practice.
A Garden of Trees.
Hopeful Monsters.
Imago Bird.
Inventing God.
Look at the Dark.
Metamorphosis.
Natalie Natalia.
Serpent.

WARREN MOTTE, *Fables of the Novel:
French Fiction since 1990.*
*Fiction Now: The French Novel in the
21st Century.*
Mirror Gazing.
Oulipo: A Primer of Potential Literature.

GERALD MURNANE, *Barley Patch.*
Inland.

YVES NAVARRE, *Our Share of Time.*
Sweet Tooth.

DOROTHY NELSON, *In Night's City.*
Tar and Feathers.

ESHKOL NEVO, *Homesick.*

WILFRIDO D. NOLLEDO, *But for
the Lovers.*

BORIS A. NOVAK, *The Master of
Insomnia.*

FLANN O'BRIEN, *At Swim-Two-Birds.*
The Best of Myles.
The Dalkey Archive.
The Hard Life.
The Poor Mouth.
The Third Policeman.

CLAUDE OLLIER, *The Mise-en-Scène.*
Wert and the Life Without End.

PATRIK OUŘEDNÍK, *Europeana.*
The Opportune Moment, 1855.

BORIS PAHOR, *Necropolis.*

FERNANDO DEL PASO, *News from
the Empire.*
Palinuro of Mexico.

ROBERT PINGET, *The Inquisitory.*
Mahu or The Material.
Trio.

MANUEL PUIG, *Betrayed by Rita
Hayworth.*

The Buenos Aires Affair.
Heartbreak Tango.

RAYMOND QUENEAU, *The Last Days.*
Odile.
Pierrot Mon Ami.
Saint Glinglin.

ANN QUIN, *Berg.*
Passages.
Three.
Tripticks.

ISHMAEL REED, *The Free-Lance
Pallbearers.*
The Last Days of Louisiana Red.
Ishmael Reed: The Plays.
Juice!
The Terrible Threes.
The Terrible Twos.
Yellow Back Radio Broke-Down.

JASIA REICHARDT, *15 Journeys Warsaw
to London.*

JOÃO UBALDO RIBEIRO, *House of the
Fortunate Buddhas.*

JEAN RICARDOU, *Place Names.*

RAINER MARIA RILKE,
The Notebooks of Malte Laurids Brigge.

JULIÁN RÍOS, *The House of Ulysses.*
Larva: A Midsummer Night's Babel.
Poundemonium.

ALAIN ROBBE-GRILLET, *Project for a
Revolution in New York.*
A Sentimental Novel.

AUGUSTO ROA BASTOS, *I the Supreme.*

DANIËL ROBBERECHTS, *Arriving in
Avignon.*

JEAN ROLIN, *The Explosion of the
Radiator Hose.*

OLIVIER ROLIN, *Hotel Crystal.*

ALIX CLEO ROUBAUD, *Alix's Journal.*

JACQUES ROUBAUD, *The Form of
a City Changes Faster, Alas, Than the
Human Heart.*
The Great Fire of London.
Hortense in Exile.
Hortense Is Abducted.
*Mathematics: The Plurality of Worlds of
Lewis.*
Some Thing Black.

RAYMOND ROUSSEL, *Impressions of Africa.*

VEDRANA RUDAN, *Night.*

PABLO M. RUIZ, *Four Cold Chapters on the Possibility of Literature.*

GERMAN SADULAEV, *The Maya Pill.*

TOMAŽ ŠALAMUN, *Soy Realidad.*

LYDIE SALVAYRE, *The Company of Ghosts.*
The Lecture.
The Power of Flies.

LUIS RAFAEL SÁNCHEZ, *Macho Camacho's Beat.*

SEVERO SARDUY, *Cobra & Maitreya.*

NATHALIE SARRAUTE, *Do You Hear Them?*
Martereau.
The Planetarium.

STIG SÆTERBAKKEN, *Siamese.*
Self-Control.
Through the Night.

ARNO SCHMIDT, *Collected Novellas.*
Collected Stories.
Nobodaddy's Children.
Two Novels.

ASAF SCHURR, *Motti.*

GAIL SCOTT, *My Paris.*

DAMION SEARLS, *What We Were Doing and Where We Were Going.*

JUNE AKERS SEESE,
Is This What Other Women Feel Too?

BERNARD SHARE, *Inish.*
Transit.

VIKTOR SHKLOVSKY, *Bowstring.*
Literature and Cinematography.
Theory of Prose.
Third Factory.
Zoo, or Letters Not about Love.

PIERRE SINIAC, *The Collaborators.*

KJERSTI A. SKOMSVOLD,
The Faster I Walk, the Smaller I Am.

JOSEF ŠKVORECKÝ, *The Engineer of Human Souls.*

GILBERT SORRENTINO, *Aberration of Starlight.*
Blue Pastoral.
Crystal Vision.

Imaginative Qualities of Actual Things.
Mulligan Stew. Red the Fiend.
Steelwork.
Under the Shadow.

MARKO SOSIČ, *Ballerina, Ballerina.*

ANDRZEJ STASIUK, *Dukla.*
Fado.

GERTRUDE STEIN, *The Making of Americans.*
A Novel of Thank You.

LARS SVENDSEN, *A Philosophy of Evil.*

PIOTR SZEWC, *Annihilation.*

GONÇALO M. TAVARES, *A Man: Klaus Klump.*
Jerusalem.
Learning to Pray in the Age of Technique.

LUCIAN DAN TEODOROVICI,
Our Circus Presents . . .

NIKANOR TERATOLOGEN, *Assisted Living.*

STEFAN THEMERSON, *Hobson's Island.*
The Mystery of the Sardine.
Tom Harris.

TAEKO TOMIOKA, *Building Waves.*

JOHN TOOMEY, *Sleepwalker.*

DUMITRU TSEPENEAG, *Hotel Europa.*
The Necessary Marriage.
Pigeon Post.
Vain Art of the Fugue.

ESTHER TUSQUETS, *Stranded.*

DUBRAVKA UGRESIC, *Lend Me Your Character.*
Thank You for Not Reading.

TOR ULVEN, *Replacement.*

MATI UNT, *Brecht at Night.*
Diary of a Blood Donor.
Things in the Night.

ÁLVARO URIBE & OLIVIA SEARS, EDS.,
Best of Contemporary Mexican Fiction.

ELOY URROZ, *Friction.*
The Obstacles.

LUISA VALENZUELA, *Dark Desires and the Others.*
He Who Searches.

PAUL VERHAEGHEN, *Omega Minor.*

BORIS VIAN, *Heartsnatcher.*

FOR A FULL LIST OF PUBLICATIONS, VISIT: www.dalkeyarchive.com